Terror

Zombie Castle 6

Terror

Chris Harris

PRESS

VULPINE
PRESS

Published by Vulpine Press in the United Kingdom in 2025

ISBN: 978-1-83919-696-6

www.vulpine-press.com

CHAPTER ONE

Huddled down in the rear of the trailer, I tried to protect myself from the bitingly cold wind and flurries of sleet and snow that swept over us. A pang of jealousy crossed my cold, numbed mind at the lucky ones whose current mode of transport had the luxury of heating, windows and a roof. Shawn, who knew how much those of us in the trailer he towed were enjoying the return trip from the Brough's farm, kept our spirits up by "accidentally" pressing the call button on his radio when asking Louise, who as usual was by his side in the cab, if she could pass him his travel mug of hot coffee, or to open the window a crack as he was getting too hot.

Those following behind in a Bushmaster also contributed to the general banter when Shawn's helpfulness quietened down occasionally, and the hot air we vented in response gave us some pretence of warmth for a while, until the next depressingly chilly and wet shower hit us.

We were returning from one of our regular patrols which served many purposes. They ensured the route between the castle and the farm remained clear of the many obstructions that nature and winter storms caused, and for us to bring supplies. The supplies included the regular deliveries of fresh fruit, meat, fish and vegetables that flowed to us from the land, sea and greenhouses on the Scilly Isles via Fort Bristol, and to drop off or pick up any swapping between the two places.

Brief glances over the side of the trailer kept me informed of where we were on the route and therefore how much longer we would have to endure such meteorological misery. We no longer kept a constant vigil for any evidence of survivors on such a well-travelled route, because if anyone was out there, we would have spotted them by now.

Our primary role was to "re kill" any zombies that the solid metal of Shawn's plough failed to dispatch if we came across them, although since the weather had turned from the wet and windy autumnal norm to the much colder winter snap we were currently experiencing, the number of zombies we encountered had reduced to near zero.

On the regular missions we undertook, travelling in an ever-widening circle around our castle home, we systematically emptied – or secured for later collecting – all places that held large quantities of foodstuffs and other essential supplies. The lack of zombies apart from the few that, through mutilating injuries, were practically immobile could not fail to be noticed.

Logic dictated that there still had to be tens of millions of them roaming the land. If they had begun to die off then we certainly hadn't come across any mass graveyards of them or any other evidence of their demise, so even though the lack of them was good news, the fact that we didn't know what had happened to them weighed on our minds.

We simply didn't know where they were, and despite many people viewing this absence as a good thing, I was most certainly looking this particular gift horse in the mouth.

As well as food and general supplies, we also combined these trips with emptying any gun shops we found in the area, which surprised a few of our number just how many there were. They were prioritised and never left untouched or merely secured for a later date due to the fear of weapons falling into the wrong hands. Not that we'd come across any survivors who wanted to do us harm since we eradicated the ones who had attacked the Brough's Farm.

Also, since rescuing Hannah from the basement of the farm where we'd found the tractor and trailer which Captain Clarke had used to rescue his and other's families a few months before, we'd had no luck in finding any more survivors.

The garrison at Fort Bristol experienced more joy in finding survivors when they too had started missions to investigate and search the land around their secure waterside base. Initially these missions were to fulfil the promises made to everyone that, if possible, they would search for their families.

The convoys from Bristol had resulted in not only four families being reunited, but also discovered three more groups of survivors. All had been holed up in remote places where they had relied on isolation to remain safe and undiscovered but not a single one of those locations, according to the reports we'd received, were or could be made defensible against a large horde. The desperate families and random groups who had managed to survive together against all the odds didn't need asking twice if they wanted to stay where they'd been found, and they all leapt at the chance to live a more secure life the explorers from Fort Bristol offered them. These few fortunate survivors, after recovering and gaining their strength and confidence that their rescuers could fulfil the promises given, were ferried to the Scilly Isles where families were reunited and the others started to rebuild their lives safe in the knowledge that they were now in a zombie-free zone.

Each report of more survivors being found always lifted our spirits and was celebrated. The numbers of the total known survivors would, if pondered, only depress someone when worked out as a percentage of what the population of the British Isles had been. The number of survivors we had in the four known communities at the castle, the Brough's farm, the Scilly Isles and Fort Bristol numbered less than five thousand in total.

No calculator was required to make the reality of our situation terribly sad, but every new survivor found still tipped the balance more in our favour. One person armed with the right weapons and trained in the tactics we were continually developing could each individually destroy the zombies that now formed the dominant population of our land by a factor of many.

Shawn's mantra on the first day the apocalypse started had been to kill every one you came across because if you didn't, that would be the one to get you in the end. We still lived by the concept that one less is still one less whenever we could, but the recent lack of them was making that task harder to fulfil.

Recognising we were getting closer to home I raised myself up from where I crouched down low against the trailer sides to try and shelter myself from the miserable weather and attempted to strike a more heroic pose as we approached the gates.

Arrivals and departures from the castle were so routine now that they didn't elicit any more response than a friendly wave from the lookouts on the walls, along with a few ribald comments about the weather from those that had left the warmth of wherever they were in the castle to open the gates following our radio call announcing our imminent arrival.

As usual, Maud greeted us as we stepped into the Great Hall shivering with cold and with floods of water streaming from our clothes, but this time she ordered us to not take another step until we stripped off our sodden clothing. We complied obediently in order to save the furniture and the need for someone to mop up after us, as we were in danger of leaving wet, slug like trails behind us tracking our progress.

Ian, following his pathological need to goad Maud, took this order one step too far in his continual comedic battle of wills to get one over her. That was something he had never managed to do yet, but it never stopped him trying. He stripped to his underwear only to be stopped when Maud shouted at him as he hooked his fingers into the waistband of his underpants and started to pull them down as well.

"If you think the sight of your privates will shock me, Ian, then you're sorely mistaken!"

Everyone knew he was about to be bested by the older woman and watched the show eagerly.

"It's just that I don't want you to be embarrassed when people laugh at how small and shrivelled they are," Maud added wickedly.

Ian's eyes shot to the audience in the room who were all beginning to laugh at him. He automatically moved his hands from the sides of his underpants to cover his front as if protecting his modesty, turning bright red with embarrassment. His usual quick wit abandoned him as he stood there momentarily shocked into unusual silence, until mumbling in self-induced outrage and with his trousers still wrapped around his ankles, hobbled as quickly as he could through the laughing throng and left the room.

Maud couldn't help herself and even she began laughing at the sight which made Ian's grumblings grow even louder until she recovered herself. With a smug smile of satisfaction on her face, she asked someone to get the rest of us some towels to protect our modesty.

Once I'd stripped and wrapped the proffered towel around my waist I went to my room and rubbed some warmth into my bones with the towel before finding dry clothes, then made my way to the room we'd converted to our command centre, which felt like a grandiose title I didn't dislike.

The inconvenience of using the dining room as our planning and meeting room, with maps and lists having to be cleared from the table many times a day, caused us to start using one of the many unused rooms in the castle. It had been a large, self-service type restaurant and dining area. Being cavernous it wasn't as cozy and homely as other places but was an ideal space for what we needed.

Tables were arranged to form separate work areas along with a large boardroom style setup in the middle to accommodate the many meetings we held. The radio had been moved there, permanently monitored by a rota of volunteers, and the walls were covered with large scale maps of the British Isles with markers pinned into them to show the last updated location of any patrols and the dispositions of forces and personnel at the three bases.

Captain Clarke was already there speaking with Captain Hammond and the Sergeants currently stationed at the castle, minus Sergeant Gallon who was presently in command of the garrison at the Brough's, discussing what other missions they could undertake. In the previous months they had secured and rescued all the survivors trapped at the various bunkers and bases around the country. All known stocks of weapons stored at military bases, police stations and other places had been found and either gathered or, if it was deemed we had no use for them or the difficulty of repatriating them wasn't considered worth the effort, they were destroyed so they would be beyond anyone else's reach.

The responsibility for gathering the remaining stores of ammunition at M.O.D Kineton had been passed on to Fort Bristol's commander, as we had many hundreds of tonnes of ammunition and huge quantities of weapons, both military and civilian, either stored in the castle's ever-increasing number of armouries or in lorries parked safely within the castle grounds. We had more than we could reasonably use in any conflict we could imagine going forwards, so the remaining stores at Kineton were being transported for storage at the Scilly Isles.

"Hi guys," I said as I poured myself a coffee from the flask on a side table and plonked myself down on a chair at the main table.

"Have you thawed out yet?" Hammond asked with a grin that could have been interpreted as sympathetic, but I knew otherwise.

"Just about," I replied, making a point of rubbing my beard thoughtfully with my middle finger. "Next time I go out I'm bagging a seat in a bushmaster. No matter how good the clothing is, if it gets any colder it's only going to get more miserable in the back of the trailer…and it may shock you to learn, but I'm not getting any younger so I vote for an age limit on winter trailer travel."

"We were just talking about the coming winter, as it happens," Clarke added, joining in the conversation. "We're not sure what jobs we have left to do. There are no more known groups trapped out there, our food stores, sundry supplies and munitions are all in excellent health. The bases are all functioning well and the supply runs between them have had no reportable issues for a while now. All in all, the good news is that there is no news and that's what we're having trouble with."

"Like the hangman said," I answered, affecting a lisp as I lifted the coffee cup to my mouth. "No noose is good noose?"

"Quite," Clarke said, ignoring how funny my joke was. "Until now we've been rather busy getting on with all the tasks we'd set ourselves, and now the list is pretty much complete, we're wondering how best to fill our time and make ourselves useful…it's not even that we can just go out there and continue dispatching the enemy as they aren't cooperating. They've bloody well gone to ground somewhere."

Clarke looked pensive, even annoyed at the mystery, so Hammond took over the report.

"Castle upkeep, apart from any labour we provide for heavy things, is being managed well by the team here. Shawn has almost finished modifying the CCTV system which should release a few more from guard duty."

I sipped the coffee and nodded. Shawn had spent much of the past weeks working on the castle's CCTV system controlled from the security office, which we'd had to clear of its unfortunate last shift on day one of our arrival at the castle. Having got the system powered up and working again, he found that a lot of the cameras were already in the correct position to monitor large sections of the walls and buildings, and had set about moving other cameras to where they would be better suited.

Cameras with motion sensors, which alerted the watcher to any movement detected, were being repositioned to cover the entire grounds so if our outer defences were breached we would know before they came into sight of the guards on the walls. Once the system was completed and tested, we were confident that we could reduce the number of guards which patrolled our walls twenty-four hours a day, safe in the knowledge that one or two monitoring the camera feeds could perform the role of many. The plan was, when we were convinced it was fully functional, to replace many of the guards with a smaller QRF or quick reaction force based in a more comfortable location than on the walls to react to any movement detected by the cameras.

The whereabouts of the millions of zombies that still had to be out there had been weighing on our minds, but so far nobody had come up with any decisive answers or theories. We still found the occasional hungry roamer, but they were usually so damaged as to be virtually incapacitated and unable to move beyond crawling or pulling themselves along on damaged limbs.

"Still no clue as to where the blighters have all buggered off to," Hammond said with a frown before turning to Clarke. "I haven't laid eyes on one for a while now, not like your chaps."

Clarke mirrored the frown thoughtfully before shaking his head as if he still couldn't comprehend what he'd seen.

"Buggers were just huddled together in a barn. Like penguins sheltering from the Antarctic wind!"

My mind filled with imagery when he said that, taking me off on a tangent as I imagined Clarke's soldiers killing off the one group they'd located in weeks with David Attenborough narrating.

We'd discussed and theorised the findings many times since but as only one group had been discovered displaying that odd behaviour and eradicated, so far it wasn't enough to pin a definitive theory on. More buildings had been cautiously searched when discovered on our travels but no more evidence had been found, leaving us perplexed.

Perplexed but not entirely unhappy at their notable absence.

"Is everything still set for next week?" I asked, knowing my question would change the subject on to more positive matters.

"Yes. No changes have been made to the itinerary agreed so far, so it's all go as far as I'm concerned," Clarke replied.

A group of us, including me, were being picked up by plane from Wellesbourne airfield the following week to attend a conference on the Scilly isles, where we were going to spend a few days discussing and planning the next steps we would take collectively going forwards, but the trip had placed me in a quandary.

Of course, I wanted to be involved in the decision-making process of what our future plans would be, but I also was concerned about leaving my family even for a few days as by modern standards I might as well have been going halfway around the world.

Even as I'd voiced my concerns to Becky, I knew my arguments were illogical.

They were safe and secure behind the walls of Warwick Castle. They would be protected, not only by a secure perimeter fence but the high walls of the castle itself. These walls were lined with a deadly array of weapons which could pour destruction down on anything that breached our outer defences, the mortar position in the centre of the castle courtyard had been extended and improved and now contained a selection of mortars from 60mm to 120mm which could provide high explosive protection in a three-hundred-and-sixty-degree radius around the castle. Many points around the castle grounds and surrounding areas had been marked and ranged to provide predetermined and accurate positions to rain down pinpoint accurate death if need be.

Also, to allay our fears, Admiral Walker had promised that the incoming flight would contain temporary reinforcements to help garrison the castle in our absence. Fort Bristol, and if necessary, the Brough's Farm could send reinforcements to our aid, so despite my reservations, there really was very little for me to be worried about. Once Becky had pointed out that it was I who was taking a risk by flying, I eventually put my fears aside and agreed to go.

CHAPTER TWO

A castle, whilst huge, grand and imposing, was by no means a modern house with high levels of insulation and double-glazed windows to keep out the cold. The cold seeped through its thick stone walls, and draughts, no matter how heavy the curtains we fixed over the doors and windows were, always found their way in.

Not that we complained much, as with fireplaces stacked with wood and coal blazing away, portable gas and electric heaters powered by one of the many canisters collected from a storage depot, and the generators humming away in the corner of the courtyard provided plenty of heat to keep the worst of the cold where it belonged: Outside.

Fortunately, we'd been saved the backbreaking work of cutting and splitting the logs needed to feed the fires by scavenging trailer loads of already split and seasoned logs, along with pallets of prepacked coal from the few businesses in the area that supplied local needs during the winter.

Maud, Willie and a few of the other older members of our community who remembered life before central heating and double glazing, enjoyed mocking how soft the younger generation had become whenever one of us moaned about the need to wear at least two jumpers and a pair of thick socks inside on a particularly cold day.

Despite this, life at the castle moved on day by day. Guards stood their post at the walls whilst others completed the daily tasks that kept the castle and its inhabitants fed, maintained and content. The knights continued training us all in medieval fighting skills and the soldiers ensured that everyone capable of using a weapon was as safe and competent as possible in their use.

Much time and attention was still being given to the four young girls rescued from the clutches of the pervert at M.O.D Kineton. Their ordeal had clearly left them with deep emotional trauma, not only from what vile acts Brian had perpetrated on them, but from the loss of their parents only days before they were kidnapped. Physically, their health improved on a regime of kindness, good food and plenty of rest but it was their mental health where we had to tread as gently as possible. Slowly, carefully, we introduced them to castle life, always making sure that a friendly face was close by. They met and got to know all the other children, who had been given quiet, firm instructions on how to act and behave around them. Even though the girls themselves weren't aware of it, a well-planned rota of volunteers was always on hand to keep a close eye on them, not only to provide a friendly face, but to intervene if things appeared to be getting too much for them. We did our best to provide them with as normal and calm an environment as possible, which without proper professional help which was just not available, was the best course of action we decided to take.

Collectively, we insisted that it would be best that when we left for the Scillies that the castle would lock itself down and no one would venture from the walls for any reason bar an emergency. I'd pushed for this decision as knowing the castle was on lock down and protected by the extra personnel who would arrive when we left, I was as happy as I could be about my family being hundreds of miles away.

Becky held my hand as I waited at the airplane steps, having insisted on accompanying me to say a last goodbye before returning to the castle with the convoy. Once the last new arrivals had left the plane and retrieved their kitbags from the aircraft's hold, I couldn't delay the moment anymore and with a quick hug and a kiss I climbed the steps to board .

We were quite a party heading off. Not only were our military residents accompanying us, but a fair few of us civilians had been invited to attend the conference. We had entrusted the command of the castle to our sergeants, so Clarke, Digby and Hammond were onboard along with myself, Shawn, Ian, Jamie, Louise, Chris, Charles the Vicar, Maud and Willie.

The choice of who would attend had been left to us and, after much debate and discussion, the lucky volunteers were chosen as collectively we could provide our experience and knowledge across a vast range of subjects.

Maud was very nervous as this would be her very first flight, which is why Willie had insisted he accompany her. She'd explained that her husband had been too mean to pay for an overseas holiday, but she suspected it was more to do with his deep mistrust and hatred for anything foreign. He'd ranted on about the safety risks of flying as an excuse not to have to go to the places such as Rome or Paris; places she had yearned for a lifetime to visit.

Even though she knew his arguments had been illogical and xenophobic, it had nonetheless instilled a deep-rooted fear of letting her feet leave solid ground.

Her usual frosty outer layer with a soft inner core was looking very ruffled and perturbed, which was a new experience for all of us. Ian had come up with an unusually subtle and cunning plan before this to wind her up during one of our regular film nights, sitting around the huge fireplace in the Great Hall watching the large television we had fixed to the wall next to it. We enjoyed the crackling, leaping flames as much as the films, although Ian had spent far too long finding every movie involving any kind of plane crash.

For once Maud's nervousness had masked her usual super-power-like perception of a wind-up going on, and we had all tried to hide our mirth as she sat with a look of sheer terror on her face staring wide eyed and silent at the screen.

Now though, actually onboard the flying deathtrap, we kept quiet as it seemed unfair to add to her terror by making jokes. She sat beside Willie holding his hand in what looked to me a painful, vice-like grip. When I caught his eye he gave a small smile and shrug as he tried not to show the pain and discomfort she was causing by crushing his hand.

It was a pleasant and unusual experience for me to be flying in a larger plane again rather than the small cockpit of the light aircraft Chris and I had been flying in recently. We'd undertaken more flights until the onset of winter and the uncertainty of the weather conditions had made us decide to not fly again until the spring came. Flying a grid pattern, we'd covered most of the countryside within range, searching for any signs of survivors but to no avail, as any likely spot we marked once investigated by a ground team was found to be empty.

Also, it was different not to have to abide by the security regulations or wait for clearance to take off from air traffic control, all of which made international travel tedious, let alone having to experience the awkwardness of a safety briefing as one of the cabin crew smiled like a maniac and did the Macarena holding an oxygen mask and seatbelt.

The fact that all of us, including Maud, boarded carrying a weapon just in case we had to make an emergency landing somewhere and needed to protect ourselves didn't even raise an eyebrow on the flight attendant's face. Her only job was to make sure we were seated and that the doors were shut and locked, then the propellors started turning and we taxied towards the runway where the engines powered up and we took off without delay.

The cockpit door was open and as soon as we had reached cruising altitude, Chris and I went up to have a nose at the cockpit and chat to the pilots as they had promised both of us a go at the controls sometime during the flight. A chance the little boy in me was definitely not going to miss.

"Trust me," the pilot said as he showed both Chris and I the controls of the plane as we crammed into the cockpit. "This baby is easier to fly than the hairdryer you've been using. Once we're up to cruising altitude I'll stretch my legs and let you have a go."

To me, the cockpit displays and controls were far more modern and numerous than the utilitarian flight school plane we had been flying, making it seem as if we were on the deck of the starship enterprise and our plane had just been used by Wilbur Wright.

"I'll just observe for a while if you don't mind, we'll have a go after Bristol as I want to see that," I replied nervously.

The flight path followed the route we had taken when escaping from Cornwall all those months before, and even though Chris and I had passed over parts of the route on our previous flights and driven by road as far as Bristol, this was the first time we'd retraced our steps fully. It was interesting to see the landmarks, such as the mass pile-ups of burnt-out vehicles in various places that had hindered our initial journey.

At our request the pilot flew us over Bristol, both to get a bird's eye view of Fort Bristol and for Jamie, Shawn, Ian and Chris who had all once called the place home to see what was left of the historic city. They all stared transfixed out of the windows as the pilot flew a wide, banking turn giving them a view of the whole conurbation. Great swathes of the city had burned and lay in tangled, twisted ruins. Seeing such destruction was upsetting for everyone, but especially for those that had lived and worked there.

Fort Bristol looked impressive from the air and it was evident that much more work had been done since we first helped establish it. A larger ring of containers had been laid out to further expand the site and protected the vehicle pool which contained parked ranks of lorries and some of the armoured cars recovered from military bases around the country. They were still gathering supplies and shipping them to the Scillies for storage, and as we circled the base we watched another convoy of lorries and their escorts enter through the gates in the outer ring of containers.

Maud had relaxed slightly and even braved a trip to the cockpit to see a pilot's eye view of the flight until, much to Ian's barely concealed amusement, a few bumps of turbulence made her rush back to her seat and fasten her lap belt as tight as it would go.

"Your plane," the copilot said after the pilot had vacated his seat and I'd climbed into it.

I settled in and gently held the controls, still allowing the copilot to fly the plane.

"My plane," I replied confirming I now had control.

The co-pilot removed his hands from the yoke. I played gently with the controls until I had a feel for it before trying a few banking turns and using the throttle, raising and lowering our altitude. All too soon it was Chris's turn, and the co-pilot retook control as we swapped seats grinning at each other in excitement.

When the view ahead showed both coasts of Cornwall tapering to where they met at Land's End, the pilot asked Chris to vacate the seat where he'd spent ten minutes flying the plane. From the look of pleasure on his face I knew it had been as memorable for him as it had been for me. We turned serious as he needed to guide the plane so we could get a view of one of the proposed projects we already knew we were going to discuss at the conference we were about to attend.

Flying at the airplanes safest slowest speed, he reduced height and banked the plane as we held the map in our hands we had been given for this purpose, and both studied the view out of the window and followed a course already marked on its large scale. We made three passes along the route until we were satisfied everyone had seen enough before the pilot turned and set his final course to St Mary's.

CHAPTER THREE

Admiral Walker-Jones was among the crowd who met us as we stepped off the plane. He shook everyone's hands warmly and even gave Maud a hug before introducing us to those we didn't know.

"Welcome," he said once the introductions had taken place, and gestured to a van and some minibuses pulling up nearby. "If you could get your luggage on the van, we'll have it taken to your accommodation and start the look around if that's ok with you?"

We were all eager to witness what they had achieved on the islands after hearing all the regular reports. The plan on the first day was to do a tour so we could put places and names to everything we had been told about.

Eagerly looking out of the windows we set off and drove through the picturesque countryside to our first destination.

"It's strange not to see people walking around carrying weapons," I remarked as we inspected a field full of poly tunnels.

The Admiral surreptitiously touched a wooden frame near him for luck as he explained.

"Since we cleared the islands not one outbreak has happened, as you know. Don't get me wrong, everyone who wasn't trained in using firearms has received tuition and—" He pointed to an open sided shed in the middle of the field where stacked weapons were visible. "—we do keep them close to hand, just in case. We also maintain quite a few quick reaction forces stationed all over the islands ready to react at a moment's notice. We do feel safe here, but as we all know complacency kills and the last event any of us want here is an outbreak getting out of control."

I nodded, agreeing silently with him as I looked around. Dozens of people were labouring away tending to the crops covered by seemingly acres of plastic sheeting. It all looked very organised and by the large volume of crates stacked with freshly picked produce waiting to be collected, very efficient as well.

Even though we did receive regular deliveries of vegetables, meat and fish to supplement our own food supplies, we also maintained our own greenhouses lined up against the castle walls. These in no way produced as much as we had given to us, but we felt it was still important for us not to be relying on others. Every meal that was announced to have been made solely with our own produce by the proud gardeners was always greeted with applause and gratitude.

At our next stop we pulled up outside a detached house. I was wondering who we were here to see when Graham and Arthur stepped outside followed by what must be their families. Those of us who had met them all those months ago on the bridge over the River Severn when we had spotted them cruising along the river in their attempt to reach the fleet in the Solent, reacted joyfully as well. It was always nice to see a familiar face in a new environment and I joined in the rush off the bus so we could reunite properly.

I'd last spoken to them when the connection between us had reached the ears of the command on the Scillies, and they'd allowed them to use the radio. It was the first time we had met the rest of the family though, so once introductions had been made and we deflected the emotion-filled thanks they kept offering, we were shown around the land which they and a few other families tended to, growing a variety of root vegetables. Being told we would see them later at a dinner being held in our honour and with the need to complete the planned tour, we said our farewells and continued.

Hugh Town, the largest village and the capitol of the Scillies, was the final port of call on St Mary's. Just offshore were a mass of ships and boats of all sizes crammed together in the sheltered waters. There were so many it looked as if you could walk across to the other islands visible across the straights without getting your feet wet. Small boats bustled between them, and I could see work parties on the decks of some still toiling to search through the stacks of containers as they were opened and any items of value found were lowered to the waiting boats to be ferried ashore.

Knowing from previous conversations that the sheer quantities of ships that had answered the call to gather in the Solent meant that safe anchorages were in short supply, especially for the deeper drafts of the container and cargo ships, so a queuing system had been organised. When a ship was searched and what it had to offer was ferried ashore for storing it was moved to another, less sheltered anchorage in the lee of one of the islands where its remaining fuel was transferred to another vessel and it was abandoned. Another waiting ship then moved in to take its place and the work was repeated.

Everyone fully acknowledged this was not ideal as a storm might cause some ships to drag their anchors and potentially run aground, and in the worst-case scenario block sea lanes and channels. Extra anchors had been fitted, with chains and lines attached to the islets and outcrops of rocks that broke the surface in many places around all the islands having been laid to secure them as best as possible and hopefully prevent this.

When time and available personnel allowed, a plan under consideration was to either take these ships to deeper water and scuttle them if no further need for them was agreed or find another anchorage in a sheltered bay on the mainland to abandon them. The nearest bays were St Ives and Mounts Bay near Penzance, and we had plans for those places so filling them with abandoned ships might hinder future projects.

A boat waited at the quayside which ferried us the short distance to Tresco, the next island largest in size to St Mary's where another community of farmers and fishermen had been established. Talking to everyone, I couldn't fail to pick up on the sense of hope and community that existed among them. Similarly to the Castle and the outpost at the Brough's, everyone was on the same page as to what needed to be done. They had survived and while the heartbreak of the losses everyone had suffered was never far from the surface, everyone knew that to ensure their long-term survival they needed to work together to achieve the common goal. A late middle-aged man, who in his previous life had been a CEO of a large international business, summed it up as he hoed the field he was working on, preparing it for planting.

"It's better than the alternative," he explained cheerfully as he sweated, despite the chill wind, pointing to the acres of land they had yet to prepare. "If someone had told me a year ago I'd be reduced to a farm labourer when for the past twenty years I've barely left my desk, hardly ever seen my family, and according to my doctor was a prime candidate for a heart attack, I would've called for security to kick them out of my office!"

His wife and son were working with him in the field, and he hugged them as real emotion showed on his face.

"Now, putting the tragedies aside, I'm the happiest I've been for decades. I'm spending real quality time with my family and I'm actually doing something worthwhile, not just analysing a balance sheet."

He patted his stomach where I could imagine a few months before he'd sported a prosperous paunch, but which now was returning to a lean and trim look.

"Also, I don't need to see a doctor to tell me I'm in the best shape I've been in for years. Buying the boat, even though at the time I did it as it seemed something a man in my position should own just so I could drink a few G&Ts on the sundeck in the marina and show off how much money I had, was the best stupid waste of money I've ever spent. I'm so glad I dragged the family out for a couple of days break so I could show off my new toy."

His wife, sniggering with barely contained laughter. interrupted him.

"Go on Noel, tell everyone about how we escaped."

"That's not fair," he replied going red with embarrassment. "I'd only bought it the week before and hadn't been on the course to drive it."

He looked pleadingly at her but on seeing a familiar eye roll from his wife he continued.

"Come on, love, don't make me."

Knowing a good story was about to be told, we all insisted on hearing it.

"Weeelll," he said, as he reluctantly realised he was about to embarrass himself in front of strangers and couldn't get out of it. "The salesman showed me how to start the engine…and that was about it. When the marina erupted in chaos and we saw zombies eating people and getting closer to us down the pontoon I knew the only escape route open was out to sea."

He smiled as he recollected the story and clearly realised it could only sound ridiculous.

"I started her up and pushed the throttle fully open, but the bloody thing wouldn't move."

"Don't tell me," I interrupted. "It was still tied up."

He shrugged and nodded.

"Yes, it bloody well was, but how the hell was I expected to know anything about mooring lines and all the other stuff you need to do to park it? Anyway, can I continue?"

We all told him to carry on as we could tell the story would only get better from here.

"The salesman told me it was a fast boat with some big horses under the deck and could do a lot of something called knots, but it all meant nothing to me…That was until the pontoon it was parked to broke and suddenly, I found myself trying to steer an out-of-control beast with no idea how to do it, which now found itself towing half the bloody dock and at least six other boats that were still attached to it behind us!"

It all sounded similar to those ridiculous videos shared on social media or tv programmes of incompetent people getting themselves in hilarious situations.

Starting to enjoy telling the story and seeing the reaction it was getting he continued, but this time with a smile of acceptance that whatever he said wouldn't make him feel any more stupid so he may as well just get it over with.

"Luckily when I ran over a small yacht a few of the ropes broke which only left me trailing four boats and a little bit of pontoon. The problem was I was panicking so much I didn't realise I still had the throttles wide open, and the bloody thing was careering around the marina bouncing off everything in its path. It was a good job it was the biggest boat in there…I mean it was bouncing around so much I couldn't even stay in the captain's chair. Anyway," he said trying to wrap the story up. "Luckily the things I was dragging behind me came loose or just broke into pieces, until eventually I spotted the way out of the maze of boats I was in and destroying a few more perfectly good boats, got out of the marina. The problem then was the boat started filling with water and by the time I'd got into open water it was knee-deep in the lounge area and I had no idea what to do next. Then I saw a big marker buoy ahead of us and headed for it so I could tie the boat to it and stop it sinking or at least we could climb onto it. How the hell was I to know it was marking a sandbank? Luckily it was, and I rammed the boat into it at full speed which at least stopped us from sinking but finished my shiny new boat off completely and left us stuck in the middle of Southampton water. We were there for a few hours until, just in time because the tide was rising, we got picked up."

Wiping tears of laughter from our eyes at the ridiculously luckiness of their escape we said our goodbyes and continued the tour.

Heartened by the whole trip we returned to the boat which ferried us back across the crowded anchorage and to the hotel where we were staying.

~

The dinner was a great success, and great fun was had by all. By previous agreement no 'work' talk was allowed and the whole population of the islands seemed to have descended on the town square to celebrate the two communities meeting for the first time. Despite the cold, the rain stayed away and the festival atmosphere created by lights hung between trees and buildings and braziers of burning wood to provide some warmth allowed the party to continue late into the night.

Admiral Walker-Jones, relaxed by a few drinks, was in a very genial mood and entertained those within earshot around him of his tall tales from his long navy career. He approached me and put a friendly arm around my shoulder which from the redness of his face was probably as much to help keep him upright as it was a genuine show of friendship.

"You know," he said waving his arm around. "We even have you chaps to thank for this."

He looked at my puzzled expression and continued.

"After spending time with you and witnessing the camaraderie and genuine love and friendship you all have for each other, we began to use this square for social events. Before we'd just concentrated on getting the job done and allocating people to where they were most suited or to whatever needed doing without considering the personal angle.

We started a social committee who dreamt up events for people to meet and get to know each other, and not unsurprisingly, morale and productivity really picked up. The old and much overused corny saying 'teamwork makes the dream work' could not be more apt. Now everyone knows each other to one extent or another and understands they are not just in it alone, but as part of a community. You see, humanity is not designed for isolation. We're social creatures, you see? We need to be a part of something larger to feel…whole…"

I clinked my glass with him as I gazed around the talking and laughing throng.

"Thank you again," he said. Taking a sip from my drink he continued talking as I tried to deflect any more of the overenthusiastic praise we as a group seemed to be constantly bombarded with.

"It's been a really interesting day, meeting old friends," I said referring to Graham and Arthur and their families, to whom I had spent a good portion of the night talking. "And putting faces to names mentioned in reports, but I'm really looking forwards to tomorrow's meeting as well. The agenda your aide handed to me earlier on looks like we're in for a full day."

Walker Jones looked at me reproachfully before he replied with an edge to his voice.

"There. You've gone and done it!"

"Done what?" I replied slightly confused.

"Mentioned work. Now I've got to get all official and break up this party to avoid everyone sporting thick heads tomorrow!"

He turned to look for one of his aides and waved the man forward before stopping when I touched his arm.

"Fancy a nightcap before we have to get all grown up again?" I asked, smiling as I reached for a bottle of whisky from a nearby table.

Grinning conspiratorially in return he waved away the summoned aide and held out his glass.

CHAPTER FOUR

After a good breakfast accompanied by a few paracetamol washed down with mugs of coffee, myself and the rest of the Warwick Castle contingent made their way to the conference room of the hotel where we were staying. The large room had been arranged such that around forty people could sit at the conference table with other desks and chairs arranged around the periphery.

Name plates had been placed by the seats, and it took us all a few minutes to find our allocated seats amongst the throng of people milling around the room.

Walker-Jones was already sat at the head of the table where he would have a good view of everyone when they were finally seated. We knew he was chairing the meeting, and as the last person sat down he stood up to gain our collective attention, causing the hum of noise and chatter to die down.

"Welcome, everyone," he began when we were all quiet. "Now we have a lot to get through today, so if we could keep the questions and chatter down to a minimum, I would appreciate it. Saying that, if you do have any pertinent questions or comments please don't be afraid to speak up, because I'm sure if you're thinking it then others around you are as well. Just direct them through me, the chair, to avoid the meeting descending into a free for all."

He stared around the table after a ripple of agreements washed around the room before continuing.

"For each agenda item I will ask for the lead of each group tasked to plan it to make their presentation and ask that we all kindly let them finish before ripping it apart!"

He waited for the good-natured laughter to quiet down.

"Okay then, let's begin with the first and the main item on the agenda. The wall."

I leant forwards as this was the main topic of the day, and following our overflight I understood why it had been proposed.

A man stood up and prepared himself to address the now fully attentive audience by shuffling his papers. He pressed a key on the laptop open in front of him, and an image appeared on the large screen attached to the wall behind him displaying a large-scale map of southern Cornwall from Land's End to Helston, a town which was about twenty miles further up the peninsula .

He began with a slightly nervous wobble to his voice that settled down as his confidence at addressing such a large audience increased.

"Firstly, can I introduce myself...My name is Tony, and I have a civil engineering background mainly based around highways development."

He then added his survival story in brief, which seemed to have become the initial icebreaking conversation when meeting someone for the first time.

"My family and I only survived due to the kindness of another family who picked us up from a jetty in Falmouth just as we were about to swim for it."

The simple statement hid a whole untold backstory of the terror they must have gone through in the seconds and minutes before deciding their only way to live was to jump into the deep, tidal waters of Falmouth harbour where survival was only a vague hope, but a better hope than not jumping.

He pressed a key again and a line appeared on the map between Hayle on the north Cornish coast to a spot just to the east of Penzance on the south coast.

"The distance between these points is approximately five and a half miles and the projected route as you can see follows the A30, which is the main arterial road in the area. My proposal is to construct a barrier made of an earthen berm and fencing between these points to stop the passage of zombies in or out of the area. Once that is complete, the area behind the barrier can be swept clean to create an approximately fifty square mile safe zone."

He looked around the room seeing nobody ready to raise any obvious objection.

"Well, that's the bones of the plan…I can go into the construction, personnel and equipment needs if you want, or we can discuss its feasibility?"

"Thank you, Tony," Walker-Jones said. "If you could give a rough timescale and the works involved first?"

"Of course," Tony replied. "We've located sufficient heavy equipment from a road widening scheme further up the A30. It'll take a day or two to get it all in-situ, but that should pose no problems as it's just a case of driving it all at their various top speeds along the main road. The barrier will follow the line of the A30 as this obviously provides the best access and the road can be used for patrolling the line afterwards. Initially we'd use bulldozers and excavators to raise and form the berm with the ditch, or moat for want of a better word, created by the excavations adding another layer of defence in front of the line. We've located stocks of suitable fencing at various locations and have also identified other places where fencing can be removed and relocated if necessary. As to the timescale…"

Tony gave a wry smile.

"In a previous life when asked about timescales on an engineering task as large as this I'd conservatively have put a twelve-to-eighteen month estimate on the project."

He raised his hands to stop the growing murmurs spreading around the table at the impossibly long timescale and raised his voice a little.

"However…I'm unshackled from the multiple layers of red tape and pointless bureaucracy, which would have bogged down any such project with environmental, traffic, pollution, noise, health and safety issues, not to mention the bat, badger, newt, and lesser spotted eight leaf clover brigades. I can confidently guess that the bulk of the works should be completed in about a month and can be improved from there."

A sigh of relief spread around the room at the far more reasonable estimate.

I put my hand up to get the admiral's attention who, when he noticed me, indicated for me to carry on so I stood up to get the room's attention and asked the question, even though I suspected I already knew the answer, but had agreed it needed to be debated first.

"This all sounds doable, but I have one question…Why? Everyone's secure here on the Scillies and we certainly are in our castle, as are the other communities at Bristol and the farm. So why do we need to create a fifty odd square mile safe zone on the mainland?"

Walker-Jones smiled at me as it was him who'd suggested I start off with that question in a conversation we had had over our final whisky of the night before. I gave him a conspiratorial wink as I sat down.

"Good question, Tom," he replied seriously and with no hint he was prepared for it. "Yes, we are all currently secure, but we're forecasting that we'll be stretching the resource capability of the Scilly Isles if we look much further into the future. We're only complementing our scavenging efforts with what the land and sea are currently providing, therefore, we're concerned that in the long term we will need more acreage planted and more livestock being nurtured if we want to feed the current population when stored foodstuffs begin to get scarcer. It just so happens that just over the sea is probably the shortest stretch of land anywhere between two patches of water in the British Isles that can create a suitable and large enough area for our needs. Also, I'm told that the mild climate of the region and the existing farming infrastructure is ideal for our requirements. Yes, fifty square miles is a lot more than we currently need, but it also opens up the coastal fishing ports at Newlyn, Hayle, St Ives and other places for us to exploit."

His tone then hardened as he leant forwards.

"Also, this is the important first step to start reclaiming our country. We know we need to, otherwise we'll just all get complacent and forget what the final aim for every one of us left standing should be."

He didn't need to tell any around the table what that was, as we all knew none of us would rest until we and our families could live without fear again.

Willie raised his hand to speak.

"You cannae just…build a fence and hope nothing gets over it. This thing will need to be patrolled and inspected regularly if people on the other side of it are going to sleep well at night. Just clearing the land is going to be a monumental job, so my guess is that you've called us here because you're going to need more people than you currently have here to do it."

"To the point and correct as usual, Willie," the admiral replied. "Yes, we will need help. and that's what we need to agree on. Completing this task will be an all-hands effort, but we cannot endanger what we've achieved so far, and that is what this conference is about."

Tony stood up and waited for Walker-Jones to indicate for him to proceed.

"Yes, Willie, as the Admiral said, you're right. My plan is to have watchtowers placed along the line with larger barracks at either end, and possibly one in the middle to provide extra security. How many people you'll need to staff this isn't my area of business, but my preliminary plans show that if the towers are placed a quarter of a mile apart and are in sight of each other, then twenty watchtowers will be needed."

I did some quick calculations in my head. Twenty watchtowers guarded by at least a minimum of two in each with larger bases at either end with at least ten in each, and adding at least three shifts per day meant a force of around two hundred needed to garrison it. Add maybe twenty percent to that to cover sickness or training and the like, and the total number of wall defenders became significant. A substantial number of our surviving population even but knowing the trained fighting forces both military and civilian we had collectively between us, it was workable taking into account that was where the bulk of any protective force would need to be based. As long as the land behind had been cleared and was known to be zombie-free, then apart from maintaining a general level of vigilance, life could carry on with the knowledge the wall was protecting them.

Still, something about that easy confidence made me feel decidedly uneasy.

The discussions continued, and after a quick lunchbreak with everyone throwing ideas into the room and contributing their area of expertise until eventually unanimous agreement was reached.

The communities at the Castle and farm wouldn't be needed until the construction phase of the wall was complete, after which we'd send a convoy with volunteers to help with sweeping the now enclosed land from end to end and eradicate every zombie we found. We knew that as we were on winter lockdown with no scavenging or any other duties except local patrols and keeping the route between us and the farm open, we should be able to send a sizeable detachment to help.

One area which invited a lot of debate over drinks after we had finished, was what to call the structure that had been given the go ahead to start in the next few days. The most corny and obvious one which most of us were very reticent to use but did actually have a note of truth to it and was hard to dismiss, was 'The Corn Wall'. No other suggestions seemed to garner as much discussion and so reluctantly it was cautiously agreed that until a better name could be dreamed up, we were stuck with it.

In the evening, when the main event had wrapped up, the work continued as everyone who'd been at the meeting ate together. More topics were discussed and agreed as we took advantage of the fact that we were all face to face and not talking over a soulless radio link. Just chatting to different people who were all striving for the same goal boosted our already high spirits. They were a community we had been involved with since the beginning but as the evening ended, they felt like more than just another community struggling to survive; they were our friends.

CHAPTER FIVE

The next morning we all, including a more relaxed Maud, said our final farewells and boarded the plane for the flight back to Wellesbourne airfield in good spirits.

Much had been achieved and we now had tasks we needed to prepare for in the coming months. The spare space around our own bags in the planes hold had been filled with fresh island produce, solely for the reason that if we had space, it may as well be put to use rather than being shipped on one of the regular supply runs. Also on its return run, apart from the returning military personnel and their gear, the plane would be filled to safe capacity with a variety of items and equipment which would have normally been sent on one of the convoys.

Two new people were also joining us on the flight. The castle inhabitants had met them collectively after the meeting yesterday, where we had the final say in whether or not they would be a good fit for our community. They were a husband and wife and had been introduced after they agreed to try life at the castle because the woman, Diane, was a midwife. Nicky's pregnancy had been progressing well but apart from many personal birth experiences, we didn't have a trained professional amongst us and therefore having a midwife staying with us at the castle was a good idea.

It wasn't just our little community, but everyone everywhere seemed to be excited about the upcoming addition to the country's population count. Nicky's was currently the only known pregnancy anywhere and everyone seemed to be taking a personal interest in her condition. Maybe the distraction of new life being brought into the world after the hell everyone had been through gave a symbol of hope that one day life would return to normal. It was often said jokingly that this birth was more anticipated than the arrival of a new royal baby or that of an A-list celebrity. In a world that had been filled with pain and suffering for so long, now that the shoots of hope were beginning to emerge, all had bought into the joy that the birth would bring and Diane would be an important factor in ensuring that the birth went smoothly.

It also wasn't that we weren't expecting any more pregnancies to follow, as the amount of blossoming romances reported between the younger members of all the communities made that fact an inevitability more than a possibility.

Diane and her husband Tim had agreed to relocate to Warwick until at least after the birth. Whether they stayed afterwards would be up to them, and us, to decide, but as first impressions went after our meeting, they seemed as if they would fit in well.

Both were friendly, and Diane certainly had the expertise and experience from her profession to become a valued member of the community. Tim, her husband, did initially seem more reluctant to leave the safe haven of the Scillies to head to the unknowns of the mainland from which they had already escaped death once before. Once we'd met them and explained how life was at the castle his fears were allayed and he readily agreed to join us. He'd served a few years in the military before returning to civvie street and now worked as a general tradesman who could turn his hands to most building work, so would be a useful addition to the mixed skillsets we already had.

Diane wasn't bringing any equipment with her from either the small hospital in St Marys or from any of the Royal Navy ships, as we reckoned we could scavenge what she needed from the hospital in Warwick, which had an accident and emergency department as well as a maternity unit. We'd seen a few wandering undead inside through the windows and decided months ago to block every exit we could find so they would stay where they were and not cause us any trouble by escaping.

Hoping the problem would go away by itself as they, with nothing to sustain them, should rot and die off, only now we had to plan a scavenging mission in the close confines of the maze of corridors and rooms the hospital would contain to stock up on what Diane would need to do her job.

Becky was waiting for me as I stepped from the airplane and gave me a quick hug and a kiss before we helped to unload everything from the plane and stack it onto the waiting lorry, before loading it with the items we had for their return journey which had already been unloaded and stacked nearby. Maud, now her feet were once again on firm ground, had regained the ability to speak and began bossing everyone around as if to make up for the last ninety minutes of silence we'd had from her. She introduced Diane to Becky, and they immediately went off into a huddle in the back of the trailer to start planning Nicky's care.

As soon as the returning soldiers boarded the plane we waved them goodbye and waited until they were airborne before embarking on the vehicles and returning home where we knew another reunion was planned.

After spending some time with my children, we all gathered in the Great Hall to officially welcome our new residents with the now traditional welcome from Charles, the vicar. This was followed by a meal in the dining room prepared from the freshly arrived produce, then drinks and a chat around the table while the children watched a DVD.

Charles had enjoyed his trip to the Scillies, where he had time to meet with the few Navy chaplains who were fortunate enough to have been aboard a vessel at the time of the outbreak. He'd admitted that knowing he wasn't alone in his multi-tasking role of pastoral and spiritual care, along with being an important part of the community had helped lift his spirits even higher.

We all understood and were grateful for the burdens of sorrow he helped lift from everyone's shoulders, but not until he spoke about how meeting other similar people had helped him, did we realise that every time he selflessly listened to and helped ease our own pain through his cheerful and grounded help and advice, he must have been adding to the weight of his own sadness. We'd taken his ministrations for granted and had agreed between ourselves that we would plan a few quiet meetings when we knew he was elsewhere in the castle to come up with ways to be a better friend to him going forwards.

Diane and Tim settled in well. After a quick refresher course run by the sergeants to reacquaint Tim with the weapons he had used when he'd served, he was allocated roles between guard duty and drawing on his construction experience, the team responsible for the upkeep and maintenance of our ancient home, while Diane drew up a care plan for Nicky and presented us with a list of equipment we needed to find to help in the birth. As she hadn't had her first scan before the apocalypse started her due date hadn't been worked out, but Diane, pulling on all her experience, reckoned she had about a month to go, which would mean a date near to the middle of January.

So, with lists in hand and the looming deadline in mind, we began preparing for a mission.

CHAPTER SIX

Warwick was deserted as we drove the short way to the hospital. Not knowing what to expect we'd gone all-in on the mission as that could never be the wrong decision for all outcomes.

"Like a condom, eh, Tom?" Captain Clarke asked me as he surveyed the convoy before we left.

I frown, puzzled for a second before I understood.

"Better to have it and not need it instead of the other way around?" I asked.

"Precisely! Overkill is underrated!" he said before ordering us to move out.

Hardly any zombies at all were found wandering around the town now the weather had turned colder, but as we had no idea where they'd gone then caution was the name of the game. Clarke, after finding the small group of zombies at a farm a few weeks earlier, had been mulling over the theory that they were sheltering from the cold; bunched together in groups until spring arrived. He was convinced that he was on to something, but as no other evidence had been discovered all he had was a theory and no proof.

His concerns did mean he insisted that every fighting person we had available should go, which included the Marines, SAS and regular soldiers and a good portion of the trained knights. The castle was left poorly defended as a result with just the children, Maud, Charles, Marc and a few volunteers remaining behind, but as we would only be a five-minute drive away, it was hardly considered a risk compared to what dangers we may potentially find beyond the walls.

Both tractors and trailers, the bus, and two armoured cars were needed to transport our large force, with the Land Rover and Volvo being left behind as their scouting roles shouldn't be required.

Clarke had been chosen to lead the mission as he and his men had the most CQB, or close quarter battle, training and experience with everyone else in a support and backup role. The hospital wasn't as large as those in big cities, but its interconnected buildings still covered a large area with many doors, corridors and rooms that needed to be searched and cleared as we made our way through it.

The mood as we made our way to the hospital was good despite the daunting task that lay ahead. Glad to be doing something different, our spirits and confidence were high as we journeyed through the now very familiar town, but on pulling into the hospital entrance our mood changed as we got our game faces on.

The car park at the front was relatively clear of abandoned vehicles, a fact we knew from the few scouting missions undertaken when planning the mission, and we positioned the vehicles in a defensive ring outside the main entrance. The many zombies that had been seen shambling around the interior on visits weeks and months before were nowhere to be seen, and with the doors and weak points blocked previously, we knew that they should still be inside. It was the specifics of where they were we didn't know.

The plan was for us to enter as one group, clearing the way if necessary, to gain access to the various locations we had to visit to find what we needed. We had enough people with us to protect the scavengers and guard the multiple doors and unexplored corridors that we'd inevitably be surrounded by.

As we got into position, Andy shouted out to everyone, giving us one last reminder in case any of us had forgotten the speech he'd given only fifteen minutes before. "Remember your training and stay in formation. Stay alert and call out everything you see."

I knew he didn't mean to treat it like an eye spy game and keep shouting 'chair' or 'window' whenever we passed one but to call out if an area was clear or full of zombies, but the child in me giggled to myself at the wind up I could but wouldn't dare to start.

Adorned in armour and gripping my melee weapon of choice, I put my stupid thought away as I stacked up behind the SAS troopers as they unlocked the padlock and removed the chain we'd fitted during a visit months ago to secure the main front entrance doors. At the command issued from Andy once he'd checked we were all ready and in position, we entered the hospital as one unit

With no maps or plans to guide us we followed the signs that, when the place was open, directed the hundreds of daily visitors to their required department. First, we headed towards the maternity ward to gather the extensive list of items and equipment that Diane needed.

When I first saw that list, I had no idea what ninety percent of it was, so she had bravely and sensibly agreed to accompany us despite her complete lack of zombie fighting experience. Treated as the precious cargo she was, Clarke insisted she was positioned firmly in the middle of the phalanx of armed and armoured men and women entering the hospital and protected at all times.

We had dressed her in the thickest leather coat and trousers we had that fitted her in place of armour as these would give as much protection as possible against bites if the worst happened. For her personal protection she was wearing a belt with a knife and a hand axe attached to it, which following a short training session she now had the rudimentary skills to defend herself if things turned bad.

Tim hadn't been allowed to come despite him obviously wanting to so he could help protect his wife. He eventually understood and agreed to help guard the castle in our absence as he didn't yet possess the time-served experience of working together with the tactics we'd developed. Having an untried and untrained but nevertheless enthusiastic extra fighter wouldn't help us if things went wrong, especially if he was emotionally attached to one specific person on the mission.

The dim mid-winter light that entered through the windows created an eerie, semi-dark space full of foreboding shadows. Knowing it was likely to be dark in the hospital we turned on the head torches everyone had been issued with, and the multiple beams sent shafts of bright white light in the directions our heads turned. All doors that led to side rooms or other corridors we passed were systematically opened and cleared as we slowly, cautiously moved deeper into the maze.

Knocked over furniture and scattered, broken items told the story of the mass panic that most likely occurred on day one of the outbreak and each piece of evidence showed the terror that had washed through what was once a place of healing. Picked-clean piles of bones surrounded by ripped and tattered clothing and puddles of now dried and cracked dark red blood were the only sign that some had not made it. Dark sprays of blood marked the white walls like some macabre graffiti art in places, marking the scenes where teeth had ripped open arteries to signify another life ended in horror and pain.

Where were the zombies? I asked myself. Surely they haven't escaped? This place is as deserted as a factory on strike day!

I'd looked through the windows and seen plenty of zombies wandering the corridors when we'd visited before and had expected to find them either shambling around aimlessly or in the stupefied, static state we'd witnessed them in before when nothing aroused their need to feast on fresh flesh, and they reverted to power-saving mode, but every corridor we walked along and every side room we checked lay empty.

Following the signs we eventually entered the maternity ward. As soon as every room and corridor leading to and from it had been checked, we stationed guards at all the entrances and began scavenging. Diane went around pointing to items, telling us to "Grab that." or "Empty that cupboard" as she identified items for us to gather, ticking them off a list she had attached to a clipboard like some kind of scavenging overseer. For ease we stacked them on the beds we needed to take with us. They had wheels and so it made sense rather than struggling carrying the items, some of which were bulky and unwieldy. The raisable sides of the hospital beds ensured that things shouldn't fall off them as more and more items were stacked up and I was surprised at the volume of items we were collecting. Admittedly, my own birthing experiences were a fair few years ago and I'd had other things on my mind at the time, mainly the experience my wife Becky was going through, but I'd no idea how much equipment was needed. I supposed that every birth was different and we may as well cover all eventualities, so we kept loading everything Diane pointed out.

As soon as Diane was satisfied we had everything, Clarke got us back into formation. Forming a bed train we made our way back to the entrance and loaded our haul onboard the trailers.

"Good work so far everyone," Clarke said as the last item was lifted onboard. "Let's take five before we decide what to do next."

He turned to Diane who was on the trailer inspecting the loaded items and double checking her list.

"How's the list going, Diane?"

She looked up and replied with a smile of satisfaction on her face.

"All good. We could just do with heading to the emergency department to get a few items, then to the pharmacy to get some more meds."

Her face then turned serious with a frown.

"But if that's going to be too much we do have enough stuff already…I'm just thinking, since we're already here we should take the opportunity."

Diane had explained the long list she had drawn up when showing it to us, covering every eventuality she'd experience in her career. She knew she was going overboard on what was most likely needed but wanted to cover all outcomes to hopefully give us all the conclusion we wanted.

Clarke jumped onto the wheelarch of the armoured car and got our attention.

"Are we all okay to head in again?" he asked with a roguish grin on his face.

"Can't see a reason why not, Boss. Place looks deserted to me," Noel, one of his SAS troopers replied.

Everyone else agreed as the place was clearly safe, and Clarke organised us to get ready to enter the hospital again.

CHAPTER SEVEN

With headtorch beams once more lighting the way, we made our way following signs along empty corridors to the emergency department. We didn't need any more beds but as they had proved such a good transportation device, we utilised a few more of them to load the items the Diane pointed out to us as we searched. When she was satisfied we'd loaded everything useful, Clarke called out.

"Great job everyone. We just need to find the pharmacy next. It was signposted back the way we came, so if we carry on as we have been doing, we'll stop by it, grab what we need and head back home."

With a muted chorus of assent, we headed back the way we had come.

"Aw shit and it was going so well," I said as I saw the sign for the hospital's pharmacy pointing down a dark stair well. The pharmacy was clearly in a basement area of the hospital. Normally with lights and lifts, its location would have gone unnoticed by most, but now the dark subterranean well looked ominous and foreboding.

Clarke took one look at the situation and took the lead.

"Nothing to worry about. My boys and half the knights will head down there. The rest of you form a perimeter and guard the stairwell," he said, peering down the black hole of the staircase before adding, "Maybe be a good time to get those lamp things out, they'll give us a wider field of vision than torch beams alone."

He turned and pointed to the group of knights, me included, who were nearest the stairs.

"You lot with me, the rest stay here."

After a few disappointed looks from those not chosen he said, "I only picked them because they were closer, so get over it. Let's get on with it, folks."

We waited a few minutes while everyone got into position and we retrieved the lamps from rucksacks. The lamps were rechargeable work lights which could either be carried or the handle used to rest them on the ground. We had found they came in useful around the castle when working in dark corners or rooms and it saved the hassle of trailing extension cables around the place when tasks were being done.

The SAS led us as we descended the stairs, torch beams penetrating the darkness beyond the ball of light created by the lamps that lit about a ten-meter radius around us, giving us the small comfort that at least we wouldn't be taken completely by surprise.

"At least it's a bit warmer down here," I said to no one in particular.

We walked down a corridor decorated by the dancing shadows caused by our bodies blocking the lights. Exhaled breaths no longer turned into steam in the cold air and our footsteps in the closed confines of the corridor sounded painfully loud as a large sign overhead told us the pharmacy was through a set of double doors coming up on the left. This was the first door on the corridor we had found so we knew that with our backs protected by those up the staircase, the only threat would come from either the pharmacy itself or the long corridor stretching into the darkness.

With a few of us blocking the corridor ahead, Clarke and his men stacked up as they prepared to enter and clear the pharmacy. Diane stood in the centre of the group, nervously looking around, her eyes peering to penetrate the darkness and her hand hovering near the comforting presence of the axe on her belt. Pushing the door slowly open they entered the pharmacy.

Thirty tense seconds later the 'all clear' was called from within and Clarke strode out purposefully.

"How do you fancy pushing the perimeter further down the corridor whilst we get what we need? I don't like the feel of it down here…it's giving me the creeps if I'm honest," he said to me, his voice echoing down the dark passage.

His comments echoed my own sentiments. Maybe it was just the darkness, but the place felt downright eerie and intimidating. I didn't really want to be there, but it made sense to get as much as we could as we were down here already.

I turned to those around me.

"Shall we?"

Normally every question asked of us got an overwhelmingly positive reply, because from experience we never would put ourselves into a situation we couldn't handle. We knew in our hearts that if we came across zombies even in the corridor's close confines, then our shield wall tactics and zombie killing experience would prevail…but there was something about doing it in the dark basement area of an abandoned hospital that set all our nerves tingling with apprehension.

Damn horror movies.

Even though most grumbled and muttered, expressing their obvious delight at venturing further into the scary darkness, they all organised themselves into formation and prepared to move onwards.

Hefting my shield higher in the front row we began walking slowly four abreast, our shields touching and filling the corridor in front of us, advancing down the corridor until a set of double doors appeared out of the gloom blocking the way ahead. The sign on the door stated, 'No entry. Authorised personnel only' and a keypad on the wall indicated it required a code or keycard held against the reader to gain entrance. Peering through the glass panel I could see the corridor beyond was clear. I pushed the door anyway – ever the optimist – and was surprised when it moved.

My surprise was evident as someone behind me offered the logical answer.

"Magnetic locks need power to work."

I kicked myself for not realising the obvious and pushed the door wider.

The corridor turned more utilitarian with painted concrete block walls showing what the rest of the hospital looked like underneath its hygienically panelled walls, causing our footsteps and metallic chinks of our armour to echo back at us even louder than before.

Ahead, the corridor turned ninety degrees and ended at another set of doors. The door was covered in a host of signs warning that entry was restricted to maintenance staff only and to the dangers of gas, electricity and high-pressure pipes, so it wasn't difficult to work out this was probably the main plant area of the hospital where the heating and electrical systems were housed.

With no glass panel in the door I couldn't see what lay beyond it. I reached out and pushed the door, it moved slightly but stopped as if something was blocking it, so instinctively I grabbed the handle on it and pulled.

My headtorch beam shone straight into a zombie's face. Shocked, I let go of the handle and staggered back as my light still shining through the now slowly closing door showed the corridor beyond it was packed with the undead who were now all turning in our direction.

"Z..z..zombies!" I stammered, the pitch of my voice raised by shock and the surge of adrenalin injected into my bloodstream. "Fucking hundreds of the bastards!"

On my shout everyone tried to step backward, pushing into those behind. Torch beams flashed unsteadily in all directions until Ian, bawling at the top of his voice stopped the initial panic.

"Hold position!" he yelled, shocking us back into calm and restoring a more dignified semblance of order.

The door in front of me began to open and, for the first time, we all heard the wheezing, growling groan emitted from dead throats. The stench of their rotting bodies washed over us like a sickening wave of putridness, causing a few in our group to retch and gag uncontrollably as the air that had been sealed in the room was released.

"Shields up, we can hold them back," Ian hollered again.

Training kicked in and nerves hardened as we found ourselves once again facing a horde, only this time in claustrophobic conditions with only one escape route. The door opened wider as more pushed forwards, the first few stepping into our lights as they approached the shield wall which blocked the corridor from wall to wall. As I had been the unfortunate one to open the door, I naturally found myself in the front line of the shield wall holding my own shield up, interlocked with my neighbours and brandishing my mace with my free hand.

The biggest problem facing us aside from the tightly packed ranks of undead was the tight confines of the corridor, and the addition of the low ceiling above our heads which made swinging our weapons difficult. Try as I might, I couldn't get enough force behind my swing to do enough damage to kill any of their front rank.

My mace damaged heads, causing rotten pieces of flesh to carve off them or eyes to pop out as my weakened blows struck them. Simon stood beside me, his preferred weapon being a sword, was having more success stabbing forwards and piercing skulls with most thrusts. The problem was exacerbated as those facing us were being pushed out of the doorway with such force by the pressure of the others behind trying to exit the plant room. Unable to hold back the mass by sheer bodyweight alone, we had to take a step back or we would be engulfed as the wave of undead washed over us.

Grunts of effort joined the hissing, moaning sounds they made to fill the tight confines of the corridor with a deafening noise.

Ian, standing on my other side, swore and screamed as he too tried to deliver killing blows, but his usual powerful swing was hampered as much as mine was, making it harder to kill one with each swipe of his heavy battle axe. It was taking him two or three attempts to damage the skull enough to destroy the brain, and our lack of speed in killing them spelled disaster if nothing changed.

He quickly appraised our situation and ordered the whole group to start stepping back in time to his shouts. Frustrated at being unable to use my mace I called behind for someone to pass a sword forwards. Holding my mace over my head a few moments later I felt a hand on my wrist and someone calling me to let go of my weapon. Opening my grip, I felt the mace being removed and another handle being placed in my open palm. I tightened my fist and lowered my arm, holding it out in front of me and quickly glanced at the sword I had been given.

I immediately began thrusting it forwards at the snarling, rotting, dead faces pushing towards me, this time killing with most thrusts as the razor-sharp point cut through eye sockets and skulls. As soon as one fell to be trampled under the masses following it, another appeared reaching out hungrily towards us. My anxiety level was rising, but so far, I'd managed to keep the panic at bay. We were holding the horde back but were in about as tricky a situation as we had been in for a long time.

"Someone, go and tell the others at the pharmacy to finish up and move out! There's no way we're gonna be able to hold this lot back with our weapons. The stairs are our only hope, tell 'em to get ready!" Ian shouted.

I was concentrating too much on my own situation to pay any attention to the reply as my sole focus was aimed at thrusting my borrowed sword at as many heads as I could. Step by step we yielded to the masses before us and retreated back down the corridor. Shields pushed up against our backs by those behind us helped those of us in the front rank stay upright as we stumbled and shuffled backwards. Ian looked over his shoulder, his height enabling him to see over heads to the rear of our too-small group.

"Fuck me this is not fun anymore! The corner's coming up," Ian shouted, his breathing now ragged and tired from the effort.

"When we get there, everyone move back quickly to create space between us and them. Then we'll use our guns to hold them back."

This was a tactic we had practised even though we hadn't found the need to use it so far. All of us had a handgun in a holster attached somewhere on our kit. The drill was, if our normal tactics weren't effective and we were threatened with being overwhelmed, we would all step back a few paces, increasing the distance between us and our enemies and open fire to quickly kill as many as we could and give us the breathing space for those with heavier weapons to step in and hopefully relieve us.

I glanced down between thrusts to comfort myself that my handgun was still in its holster strapped across the front of my chest. Our marksmanship and proficiency with them was improving steadily thanks to the regular training sessions we all attended at the newly created firing range in the castle grounds. Even though they had an effective range of fifty meters, in reality it was hard for even the most proficient marksman to make consistent kills at that range. Most of our training was at a range of twenty-five meters or less, knowing that if we were forced to use our primary backup shooting weapon it was because either our main weapon had failed due to a stoppage or was out of ammunition and the user had no time to reload, then whatever we were shooting at would be much closer, so a quick draw-and-fire discipline with our hand weapons was essential.

Slowly we retreated along the corridor leaving a trail of bodies instantly trampled under the shambling feet of more undead behind them.

"We're at the corner!" someone shouted from behind us.

"Get ready to disengage on my command!" Ian bellowed breathlessly.

I sensed rather than saw the corner approaching as the light emitted from some torches changed as those at the rear went round the sharp bend.

"All ready?" Ian screamed.

Those of us in the front line seemed to redouble our killing efforts as we knew the end to our current predicament was close. When the shouts of affirmation from eager throats washed over us, I felt the pressure of the shield pressed against my back ease as whoever was behind me changed their stance in preparation for our quick dash backwards.

"On three," Ian shouted between swings.

The weight of the shield against my back disappeared entirely when the count reached three and following Ian's quickened cadence calling the step on our retreat, we shuffled awkwardly but quickly round the corner until we had created a five-meter gap between ourselves and the zombies.

I dropped my shield on the ground for it to lean against my legs, shouted for someone to grab my sword as I held it behind me whilst reaching for my pistol. With a much-practised technique I drew it and as soon as I felt the sword leaving my grip, charged it, got my feet into position and pointed it downrange.

The five-meter gap we had created had already closed in the few seconds it took for me to get ready. The shooting was at point blank range and as soon as a head was in my sightline I pulled the trigger, punching a neat red hole in the forehead of the one closest to me.

Simon, Ian and Dave who formed the front rank with me all fired at virtually the same instant and the zombies facing us collapsed as lead mashed brains. At such a close range the bullets smashed through skulls and punched into more behind. One fell as its brain was also destroyed and the other two staggered with the impact but remained upright, pushed towards us by their undead comrades behind.

I moved my aim a fraction and pulled the trigger as soon as I was lined up on the next snarling face. The concussive crack of the weapons discharging in the confined, hard-walled corridor was punishing on the ears and senses, but it was either suffer that noise or get eaten so we kept firing.

At that point-blank range it was almost impossible to miss. With every shot fired another fell which hampered the progress of the others behind. Zombies fell over the twice dead corpses now collapsed on the floor, but the force of yet more still pushing from behind continued to propel the rest towards us. The Glocks we all carried held seventeen rounds and our extensive training showed when I subconsciously knew I only had a few rounds left in the weapon and was reaching for another magazine to swap them as soon as it clicked empty.

I was halfway through my next magazine when a firm tap on my shoulder and a voice I recognised as Clarkes told me that as soon as I was ready, he would take my place. Looking ahead I could see that our sustained close-range fire had started to hold the pack back as the bodies were building up, forming an obstacle that finally began to slow their rate of advance.

"Two more shots," I yelled in reply, taking aim and snapping off another round.

As my pistol clicked on an empty chamber I pushed backwards, keeping my eyes fixed on the threat and trusting that Clarke was ready.

He was, and he pushed past me to take my place in the line with his rifle already raised, finger on the trigger, to begin firing into the mass facing us.

I stood there, more than a little in shock at the events of the past minutes as one by one, Ian, Dave and Simon backed out of the line and were replaced by one of Clarke's men standing behind them. The muted sounds of their supressed weapons firing rapidly gave instant relief from the sharp, concussive cracks of our handguns that had been abusing our senses. Shaking my head to try and rid my ears of the cotton wool that had seemed to fill them I looked around as my senses started to return slowly. We were still in an underground corridor facing hundreds of zombies and needed to get out of there and back to the castle as a matter of urgency.

A second rank of soldiers stood ready to relieve those on the front line but everyone else had moved back, and in the light cast by their torches and lamps I could see they were making their way up the stairs. Pete Newman, Clarke's sergeant, was with the second rank of soldiers standing ready and patted my shoulder to get my attention.

"Good work!"

He smiled and issued one of his stock phrases which all NCOs seemed to be able to produce from their back catalogue at such times to calm and focus minds, but this one was adapted to our current situation.

"Makes me wish I'd joined the submarine service! No z's at the bottom of the sea!"

Once my brain, which was still slowly resetting itself, comprehended what he'd said, I grinned at the stupidness of his remark which clicked my recovery rate up a few notches.

"What now?" I asked, back in business mode again.

Newman pointed to the gun still in my hand with its slide locked back.

"Try reloading that for a start, then stay behind us in case we need you boys again. I've told them up top to find anything they can use to block the stairwell," he said, pointing to the wall where my borrowed sword was lit in the beam of his headtorch. "Grab that and get ready."

Feeling like a raw recruit for having not immediately reloaded my weapon I grinned an apology at him, swapped out the magazine, and holstered it before grabbing the sword and positioning myself at the back of the fighting line.

Rifles handled by experienced soldiers had already succeeded in dropping enough of the first rows of the mass of zombies illuminated by torchlight, but they had more than ample reinforcements. The horde stretched into the distance, filling the corridor completely with an innumerable advancing wave of undead corpses.

The barrier of their fallen comrades failed to hold them back, and I watched as the pressure of their combined bodyweight began to force the pile forwards like a bulldozer pushing an ever-growing pile of dirt onwards in front of its blade.

Shouts of 'changing' were the only words issued by the front rank as they maintained a withering rate of fire, expertly swapping empty magazines for fully charged ones before resuming their relentless defence.

Clarke calmly called the retreat step by step, slowly backing us up the corridor to maintain a safe distance from the leading edge of snapping death until we reached the stairs where Newman had positioned others to act as a rearguard ready for when the front rank disengaged.

"Captain! We have you covered," he bellowed over the sound of gunfire.

Clarke glanced behind him to check their escape route.

"Break contact front! Break contact front!" he roared, and the gunfire rose to a crescendo.

They had been firing controlled single shots, each one finding a target, but on the order to break contact his troopers selected fully automatic with a flick of their thumbs and poured torrents of red-hot lead into the mass facing them in just a few seconds.

We were told never to use the full auto function on our weapons unless you were in an absolute dire situation as it was just a waste of precious ammunition, but the purchase of precious seconds at the cost of plentiful ammunition was simple mathematics.

In seconds magazines had been emptied and the men turned and with Clarke bringing up the rear they ascended the stairs past Newman and the rear guard. The devastating automatic fire had overwhelmed the front rows of zombies causing then to pile up, stopping the advance of the others behind for about ten seconds, but that ten seconds was all the time we needed to prepare for what was happening next.

CHAPTER EIGHT

Everyone at the top of the stairs had grabbed whatever was close to hand to make a barricade, so when the last person reached the top they began throwing chairs, tables, signs, basically anything they could find that was heavy and not bolted to the floor down the stairwell. The more that got thrown the more they tangled together to form a solid mesh of a barrier. When the last item, a vending machine, had been heaved over the edge, we gathered at the top and shone our torches down the dark well of the staircase to see it blocked from floor to ceiling.

I could hear the zombies below and waited to see if the barrier would hold, unaware I was holding my breath until a wave of dizziness threatened to wobble me. The barricade shifted and heaved as the mass of enemy surged against it but all that seemed to do was compress it tighter together.

The group stood silently together for a few seconds all absorbing the fact that we had survived another close encounter when Clarke summed up our escape in his own individual manner.

"Gentlemen, I believe the unstoppable force has met the immovable object! Well, that was all rather exciting…shall we head home for a cup of tea?"

With a ripple of eager positive affirmation we gathered up all the bags of supplies and pushed the beds full of equipment along the corridors to the hospital entrance, eager to put the hospital and the subterranean horrors far behind us. Once we'd securely chained and padlocked the doors we loaded up the vehicles, abandoned the beds we'd used as shopping trolleys in the car park, and made our way back home.

Looking back at the padlocked doors my mind wandered to the sheer force so many undead bodies could generate, and I knew that if they somehow freed themselves from the lower levels then no mere chain and padlock would keep them inside.

Gathered in the Great Hall with a steaming mug of tea in my hand we discussed the day's adventure. It had, on the face of it, been a complete success, having retrieved everything, and more, from Diane's list, so hopefully when Nicky's time came we'd be as prepared as possible.

"I knew it. They must be sheltering from the cold. It's the only explanation as far as I can see," Clarke blurted out with a note of triumph, unable to contain himself any longer as he interrupted my account of the underground battle to a group of eager listeners.

"Now we know where they're most likely to be, we can go get the buggers," Clarke added with bloodthirsty relish.

This drew a sharp intake of breath from everyone who heard his words, but Becky was the first to respond and summed it up in her characteristically blunt way.

"So…after just about escaping from a massed horde of them, resorting to blocking a stairwell so you could get away, you want to risk more lives by going into every pitch-black basement you find and do it all again?"

He nodded warily at her, not sure where the conversation was going. Becky smiled sweetly, disarming the officer.

"Captain, may I ask a personal question?" she said sweetly.

"Of course, please d—"

"Are you bloody stupid or just plain thick?" Becky snapped venomously.

I winced inwardly, recognising that particular tone as announcing her 'don't even think about it' mood.

"Yes, we kill them when we can," Becky continued, "but it must be done on our own terms. It's far too dangerous to go into every dark hole you find just to see if anything in there wants to eat you."

I could see Becky was building her way up to really giving him her opinion, when Tan, Clarkes wife moved to stand beside her.

If Clarke was ignorant of Becky's glare and what it foretold, then he understood Tan's matching look.

"Andy," Tan said sternly. "I don't know what the hell you're thinking right now, but you've all just had a close call and the only thing as far as I can see you've gained from it is information. Now correct me if I'm wrong, but you're always telling me information is key to any successful operation you undertake. Now…take a minute, dial back your bloody ego, and let this new information sink in before you run off and get someone killed. The one thing we need to do right now is tell all the other groups out there to avoid those kinds of places. If we don't tell them and they aren't as lucky as you lot and all get out alive, then it's on us. It's on you, Andy."

Clarke demonstrated an instinct for survival by not disagreeing with his wife and nodded reluctantly.

With a more subdued atmosphere filling the room we finished our mugs of tea with more general chatter, unloaded our haul, and began transforming the room allocated to be our new maternity hospital.

By the end of the day Diane was satisfied that everything was in order, and we now had a facility that was more than fit for purpose.

After dinner, aside from those on guard duty, we gathered in the Great Hall for our end of day debriefing and socialising. Clarke had informed all the groups about our basement zombie ordeal, but he had obviously been mulling over the situation while working and he called out for some attention amidst the jovial chatter the room was full of.

"I've been thinking about today," he announced, glancing at his wife before continuing.

"And now that I have… reconsidered immediate action…"

He waited for the chuckles to subside before continuing.

"I believe running off and hunting them down in whatever dark corner they're hiding in is probably not our most appropriate course of action. We now have a good idea where they've disappeared to, and that gives us an advantage in that we know where they definitely aren't, which is wandering around in the open. We haven't come across any serious groups of them since the weather turned cold, and now we know why."

I frowned, having given the issue some thought of my own. We knew where they were hiding, but I didn't see a reason why.

"They are hunkering down, just as we are for the winter. Call it a hibernation of sorts. What'll happen to them in the spring is anyone's guess, but for the first time we can plan around them not being a threat for at least the next few months," Clarke said.

He paused for a few seconds as he waited for us to second guess him, but when no one responded he continued.

"What I propose is we start looking for areas where they might be hiding, not to kill them," he added hurriedly, raising both hands as a murmur of dissent grew rapidly.

"Not to hunt them, but simply to trap them where they are. Then, when the warmer weather arrives, if they haven't rotted away, they won't be able to escape. If we go out armed with locks, chains or whatever we'll need to stop them getting out from wherever they are then it can't do any harm."

"But…Andy…" Jamie said. "There's got to be thousands of places they could be at! How do we get round them all?"

Clarke shrugged.

"Good point. It's only an idea for now, and in all honesty I was only thinking of our immediate surrounding areas, but I do see your point about thinking further afield. What do you suggest?"

"Weeeeell…" Jamie said, drawing out the word as he gave himself time to think. "I can't see a problem with trying it locally to start off…when we go further afield we can just secure any place we find when passing. We'll never get them all but at least it's a step in the right direction?"

Ian lumbered over after helping himself to another drink from the table.

"I don't think it'll do any harm," he said affably. "But what about the land we're meant to be clearing behind this wall thing they are building? Wouldn't now be the best time to do it? We know where they won't be, which is out in the open, and apart from a few smaller towns, the place is mainly countryside and small villages where we could identify any potential hiding places without too many issues."

We all looked at Ian who, for once, had actually come up with a good idea and not just a prank or general tomfoolery which was his usual contribution to the group.

Since the meeting in the Scillies where we had promised to send a detachment to assist in the clearing once the wall was built. The project had started, and we were following its progress avidly on our regular radio calls to the Scillies. The diggers and earth-movers were continuing to raise and extend the berm, following the line of the main road while along its top, other gangs of work-ers toiled to build the secure fence. We were told the work was going to plan and speeding up as everyone became more profi-cient, solving problems as they arose. Their aim was to complete the basic construction first and then to improve it along its length, adding the guard towers and utilising existing buildings along the route as barracks for the sentries.

Ian's suggestion had merit. Now we had the maternity unit set up, apart from local patrols, shift changes at the Brough's and general maintenance around the castle, we had no big jobs planned until the weather improved. So the general consensus was one of, 'why don't we get on with it?'.

On our evening radio call with the Scillies the plan was approved, and we were told to get on with organising things our end while they made similar preparations.

In the morning we held a meeting to discuss and plan the logistics involved in taking a convoy of vehicles and personnel all the way to the tip of Cornwall, and once a map had been spread on the table the route became obvious. It retraced almost exactly the route that had started our adventures all those months ago when Becky, our kids and I had escaped St Agnes, finding first Shawn, then Eddie, and all the others on the way. The end of the wall at Hayle, near St Ives was only thirty or so miles further down the road from where we'd started out.

It gave me an odd sensation of nostalgia, as if returning there would bring my story full-circle, and something about that bothered me.

On a map it all looked simple: drive to Bristol on the well-established route, continue down the M5 motorway on a route we and others had travelled so we knew where to divert off it due to blockages, then continue along the A30. We chose not to use the A38, the road we'd used before, as that had more single carriageway sections and also passed through the larger city of Plymouth where previously we'd turned off it to get to Bickley barracks.

The issue was the distance. Even back when the world was normal and you timed your journey right to avoid the usual holiday traffic snarl-ups, the trip would probably take four to five hours.

Now we would be in a slow-moving convoy, diverting around known obstacles and probably encountering others on the way, the journey was going to take much, much longer.

At the meeting in the Scillies it had been agreed that we would have the say on how many people we could spare for the operation. We'd be a long way from home and our own security was naturally top priority, but the more people we could provide to help then the quicker the job would be done. Between the Brough's and the castle we had a formidable and sizeable force of trained personnel, both military and civilian available, but how many we would need to ensure the safety of those that remained behind was a difficult question to answer.

We were reasonably sure that zombies wouldn't be a threat, as we had a good idea they were all sheltering, as we were, from the cold weather, so the threat of a large horde penetrating our formidable defences was minimal.

It was the threat from the living we couldn't predict.

Since the attack at the Broughs we'd encountered no other rogue bands, but it didn't mean they weren't out there searching for someone to raid. We were reasonably confident that the defences we had in place with mounted machine guns and grenade machine guns that lined our high walls, to the mortar positions both settlements now had set up, that any attack, unless they had heavy weaponry would be repulsed. Still, we couldn't ignore the risk, so after much debate we agreed that sending fifty percent of our fighters would be an acceptable number.

We did briefly discuss the notion to evacuate the Brough's entirely which would enable us to provide more fighters, but the effort to relocate all their equipment and stores back to the castle was deemed too much for the benefit of just a few additional people. Besides, our numbers were only complementing the hundreds of fighters the Scillies and Fort Bristol were capable of providing, but we'd been asked to help, so we wanted to do the best we could.

Next, we decided what vehicles we'd take to get there. Earlier that morning we'd been told that Fort Bristol would send out a patrol to check and, if necessary, clear the route all the way to St Ives. The route to the furthest tip of England was, in the future, going to be an important road once the safe zone had been created as it would provide the most economical way to transport goods and people between the bases. Clearing that route had always been the plan, therefore it was just being brought forward.

The engineers at Fort Bristol had already got plans underway to clear the few large blockages we'd encountered on our initial journey that still prevented travel down sections of the M5 between us and Bristol. Large bulldozers had been located, and they were on the hunt for some heavy transport lorries to move them to where they were needed.

It wasn't just the places where the motorway was blocked completely which required attention. On our journey up we'd cleared narrow lanes through some jams, and it made sense if these were widened as well, future convoys wouldn't have to slow down to navigate through the tangles of vehicles. When all that was done, it should decrease the journey time between Bristol and Warwick by a good amount.

This was great news as we wouldn't need to plan for that, just the quickest and safest way to transport over thirty of us through over two hundred miles of, hopefully, zombie and obstruction-free country. The obvious choice was to take a selection of our zombie-proofed armoured cars as they were armed to the teeth with the addition of many mounted weapons and would provide a fast and reasonably comfortable ride for the drivers and passengers. An army lorry towing a fuel bowser would accompany us to carry our supplies and extra equipment enabling us to survive independently.

With all the decisions made we informed the Scillies we'd be ready to go when they gave us the green light. Christmas and New Year were fast approaching though, so we were told it would most likely be in early January.

Over the next few days some of us prepared the vehicles and arranged who from the Brough's were going to come with us. Clarke and Digby also started to conduct expeditions around Warwick and the surrounding areas to secure any buildings with the potential to be sheltering zombies in their dark depths as a means of checking the feasibility of the idea.

Taking chains, padlocks, timber and tools for boarding up they finessed the best way to barricade the buildings they decided needed securing.

However, after only a few days of effort, we decided to scale back the idea as the sheer number of potential places discovered in the relatively small town of Warwick made the job too daunting and time consuming to consider rolling out on a larger scale for what was only a theory.

Besides, we decided, if the zombies emerged in the warmer weather, we could deal with them as we had many times before with our tried and tested routines.

CHAPTER NINE

"Heave! Put your backs into it!" Maud commanded as ten of us struggled with ropes and lengths of timber to pull and push the massive Christmas tree upright and into the bracket we had fabricated to hold it into place.

"It's going!" someone shouted as it started to overbalance and tilt alarmingly to one side. Gravity took over and those in the way of the rapidly descending tree let go of the ropes and desperately tried to scramble out of its path in a pure act of self-preservation. It fell with a soft rush and a creaking of bending boughs.

"Bloody hell, Maud," I exclaimed, wiping sweat from my face. "Can't we just chop a smaller one down? Someone's going to get hurt!"

"It'll be you fetching a mischief if you suggest that again, Thomas! No. This beautiful room deserves a beautiful tree, and this is it," she said waving at the fallen article.

I didn't argue, as I'd heard how long she'd spent wandering the grounds with Willie until declaring she had located the perfect tree before ordering it cut down and brought to the castle.

"I'm sure this room would have had similar trees here in the past. It's just that it would have been put up by real men and not a load of moaning ninnies like you lot. Now get on with it and try ag—"

She was cut off by a muted call from somewhere in the green pile that now lay across the room in a voice that was unmistakenly Ian's.

"Errr…help? Can someone get me out please. I've got a branch poking up my arse and it hasn't even bought me a drink yet!"

We all burst out laughing and Jamie called out, pointing to the waving branches indicating where Ian was struggling to free himself.

"Bugger me. I thought the fairy was meant to be on top of the tree, not underneath it," Jamie said.

We considered leaving him there for a while as payback for his continuous pranks, but Maud was more concerned about the damage he might cause to her tree than to any harm that may befall Ian.

Lifting an end up with some effort a very bedraggled Ian, covered in pine needles, rolled out from where he'd been trapped. He took the ribbing we gave him about being too fat to move out of the way with his usual smirk and shrug of the shoulders as he lay on the ground like an elephant seal, as he comically tried to roll over and regain his feet.

"That's enough of that. Now stop messing about and get this tree up," Maud commanded before Ian had managed to regain his feet.

She was on a mission, and we all knew better than to mess with her when she was in that mood, so we all got into position to try again. The experience gained from our last failure had taught us the vagaries of dealing with an unwieldly, obstinate tree that just wanted to lie on the floor and not be upright ever again.

With much effort and colourful language we eventually had it secured in position.

By the end of the day and with help from excited children, the castle was fully bedecked with Christmas decorations. The last act was to put the star on top of the tree. Maud, despite our protests about the safety of her ascending the tall ladder, insisted that it was her job.

"I've put the star on every tree I've had since I was old enough to walk, and I'm not stopping now," she stated obstinately as she headed to the ladder.

Willie hovered beneath her nervously as she climbed, ready to catch her if she lost her balance. We all watched with trepidation as she reached the top and stretched out precariously over twenty feet in the air to balance the star on its peak.

The cheer we let out was more of a sense of relief she hadn't fallen than seeing the large star in position.

None of us had considered it, but the reaction to the lights being turned on and filling the hall with sparkles that illuminated the room as darkness descended outside seemed to reach to most of us on a deeply emotional level.

Putting up the Christmas decorations was such a traditional family event most households kept up, that the sheer normality of it all hit home. After months of fighting to survive, seeing friends and strangers alike ripped apart before our eyes, counting our survival hopes in minutes rather than hours until our group grew and hours became weeks and months. After everything we'd been through, after all the suffering and violence, something so simple was suddenly very meaningful.

Decorating a tree surrounded by our new family, safe and well in the grandest of surroundings prompted emotion-fuelled tears to flow, and hugs were exchanged as we marked another milestone.

Apart from guard duty all other work was stopped as every available hand was commandeered by Maud for a multitude of jobs. All had to be completed by the unmoveable deadlines she announced as she bustled everywhere, determined to make the fast-approaching Christmas period as good as it could be.

By mutual agreement all adults agreed to forgo the expectation of getting any presents. Every house in Warwick would have yielded a host of suitable gifts if raided, but receiving a gift that belonged to a most likely dead person would put something of a stain on the item. We all agreed that just being alive was the best present any of us could ask for, but the children were a different matter.

We had all ages to think about, from Sarah who was under one to teenagers, and the best solution we could think of was to dispatch an expedition to a local retail estate that contained a toy superstore. When it had been declared zombie-free, the mothers in the group in charge of selection bustled around pushing trollies, armed with lists of ideas while the men mainly goofed around with bigger toys as they pretended to be on perimeter security. The one good idea the men had while playing on a pool table was to create a games room for the children.

When the weather was bad the children, when not doing the various chores they were expected to perform depending on their age, mostly played games like hide and seek to fill their time when not under direct adult supervision. This did lead to things occasionally getting damaged by being knocked into, or a tribe of charging about children getting under the adults' feet, or disturbing the sleep of someone who was trying to get some rest following a late night or early morning guard shift.

Creating a room which they could use as a club house and entertainment area was quickly deemed a good idea and there was a large room we knew of that was sitting empty far away from the living quarters that would be ideal for such a purpose.

We selected pool tables, table tennis tables, table football tables and other items for the older children and a big range of large toys suitable for the younger age group to enjoy. It really was like setting children loose in a sweet shop. We'd come up with an idea and as everything was free for the taking, we got a little carried away and the trailer started to resemble a smash and grab at a toy shop, which it basically was. Eventually the group drove back to the castle in high spirits discussing the best way to distract the children as we snuck everything inside.

The future games room mysteriously had a lock fitted overnight to stop our surprise being discovered and a shift of volunteers began wrapping the mountain of recovered gifts while others built and positioned all the games rooms items for the big reveal on Christmas Day.

The importance of the fast-approaching big day electrified the whole community with more than the usual Christmas cheer anticipation of a few days off work, spending time eating and drinking too much while putting up with extended family dynamics.

Carols were spontaneously sung as one person hummed a tune which soon turned into a choir made up of whoever was in earshot.

The mood was good. The mood was festive. The mood was full of hope.

"Mom! Dad! Get up!"

The children shrieked far too early in the morning, the excitement of Christmas making their internal alarm activate way too early.

I groaned and opened an eye, noticing the lack of light seeping around the edges of the curtain of our room indicating the early hour. I pulled the duvet over my head and gave Becky a hug as she too squirmed in protest at the way too early and very loud wake up call.

"Happy Christmas, darling," I whispered in her ear.

I let out an explosion of breath as three overexcited bodies launched themselves at the bed, elbows and knees hitting parts of my body I'd rather they hadn't, just to make sure we'd heard them and weren't still sleeping.

We weren't the only ones up early and as we trudged bleary eyed downstairs, attempting to sound cheerful as the last vestiges of sleep left us. Voices from downstairs and emanating from other rooms told a similar story being played out as the excitement of the day woke up all the other children in high spirits.

Maud, as always awake before most, was already bustling around. Cheerfully assisted as ever by Willie, who was wearing a

Christmas hat and a big smile, she hugged everyone that emerged and indicated the trays of tea and coffee she already had set up for those who needed the early morning caffeine rush to feel fully alive. It was hard not to be affected by the buzz of excitement filling the place, and as the drinks did their job the room began to fill with people, laughter and conversation.

The schedule for the day had been dictated by Maud, and as no one dared to disagree with her, we followed her plan.

Once breakfast had been consumed in shifts the whole community gathered in the chapel for a church service conducted by Charles. A sweep of the grounds beforehand gave us the confidence to briefly pause our eternal guard duty as it would be unfair to exclude anyone from the service.

As expected Charles delivered a humorous sermon, which though it gave a nod to the religious significance of the day, was mainly about giving thanks for what we'd collectively achieved. The children were ushered back into the Great Hall as those on guard duty headed to their allocated posts and the main day began.

Presents were distributed to the very excited youngsters including a very overexcited young Sarah who, the same as most babies from memory, seemed to prefer the wrapping paper more than the actual present. The excitement level reached a climax when the games room we had created for them in secret was unveiled.

As we'd all hoped, it was a great hit and congratulating ourselves for the idea, we retreated back to the main rooms leaving the children to noisily explore their new space to prepare for the

Christmas dinner which a lot of planning and preparation had gone into.

Again, it had been agreed that if we made sure we monitored the CCTV system then we could forgo guarding the walls for the duration of the meal. The renewed system gave those watching the screens complete coverage of the grounds and castle, and therefore ample warning of any danger approaching. The two people monitoring the banks of screens would change regularly so no one missed out on the fun.

The meal was a great success as we all crammed around the main table and extra tables that had to be set up to accommodate us all in the dining room, eating far too much food and for those excused duties for the day, drinking far too much.

Horace and Princess both stole so much food that they were incapacitated for a while and lay sprawled by the roaring fire in a food coma. That was until they were both ejected for a while, as the rich food had had an effect on their digestive systems that was bad enough for those caught in range of the noxious clouds they kept producing to have trouble not gagging.

We had struck a deal among the community that those with children, or those not of a partying disposition, would have Christmas day and Boxing Day off and those who didn't or were known for their love of socialising, would be excused duties on New Year's Eve and the following day to recover.

The agreement worked and everyone had chance to take some time away from the reality that would soon face us outside the walls again when the festive period was over.

CHAPTER TEN

Waving through the windscreen of the armoured car I drove at the people ready to close the outer gate, I followed the lead vehicle in the convoy as we set off. Becky sat in the passenger seat next to me and wiped away a tear as she took one last look back at the castle disappearing from view.

This was the first time we'd left the children in the care of others, but she'd insisted on joining the expedition. Even though she had proved her bravery and fighting skills on many occasions, recently she had found herself spending more time in the castle as the need for action was replaced by the need to make it a home for us all.

She was conscious of this, and the fact I had spent just as much time away from the castle as others made her decide it was her turn to do her bit outside the walls. She was upset about leaving the children but knew that they would be well cared for under the supervision of Maud and, more importantly, well protected by those chosen to stay behind.

The mix of knights and soldiers behind us chatted and laughed between themselves, excited after the break we'd all had over Christmas to be doing something again. Their laughter brightened the mood, and in the front of the vehicle Becky smiled at me as I asked her for the umpteenth time if she was okay.

"Yes, love. I'm fine," she said wiping away her last tear. "The kids will have a whale of a time with everyone else. I know Maud has plenty planned to distract them. Anyway, it's not like I won't be able to speak to them every day."

She paused in thought, then looked sternly at me.

"They understand it's more important for me to come along to stop you doing anything stupid than it is to stay behind. They've only got one dad, who seems to think he's some super-hero special forces knight who can keep up with young men half his age…"

"Whoa!" I interrupted her laughing. "You were admiring my new physique last night if I remember correctly."

She sent a half-hearted slap towards my arm with an embar-rassed look over her shoulder in case I'd been overheard.

"As I was yours," I added in a low voice.

She blushed and glanced behind again to make sure nobody in the back was eavesdropping.

"SShhh!" she hissed, then tried to get the conversation back to where she wanted it.

"Eyes on the road, Romeo. You're getting too close to the car in front."

I smiled and paid attention to the road.

"I'm so glad I met you. I was forever crashing into cars be-fore…"

She treated me to a dazzling display of side-eye, so I decided to change the subject.

"I'm glad you're coming along, really I am…and yes, I prob-ably do need you to keep me from doing something stupid." I jerked my thumb backwards indicating the young men and women who were still bantering behind us. "They're all younger and fitter than us, so with our old heads to guide them we can get the job done and get back home before Nicky gives birth."

"OI! Enough of the old," Becky replied with a fake edge to her voice. "I prefer to call it wise…and yes, I really want to be back for the birth so that's why I'm here. To make sure you lot don't get carried away so we can get back when we need to."

This was the first time Becky had made the trip to Bristol, retracing our original journey north, and she enjoyed spotting and pointing out landmarks that sparked memories. I was just enjoying being in the warmth of a heated vehicle and not standing in the back of a trailer being towed by a tractor, being blasted by rain, snow or freezing air made worse by the addition of the wind-chill factor.

Cruising at a comfortable speed the journey to Bristol passed quickly, helped by the fact that the engineering crews from Bristol had done a good job in clearing the few blockages that had slowed our previous journeys and sometimes forced us to divert off the motorway to use the slower and narrower A roads before we rejoined the wide motorway.

As the Avonmouth bridge, the modern suspension bridge built to carry the tens of thousands of vehicles that used to travel up and down the M5 daily, rose ahead of us I looked at Becky.

"In or out?" I asked

For a few seconds she looked at me in confusion until she realised what I was on about. In the past it was my 'Dad move' when crossing the bridge. Everyone had to guess if the tide was in or out, either exposing the muddy tidal banks of the River Avon or filling it with water.

"Out," she said after a brief contemplation.

She was right of course, and as we crested the bridge I saw a column of mainly green vehicles ahead filling one carriageway of the motorway.

"There they are," Clarke's voice said over the radio. "Prepare to stop."

Lifting my foot off the accelerator I slowed and eventually stopped alongside the massed ranks of vehicles waiting for us.

The convoy from Fort Bristol was meeting us on the motorway so we could complete the journey together. They were providing more personnel and equipment than us, being a larger, military garrison.

I stepped from the armoured car to stretch my aching muscles, looking at the long line of armoured cars and supply lorries lined up on the side of the motorway to marvel at the impressive sight.

The plan was to have a break there while the two convoys merged, and everyone dismounted the vehicles for the two groups to greet each other, combining into one. I recognised a few familiar faces from trips to Bristol and ones made to us in Warwick, and greetings and introductions to the ones who didn't know each other were made.

Thoughtfully and thankfully, they'd set up a mobile canteen and friendly conversations continued as we queued up to get a warm drink and some food to sustain us for the remainder of the journey, but I noted many of them on top of vehicles keeping watch.

Not much extra planning was needed between the military officers leading the mission, so once they'd had a quick meeting and everyone had eaten and answered the call of nature, and conscious of the journey we needed to complete, the much-enlarged convoy set off to the roar of engines and black smoke billowing from exhausts as we built up speed.

More landmarks from our initial journey were passed.

The place where we'd met Steve and his men as they were making their way to Exeter to fruitlessly find their families.

Where I'd blown the tyre on my Volvo and the fight that had taken place to protect us as we were changing the wheel, and many others.

All memories that reminded us of the trials, terror and moments of good fortune that had marked our journey north. The one noticeable change was the absence of massed tangles of vehicles that Shawn had used the power of the tractor to push narrow lanes through.

The engineers had done a great job. The pile ups had been moved out of the way, either pushed down embankments or crushed to the side of the carriageway where they would undoubtedly lie until they rusted away to nothing. I noticed they'd even taken the time to sweep the roads clear of any debris left behind to protect the tyres of the vehicles that would hopefully travel the route in the future.

In no time it seemed, the M5 changed to the narrower, two-lane A30 which was usually a tiresomely hectic road to drive in the busy summer months, but devoid of traffic was now a treat. Cleared of every blockage and with all the abandoned cars and lorries now moved to the side of the road, the convoy kept a steady speed as we drove in a long column of military might and power. I couldn't help smiling to myself as we drove along.

"You're actually enjoying yourself, aren't you?" Becky asked with a hint of mockery when she noticed my grin

I smirked in reply, not wanting her to say any more as she knew me better than anyone else. Pride wouldn't allow me to admit it, but I was very much enjoying myself. I was driving an armoured car in a convoy, at speed, along empty roads with a force of well over two hundred heavily armed people to back us up if anything happened.

"Nope," I lied, not even convincing myself.

"Child!"

Her one-word response made my grin widen.

The hours and the miles passed as we drove deeper into Devon and then Cornwall as our destination grew closer. We shared a look when we saw a sign to St Agnes; the place where it had begun for us all those months ago. I reached over and squeezed her hand in silent acknowledgement of our terrified first few hours as the world fell apart around us.

An hour later we slowed as we approached the scar of newly dug earthworks stretching away into the distance ahead of us indicating that we had reached our destination. I'd seen the plans for it and flown over it on our visit to the Scillies, but that didn't prepare me for seeing it in person.

Bulldozers, diggers and trucks, foreshortened by the distance, looked like Tonka toys scattered around a child's sandpit as they slowly crawled along, scaling the sides and traversing the top of the raised berm. Even from a distance it looked impressively high, and I let out a snort of surprise when I noticed that everyone was wearing high viz vests, surprised that health and safety was a concern in the new world we were living in.

Then again, I realised a few seconds later, that as camouflage was the new fashion trend most of us now wore, it made sense for someone on foot not to blend into the background when hundreds of tonnes of metal was moving around you.

Becky seemed to intuit what had prompted my amusement and pointed at the nearest man dressed from head to toe in camouflage uniform with a bright orange reflective vest over it.

"He needs to make up his mind…I mean, does he want to be seen or not?"

More of what had been achieved so far became apparent the closer we got. Where the A30 cut through the wall, a team of workers were busy constructing a gate to defend it. Hundreds of earth and rock filled gabions had been stacked on either side of the road to shore up the earthen bank that already, after only a few weeks of work, stretched away in both directions. I was impressed by the progress that had been made in a relatively short time, and could see now that Tony's estimation that the bulk of the work would be completed in about a month wasn't a bad guess.

An officer was waiting for us at the gateway as our arrival time had been regularly updated enroute and he was standing waiting for us. We'd been told that we wouldn't disembark at The Wall but would pick up a guide who would take us to the accommodation prepared for us. I watched as he climbed into the front vehicle of the convoy, and seconds later the order came through the radios to get ready to proceed.

The Corn Wall, as we knew, was following the route of the A30. We weren't involved in the construction, but all of us avidly inspected it as we drove slowly along what had been completed so far. By now every hatch was open on the armoured cars enabling those in the back to get some fresh air as well as to have a look around and see the raw, brown-earthen berm that had been raised cutting a swathe through the bleak mid-winter countryside. Armoured cars passed us as they patrolled its length, ready to react to any threats spotted by the armed soldiers standing watch on top of the manmade hill.

If any environmentally minded people from the pre-apocalypse days had seen it I'm sure there would be protests, with camps and people chaining themselves to trees all along its route, all in a bid to halt its construction.

It was an ugly, stark, massive blot on the landscape, and I couldn't get enough of it.

Its construction was for one purpose: to help humans survive, and that outweighed any environmental or ecological argument.

In places where construction had yet to begin, wooden pegs with tape strung between them marked its route, ready for when the machinery reached it.

CHAPTER ELEVEN

Not knowing where we were going to be staying, I followed the vehicle in front and drove towards Penzance as the day began to darken with the approach of the early winter night.

As Mounts Bay came into view the logistical effort involved in the wall's construction was displayed in the mass of shipping, both Naval and civilian, that filled the bay. The tide was in and even on the cold, cloudy day we were experiencing from the shelter of our heated vehicles, the view over the expanse of the bay was beautiful. A large passenger ferry was moored in the bay and my first thought was that was where we were going to be accommodated.

I pointed it out to Becky.

"Look over there. I always promised you we'd go on a cruise one day! Don't say I never deliver on my promises…"

Becky didn't reply and I avoided looking at her as I knew her eyes would be trying to burn a hole into me.

To my surprise we didn't follow the road to Penzance but turned off at a roundabout just outside the town. Having been to the area on holiday before I was vaguely familiar with the road but was confused as to why we were heading that way. Becky, who was always quicker on the uptake than me, sat forward in her seat with excitement evident on her face.

"What is it, love?" I asked, slightly confused by her mannerisms.

"Nothing," she murmured as she continued leaning forwards and staring out of the window wearing a look of anticipation.

I followed the convoy into a large car park which was surrounded by a new looking fence with manned, wooden guard towers built in each corner, each sprouting the barrels of heavy machine guns. We were marshalled into some semblance of order and at a cutthroat signal from the man directing me, I turned off the engine.

Stretching in the seat I tried to force some movement back into my tired body after a full day behind the wheel of not the most comfortable driving experience I'd ever had.

I opened my door to climb out stiffly, and after waiting for Becky to join me I hobbled, slowly at first, before I loosened up and my legs started to work again, towards the crowd that was growing as the other vehicles emptied of their occupants.

A naval officer walked towards us and, after exchanging salutes with his army counterparts of superior grade, introduced himself as Lieutenant Corrall and our liaison while we were there.

He climbed on to a step on an armoured car and raised his voice so we could all hear him.

"If you could gather your kit bags and personal weapons and follow me, I'll show you how to get to your accommodation before the light leaves us altogether."

A few minutes of confusion reigned as everyone found and gathered their personal kit from our logistics lorry, then, with weapons slung over shoulders, we followed the officer across the car park towards the beach.

Then it became clear, and my excitement went through the roof.

"We're not, are we?" I whispered to Becky.

"Quick on the uptake as usual I see. I guessed it when we turned off the main road," she laughed in mock exasperation.

"Why didn't you tell me?" I whined in a sulky tone as, once again, it became clear that nothing got past my wife.

"Darling," she replied, smiling excitedly at me. "I realised long ago that unless it's staring you in the face you never know what's coming next."

As we rounded the corner of a building, she spread her arms wide.

"And there it is!"

I stopped, causing those following behind to bump into me, as before me was the splendid view of St Michaels Mount. The tide was in, and it stood in awe-inspiring isolation, surrounded by the wind-whipped waters of Mounts Bay. It looked so magnificent that even the chill wind couldn't dampen my spirits.

We'd visited it before as it was one of the must-see tourist destinations in Cornwall. Managed by the National Trust, it was still occupied by the family that had owned it for hundreds of years.

Rising from the bay, its steep sides climbed up to the beautiful castle that surmounted the peak looking like something out of a fairy tale, and the fact we were going to be staying there was a heck of a lot more than I'd been expecting.

Gathering in groups on the road that ran down to the shore and submerged itself under the waters of the bay, I could see a fleet of open boats heading towards us from the harbour on the island. When the tide was out the causeway emerged from the waters of the bay, enabling vehicles and pedestrians to reach the island. In the early days of the apocalypse we'd briefly discussed heading to St Michaels Mount, but had quickly discounted it as, twice a day when the tide was out, it would be accessible by foot and so the dangers of a horde of zombies reaching us made the idea unwelcome.

The naval lieutenant stood on a wall this time to make himself more visible, and once again got our attention back from the view before us.

"The boats will ferry you across," he began." It will take a few trips, so if you could form a queue it won't take long. I'm going on the first boat to show the first to arrive the way. Once everyone is there I will allocate your accommodation, so if you could bear with me until we are all together again I would be most grateful. Now, as the light is fading, could those behind please wait to be escorted by my staff, who will be waiting with torches to light the way. The path is steep and a bit rough in places and I would hate for anyone to hurt themselves."

I remembered the path from my previous visit so could appreciate what he was saying. It weaved its way up its steep sides through woods and gardens before reaching the castle itself.

Becky and I were near the front of the queue and didn't have to wait long before we stepped on to a boat to make the short journey across the water. Motoring into the harbour the extra defences that had been created impressed me. They had more the air of permanence than temporary about it which got me wondering.

Well-constructed, roofed machine gun posts covered the harbour entrance and road that was exposed at low tide while layers of razor wire-topped fencing stretched away as far as the fading light allowed me to see. If a horde of zombies crossed the shallows at low tide, they would be caught not only on the fence but by deadly interlocking arcs of fire from the many guns pointing outwards. It was all very comforting that our safety would be more than looked after while we were there.

The Great Hall of the castle was lit with strings of festoon lighting and its fireplaces were blazing with stacked wood. The temporary lighting and furniture stacked in corners didn't give the room the feel of permanence and homeliness that our own Great Hall did, but it was still the Great Hall of an important place in English history so it remained impressive, especially given its location. The Warwick Castle residents were accustomed to the grandeur of our own surroundings so we didn't gawp like tourists at seeing the unimaginable splendour, but those from Bristol who hadn't visited our own home stared. Excited voices grew as features were pointed out and groups began exploring on their own accord until brought to attention by the lieutenant climbing onto a large dining table for our attention.

"Welcome to St Michaels Mount," he began formally. "We decided to use this place to accommodate you as it can easily absorb your numbers. With the defences in place and the help of the tide twice a day, it makes an impregnable and not to mention rather impressive fortress. After the wall is completed we plan to establish our mainland base of operations here, so all the work you see that has been done so far and is planned going forwards is for the long term."

I smiled to myself as that answered my previous thoughts.

He glanced at the clipboard in his hand before continuing.

"As to your room allocation. Unfortunately, most of you will be accommodated in barrack-type rooms where we have cobbled enough beds together to sleep you all."

My heart sank at the thought of either being separated from Becky if I was to be put up in a male only dorm, or having to get used to communal sleeping again as we had done before arriving at our castle. He then smiled as he glanced up.

"But this place does have an impressive number of bedrooms and rooms we have converted to that use. I will allocate them first so if you could step forwards when I call your name please. Once you have settled in, please return here and food will be served in the dining room. After we have eaten, Admiral Walker-Jones, who is on his way here now, wishes to hold a final planning meeting about the work that will begin tomorrow."

Happily, Becky and I were one of the first names to be called and we followed an able rating to an impressive room, which in daylight I imagined had commanding views over the bay. I thought this must be a privilege of my supposed ranking in the new society we lived in, as I inspected our very well appointed, luxurious room. Putting our bags on the floor and leaning our weapons against the wall we had a look around the room that was lit by a few propane lamps. The room was cold, which was nothing we weren't well-accustomed to living in our own castle, but the bed looked warm and inviting with a thick duvet and extra blankets laid on top.

I raised my eyebrows at Becky and smiled, glancing at the bed.

"Oh no! It is going to be a cold night...however are we going to cope?" I asked woodenly with mock horror, punctuating my chanced luck with a suggestive bounce of my eyebrows.

Becky sidled up to me and ran her fingers up my arm affectionately, leaning towards my face with a mischievous smile of her own. When I fell for it and turned my head for our lips to connect, she moved to whisper in my ear.

"I've brought some thick socks. I'll be fine."

My puppy dog look of dejection made her laugh, but it was mostly annoyance that I'd been so expertly played.

"Now I'm starving," she said. "Let's eat!"

CHAPTER TWELVE

We huddled in our coats against the early morning gloom and drizzle as we waited for our turn to be ferried to the mainland. We'd finalised our plans the night before and knew what we needed to achieve today, having been assigned an area that was our responsibility to clear. The whole of the Cornish peninsula was split into zones which each team had a responsibility to check and clear every village, home, barn and shed or anywhere else where zombies could possibly be sheltering.

We had been issued with detailed maps and overhead imagery courtesy of the comprehensive aerial survey the Navy had undertaken in preparation. Our group from the castle would be operating in their own sector independently from other groups, but with the added reassurance that if any large concentrations of zombies were found that we couldn't deal with ourselves then a QRF could be summoned. The relatively small land area we were all working in meant that help wouldn't be far away if called upon.

The larger towns of Penzance, Newlyn, St Ives and Hayle and some of the larger villages were going to be cleared by much larger formations comprised of military personnel and Scilly Isles volunteers.

At the meeting last night we'd been told that as the wall's construction was already taking up a lot of the available personnel, every other task had been put on hold to free almost every able bodied and trained hand available for the clearing task. They were being accommodated on the fleet of ships in the harbour which made me feel slightly guilty, as for some reason, we'd been given the best accommodation available.

As I held Becky's hand and waited for the next boat to ferry us over the short stretch of water, I decided I didn't feel that guilty after all as the bed had been comfortable, warm and cozy with the extra blankets laid over it.

Over breakfast our group had finalised our own plans and procedure for the day, so as soon as the last of us had been ferried across on the waiting boats, we wasted no time to board our vehicles and head out to our first destination.

When we joined the main road, from my position in the driver's seat, I could see convoys of other vehicles ahead of us as other groups began their day. Beside me Becky navigated and as other convoys turned off the main road, we continued until our turning came up.

Everyone was starting with their backs to the wall, literally, and over the next days would check everything in our path as we wound through the lanes until we reached the very end of mainland UK at Lands End.

Our detailed maps and aerial photos gave us the location of every possible place we needed to check, and for administrative purposes every location had been given a reference number which could be marked as clear on a list at the end of every day by a team back at our temporary island home. We had also been issued with cans of spray paint to clearly mark every property as checked and clear. Everything seemed to have been considered, and all we needed to do was get on with it.

During the day we perfected the routine we had planned over breakfast. The size of the property or properties we checked at each location dictated how many people cleared it or stayed outside on overwatch. Our previous experiences at scavenging made us all confident at this and very little communication was needed, as we all knew our roles and simply got on with it. Every hour that passed saw more buildings cleared and marked ready for the final day's tally.

The one obvious fact that became apparent after a while was that most houses we checked contained a cache of supplies both in food and other equipment that would be useful for all communities in the future. Our mission didn't afford us enough time to scavenge any of it, but nevertheless if a notable quantity of useful items was discovered then we marked the location for future collection.

On the first day we encountered no zombies. None. Zero.

Overheard radio calls informed us that other groups had discovered some small groups of zombies hidden away. I guessed they were probably families who, once turned, had been unable to leave and became trapped forever in their homes. Exterminating them had caused no issues, but it did prove that everywhere, no matter how unlikely a hiding place, needed to be cleared if the land was going to be repopulated by the living in the future.

In good spirits after having a non-eventful, but nevertheless – according to our mission parameters – successful day, we returned in the fading early evening winter light to the carpark seeing the tide far enough out for us to be able to use the road to reach the castle. A few minibuses had been found, and in no time we were rumbling over the stone causeway stretching across the sand and climbing the path to our temporary home.

After dinner we spoke to Stanley and Daisy, who happily were reported to be behaving themselves and having a great time under the care of Maud. We then met the others from our group in the room set aside for the planners to get an update on the day's progress, seeing the information from other groups displayed on a large-scale map fixed to a wall. Stretching out from the wall and going west, all the land that had been checked and cleared was marked, and I couldn't help thinking that even though we'd worked hard all day, relatively little of the mission area was showing as cleared. Determined to do better the next day we had an early night so we'd be ready to go at first light again.

Over the following days the cleared areas lazily crept across the map like a slow tide advancing up a beach. Apart from a few small groups we encountered and eliminated, the mission was going well.

Only one serious concentration of zombies had been found so far in the basement of a large warehouse in Penzance. At our evening meeting we were read the report from the ones who had discovered it. To avoid any potential dangers with dealing with what was reckoned to be thousands of them, and because the warehouse had no other buildings nearby, the decision was taken to pump petrol into the basement and let fire consume them.

The explosion and subsequent fireball were reported to have been impressive, and it took two days for the fires to extinguish themselves.

For ten days we continued working our way across the peninsula, continually reducing the square mileage of hostile territory, and throughout our group's spirits remained high. We could mark ours and everyone else's progress daily on the map, and we all knew we were making a difference as the remnants of the whole country pulled together on the monumental task at hand.

Cornwall was also riddled with old mine workings from its industrial past. Some of these had been turned into tourist attractions which provided an insight into the terrible conditions suffered by the miners who, for a pittance, risked their lives daily to extract the minerals needed to fuel the industries that needed them.

The first of these mines that needed to be checked proved to be a deadly experience for a team from the Scilly Isles. Entering the mine with torches and lamps they cautiously went deeper into the maze of tunnels and caverns stretching for miles underground. Their penetrating torch beams failed to find any zombies at first, but they knew the whole place needed to be checked before it could be declared safe, so deeper they went.

The temperature rose the further they went until a huge huddle of zombies was discovered in a cavern. As these zombies noticed the team and switched from power saving to attack mode, other zombies appeared from side tunnels swelling their numbers further.

Left with no choice as they faced more undead than the number of bullets they carried between them, they retreated only to find themselves surrounded by others emerging from more tunnels.

Desperate calls for help via radio went unheard as the surrounding rock blocked the signal.

They opened up with their weapons and fought desperately along the tunnels, shooting, kicking and hacking their way through the living dead in search of the surface. Disorientated and panicking as they were experienced the stuff of nightmares, wrong turns were made and they continually found themselves at dead ends and needing to fight their way back through the horde.

Outstretched arms and hands clawed at the terrified defenders, pulling them screaming into the throng as each step took them closer to the exit.

Only five out of the twenty that entered the mine saw daylight again.

Calling for urgent reinforcements as soon as their comms were restored, they resupplied with ammunition from their vehicles and desperately tried to keep the zombies from escaping the mine. Packing the entrance with so many bodies they thought they'd won the battle more than once, more kept pushing their way through risking another outbreak.

When reinforcements arrived, shoulder mounted rocket launchers soon turned the mine entrance into a pile of impenetrable, smoking rubble and rock, sealing those left inside forever.

Command at St Michael's Mount were appalled at the losses and some members of the mission planning team found themselves under significant scrutiny for the massive oversight.

Issuing orders that no more mines would be entered, word quickly spread that when one was found it was to be sealed using explosives without exploration.

Most mines had more than one entrance however, and those weren't always clearly marked or even shown on any map or plan, so they were forced to scour the area around them to ensure all entrances were blocked. The crump of explosives sounded around the peninsular as every mine or hole in the ground discovered was treated to a gift of high explosive.

Seeing the daily progress each evening began to feel like we were achieving something, like we were making a difference, even though the task was so monumental it required a combined effort from all surviving communities.

More large groups of zombies had been discovered huddling together in dark, underground areas had been dealt with utilising a variety of methods such as fire, explosives or simply dispatched with personal weapons.

We'd never know the true numbers exterminated in those hordes, but we could keep a count of those smaller groups found mainly trapped in houses. An estimate in the many thousands was guessed at which only proved that what we were doing was essential.

That evening Walker-Jones, accompanied by his usual entourage of aides, visited us as we ate our evening meal. He had a serious look on his face and walked immediately over to Becky when he spotted her in the crowded room.

"Becky. Tom," he said seriously. "We've just received word from Warwick that your lady has gone into labour."

A panicked look descended on Becky's face. She'd really wanted to be there for the birth, and I knew she'd be mortified if she missed it. She rose in her seat and looked at me.

"Tom, we are leaving. NOW!" she said before walking off.

The one thing I knew we couldn't do was leave straight away. It was a long journey, and our steadfast rule was that we didn't travel at night.

Walker-Jones put his hand on her arm to stop her leaving, earning a stern look as she rounded on him.

"Becky, I understand how you feel," the admiral said carefully. "But I'm afraid I simply cannot permit you to travel by vehicle, it's just too dangerous at night."

If the admiral didn't recognise the way she drew herself up and sucked in a breath, then I certainly did. I was torn between saving him and watching for enjoyment.

"Which is why I have a helicopter warming up this very moment to take you home!" Walker-Jones finished hurriedly, proving that he did recognise the signs of an imminent detonation.

She stopped abruptly, every argument she had simply dying on her lips.

"Oh?" was all she could splutter in response.

"I'm also afraid there's only sufficient space for you, Becky," Walker-Jones continued with an apologetic glance in my direction. "If you could collect your belongings and say your goodbyes, it'll be landing on the lawn outside in a few minutes."

She looked at me and I smiled.

"Go. The deal was we'd help until the birth, so it looks like we're all going home now. It's just that you get to travel first class. Grab your bag and I'll walk you to your ride, then I guess I'll start organising our trip home."

As she strode purposely away Walker-Jones turned back to me.

"We'll be sad to see you go, Tom. You've all been a great help and really advanced the programme."

"Glad to help, but I can't say I'll not be happy to get home and see the kids."

I paused as I thought about why we were heading back.

"A baby…after all we've been through…It's quite something, isn't it?" I asked him, my voice filled with wonder and emotion.

"Yes, it truly is," he replied, his own tone softening at the thought. "It's probably the strongest message there is to prove that amongst all the pain and loss we've suffered, that life still goes on."

He laughed, and his sombre wonderment evaporated.

"And anyway, with all the shenanigans I hear going on between the youngsters which I'm not supposed to know about, I'm sure there'll be many more new arrivals in the not too distant future! But, as this is our first, all assistance we can provide will be given."

He snapped his fingers as he remembered what he'd forgotten to tell me.

"Oh, and the reason there's only room for one on the helicopter is that I'm also sending one of our ship's surgeons along, just in case. Hopefully you won't need him and can send him back soon, but it's better to be safe than sorry."

"Couldn't agree more!" I replied immediately. "A surgeon would be far more useful than me…All I'd be doing is handing around the cigars and planning to wet the baby's head."

Walker-Jones laughed.

"A party!" he said thoughtfully, rubbing his chin as though pretending to consider the matter deeply. "You know…I may just have to have my staff arrange a congratulatory visit…"

He winked as he turned to walk away before glancing back at me.

"Keep me in the loop, Tom."

Sensing her nervousness about a helicopter ride at night I tried to make her feel better about it but, as usual, couldn't find the right words. Saying as much to the pilot who was stretching his legs and enjoying a smoke as he waited for us to arrive, we both felt reassured at his easy chuckle and confident words.

"If I can land that thing on a ship in the pitch black, in thirty-foot swells using night vision, I think you can trust me to Uber you up the road a ways, my dear," he said in a strong Devonshire accent.

Waving her off and trying to shield my face from the stinging wind whipped up by the blades as the helicopter took off and disappeared into the night.

It had all been a bit of a rush, as barely twenty minutes had passed since the news first broke and she'd left. I took a moment to get my whirling emotions together before I went back inside and gathered the Warwick contingent so we could discuss what to do next.

Before leaving we'd all agreed we wanted to be back for the birth. After all, it was an event the whole community had been eagerly anticipating, but we were also disappointed we hadn't finished the task set for us in Cornwall.

We'd achieved much and knew we'd contributed a great deal to the mission as a whole, but leaving the other teams to carry on without us felt like we were ducking our duty somehow. The planners had already estimated it would take approximately another two weeks to conduct the initial clearing, and once that was done the teams would patrol their areas for any sign of stragglers. When the wall was complete, a final sweep would be completed to make sure nothing had been missed before the repopulation efforts began.

We hadn't bought much stuff with us aside from our own weapons, kitbags and the supplies in the lorry along with the fuel bowser it towed, so packing up to leave was no major logistical nightmare. At first light we'd give the vehicles a quick once over, fuel them up and load up to head back knowing it would take most of the day to get home at a steady pace on the freshly cleared roads.

With nothing more to plan we headed to bed for an early night, in anticipation of a very early start in the morning.

CHAPTER THIRTEEN

With fuel tanks topped off and oil and fluid levels checked in all the vehicles, we closed bonnets and climbed onboard our respective vehicles to begin our journey. Digby had chosen to take Becky's place in the front seat of my armoured car, which didn't disappoint me as he was becoming a close friend and someone with whom it was a pleasure to spend time with. When at the castle, his nephew Eddie was rarely far from his side and he really seemed to enjoy spending time with the young man. Eddie clearly idolised his uncle and in return Diggers took his role as substitute parent very seriously out of honour and respect for his sister as well as a genuine fondness for his nephew.

With headlights on full, cutting through the darkness which would soon disappear as the eastern sky lit up, we began our journey north following the construction line of the wall.

Even in the dim morning light it was clear that more progress had been made since we first laid eyes on it. Every day the teams of bulldozers and diggers excavated, pushed, and formed the earth and rock into a high bank that would soon form a complete barrier. It was a monumental construction project that, when completed, would hopefully provide an effective safety net for those living and working behind it.

Becky had arrived safely at the castle last night, and via radio had reported that Nicky's labour, according to Diane, was going slowly but to plan. Nicky and her baby were in good health and both Diane and the ship's surgeon had no concerns for their well-being. From my own limited childbirth experiences I knew that it happened when it happened, and each time was different with little anyone could do to influence the timing or the outcome. There was going to be a baby, that much was undeniable, it was when that nobody could predict with any form of accuracy. Still, we all felt a sense of trepidation as, until it arrived, there were still dangers to both mother and baby.

The mood was quiet as those in the back with much less to see in the windowless compartments tried to grab a few hours extra sleep. Digby and I chatted as we sipped on our travel mugs of strong coffee we kept topped up from flasks.

An hour later and my bladder wished to see the manager about the amount of coffee it had been forced to deal with. After announcing to the convoy over the radio our intention to take a quick comfort break at the side of the road it was apparent I wasn't the only one with the same issue.

As a line of us directed our steaming streams to irrigate the nearest bushes and the women found a thick hedge to hide behind, I looked around and saw a sign ahead that directed you towards St Agnes, and a sudden thought hit me.

All that time ago, when we'd fled the camp site and abandoned our caravan, we'd left a few personal items behind in our rush which Becky said she missed. They just hadn't been thought about in the panic of getting the hell out of there.

"Penny for them, Tom?" Digby asked when he saw my expression.

"Hmm?"

"You looked rather vacant just then. What's on your mind?" he asked.

"I was just wondering if it would be okay to be slightly selfish," I answered ponderously, still looking at the sign.

"In what context?" Digby asked.

"I was just wondering if we could make a quick detour."

I explained where I wanted to go and why, arguing that it was only a few miles off our route so shouldn't delay us too much. As soon as I spoke the words I felt foolish, risking lives and delaying our return for things that, logically speaking, didn't matter so I was surprised when everyone agreed. We climbed back on board and with me leading the way, we headed for St Agnes.

Memories flooded back as we drew nearer to the camp site. Shawn and Louise, who were in the back of the vehicle, came to the front to peer through the window as I pointed out where we'd first met.

The Range Rover was still there, along with the devoured and decayed corpses of the family surrounding it. Just beyond was where we'd rescued Eddie from the zombies pursuing him, Shawn proudly pointed out to Louise the tyre marks on the tarmac where he'd used his car to smash the closest undead clean out of the way to give me the time to grab the boy. We passed the garage where we'd both seen our first Zombie, feeling once more the stab of fear and revulsion when life first confirmed the impossible had happened.

The fireball we'd seen rising over St Agnes that day now explained itself as we had to slow to push a few scorched vehicles off the road which surrounded the shattered remains of a tanker on the outskirts of the village.

The place looked much the same as every other abandoned small town or village we'd explored countless times on our travels. The evidence of the panic of the first days of the apocalypse unmistakable in the form of crashed cars, unsecured houses surrounded by scattered belongings and clothing-covered corpses eroded down to white bone lying everywhere. We were immune to such sights now, so barely glanced at what would have given us nightmares before it began.

Leaving the village I followed the well-remembered road to the camp site, turning into the entrance to witness evidence of the chaos that had occurred on that fateful morning.

Abandoned cars, some with caravans still attached, blocked the road. The only easy option to me was to drive through a wooden fence, across overgrown flower beds, passing what was once the playground where the kids had played with their holiday friends.

As I drove through the field I steered around the scattered remnants of bodies that lay everywhere, proving that true horror had found the place not long after we'd left.

Filled with emotion I stopped outside our caravan. The awning had suffered during the winter gales and lay in a tangle of twisted poles and ripped fabric still stubbornly attached to the van. I looked at it sadly as it was a new awning I'd purchased for the holiday, and had cost me a small fortune, as if such trivialities mattered now.

"Oh well," I said to myself ruefully. "Won't have to struggle with that again with no one helping me."

I smiled nostalgically, recalling the amount of times my family had promised to help me set it up on arrival, only to vanish not long after to explore.

I'd thought returning to where it started would just be a routine event. I had some personal items to collect and just needed to do it, but I found tears streaming down my face as I entered the caravan.

It held so many happy memories of the normal life we'd lived before it all happened; a life that seemed so long ago and unreal now that it was almost impossible to remember.

Stepping into the caravan brought it all back.

Through vision blurred by tears I found a bag and looked around for the things I wanted. I picked items off the side, opened draws and cupboards to find the stuff I knew Becky missed not having, like some pieces of sentimental, if not valuable jewellery and some photos she always insisted on decorating the caravan with to give it a more homely feel.

I moved through the small space like a ghost, picking up items of clothing such as her favourite walking boots she was always moaning she missed as she had spent years breaking them in and were the most comfortable she'd ever worn. I knew if Becky was with me she would have probably wanted to take more, but as I scoured the small space nothing else came to my attention. I just hoped that when I got back she would appreciate me doing it and not moan about what I had forgotten; that she would focus on the positive instead of criticising the negative and maybe recognise that returning there had been difficult.

A few minutes later, after taking some time to compose myself, I fought my way back outside through the damaged awning to find that the others had not been idle in my absence and had taken the time to gather gas bottles from the caravans closest to us. We used a lot of them to heat the castle's rooms with our scavenged portable gas heaters, and even though we had a plentiful supply back home the mindset of 'if it's there, take it', was deeply ingrained in all our collective psyche now.

I looked at the caravan opposite, once proudly owned by my chain-smoking neighbour who had first alerted me to what was happening. It was he who had probably saved us by telling me what was being shown on TV, otherwise we would've just left to go to the beach for the day and probably died there, or at least later on as chaos consumed the country. I wondered where he was now, then glanced around the field full of corpses of all sizes, reckoning he was probably among them somewhere.

Again, with tears in my eyes I walked over to his caravan and reverently placed my hand on it.

"Thanks mate, I...I owe you my family's life."

I couldn't say any more as I bowed my head and a sob escaped, trying to hold it inside until Diggers approached to put a comforting arm around my shoulders.

"Come on mate. You've got what you need and there's no point dwelling on what could've happened. You and your family are alive and that's all you need to focus on, not the what ifs, okay?"

I turned to him and nodded my agreement, still unable to speak for fear of opening the emotional floodgates.

"Come on, I'll drive to give you time to recover," he said, slapping me on the back to get me moving in the right direction.

CHAPTER FOURTEEN

"Are we too late?" I shouted as the gates opened for us.

During our last communication telling them our ETA, we'd been told that Nicky was getting close, prompting us to speed up and for me to feel a little guilty about the diversion I'd made us undertake.

"Last I heard it wasn't here yet," came the shouted reply as we sped through the gates and headed to the castle.

It seemed that our entire community, apart from those on guard duty, had gathered in the Great Hall awaiting news. I looked for Becky but she wasn't there, nor could I see my children, or indeed any children.

"Where's Becky?" I asked.

Willie approached and offered a handshake I accepted on autopilot.

"She's with Nicky, along with quite a few of the women," he chuckled, waving his arm around the room to show it was mainly filled with men.

"Are they all in there?" I replied, thinking that was a little too much.

Giving birth was normally a private affair attended usually by just the partner and medical professionals, so the idea of a crowd cheering Nicky on made me feel uneasy.

"No, laddie," he replied cheerfully. "They're all hovering near the door waiting to be needed, or if y'ask me they want to be the first to hear the baby cry! It's just Chris, Becky, the midwife and the doc in the room with Nicky. My Maud's doing her level best to keep them from all interfering, but I fear she's fighting a losing battle."

"What about the kids?" I asked, earning a chortle from the old Scotsman.

"We banished the bairns to the games room a while back. They were bored and getting under our feet as they do. I promised them if they didn'ae cause any more trouble, they could have a late night as most likely people would forget about them so long as they stay quiet."

"You're going to get into trouble with Maud," I told him with a grin.

"Och no, laddie! She's in full baby mode and isn'ae thinking about anything else, so I reckon I'll survive."

As I turned away, I gave him a 'you really think so?' look, but he just smiled and shrugged to indicate he lived in perpetual hope.

Myself, Diggers and the other parents who had been on the mission made our way to the games room to say hello to our kids, feeling disappointed that they were having a wonderful time and saw our return as a mere interruption. The older ones had organised a pool, table tennis and table football competition which was in full swing while the younger ones were in the TV corner watching a movie, lying on the extremely comfortable looking cushions and bean bags arranged on the floor.

Once I had the attention of my two I hugged them, but when the initial excitement of seeing me had quickly passed they wanted to get back to what they were doing. It was the same for the other parents and carers, so we headed back to the Great Hall where we all sat around and waited for news.

Willie decided that it was late enough in the day for those who wanted to relieve the stress they were under to do so.

"And in ma humble opinion," he added mischievously. "Whisky's the best remedy I know of for occasions such as these."

In no time the glasses and bottles appeared, and we sat in companionable but tense comfort to while away the hours, chatting and updating people on the mission to Cornwall. Every time the door leading to the maternity ward opened we looked up expectantly, but it was usually someone bustling in and out just needing to get something. After annoying the wrong woman once too often for news, we sensibly stopped asking.

Then, eventually, we heard the faint cry of a baby.

We all stood, silence gripping us as if we waited to see if a penalty went in, then when a far more distinct sound reached our ears we erupted in cheers, hugging each other as if it was our own that had been born.

Willie approached me wearing a wide smile, offering up his glass. I clinked my own to it and smiled back.

"Willie, did I ever tell you I was a doctor?"

He frowned, well aware he was being set up for a joke but shook his head to play along anyway.

"Doctor of mathematics…you know what I mean?"

"I do not, but I'm sure you're about to tell me!"

I raised my glass again and smiled warmly.

"Plus one," I said, feeling the first addition to the UK's population deep in my soul.

Willie's smile turned into a pained expression and I walked off before I heard the groan.

Maud walked into the room a few minutes later with tears of joy running down her cheeks. She was so excited that she didn't even notice most of us were slightly drunk, nor did she seem to notice the empty whisky bottles abandoned on tables.

"It's a girl," she declared.

That was all we heard before any other words were drowned out by more cheering and clapping. Willie hugged her and tried to press his glass of whisky into her hand, but she took only a fortifying sip before rushing back to the maternity ward before we could ask any more questions.

Thirty minutes later we looked expectantly as the door opened and Chris walked in, followed by the others who had been loitering outside the delivery room. He held a blanket swathed bundle in his arms carefully, as if he was transporting a priceless artefact, but there was no disguising the pride radiating from him.

I immediately went to hug Becky who was beaming fit to burst.

"Is Nicky okay?" I asked.

"Yes. It was a long labour, but it all went well in the end. She's already fed baby and needs rest as she's exhausted, so we thought we'd bring the little one to see you all."

We crowded round to get a glimpse of the tiny, red face. She had the look and temperament of all the newly born babies I had seen. She'd been through a traumatic time leaving the warmth and comfort of the womb only to be thrust into an alien and strange world, and she wasn't shy at letting it show.

It was always surprising how loud a baby's crying can be coming from something so small as she complained to the world in general about her treatment.

"Och! Wee lassie would like to speak to the manager!" Willie announced, prompting laughter that only made the baby cry louder.

"Isn't she beautiful?" Becky asked in a tone that was worryingly adjacent to a discussion about having more children.

"Yeah," I said, evidently not convincing Becky who aimed a weak slap at my chest.

"What?"

"I know that face. Spit it out!" she demanded.

"Okay," I relented. "She's beautiful, but don't you think all newborns look like Winston Churchill chewing a wasp?"

The slap came again, harder this time, but her laughter more than made up for it.

"Does she have a name yet?" I asked, looking at Chris for an answer.

Chris, still holding her close despite the multiple requests for cuddles, rocked her gently in a futile effort to calm her down.

"Yes…" he answered, raising his voice for the announcement. "Ladies and Gentlemen…I'd like to introduce you to our daughter, Hope."

On hearing the name the room lowered into quiet contemplation. Hearing the name they had chosen immediately made me emotional.

It was a powerful name that could not have summed everything up better.

It was a perfect name.

Still with an arm around Becky and both of us with tears in our eyes, and with a shaky voice, I raised my glass in the air and said, "To Hope."

"Hope!" came the echoing reply from others raising their own glasses.

True to form, Charles got our attention, offering a short prayer to give thanks for the safe arrival of our newest member, before once again raising a glass and toasting Hope.

The mood was positive. The mood was good. The mood was full of Hope.

~

Nicky was on her feet the following day, enjoying all the attention, praise and constant looking after she was receiving from everyone, but especially from Maud.

Chris, by unanimous agreement, was given a week off all duties to spend time with his wife and daughter, but that didn't stop him wrapping the baby up warmly and carrying her in a sling across his chest to walk the ramparts, giving Nicky time to rest and recover away from the exhausting baby duties new parents just have to endure and get through.

Another advantage for them caused by the communal living arrangements of castle life was that there was always a willing volunteer to look after Hope when both parents needed the chance to catch up on sleep after another night with little of it.

Once the excitement of the new arrival had calmed down, the days once again filled with training, repairs and maintenance on both the castle and our fleet of vehicles. The winter weather hit again with full force and most mornings the castle was covered in a heavy layer of frost. The snow that fell did not melt during the day as it had before, and while it made the place look beautiful and seasonal, it also made the external stone staircases treacherous and watch duty very uncomfortable.

Fed up with the conditions we conducted an expedition to find some rock salt to treat the most dangerous areas, which helped to reduce the bruises both to the body and ego of those who landed on their backsides before an audience.

The regular communications with the Scilly Isles kept us informed of the wall's progress. All still proceeded to plan and construction was due to be completed by the end of January, but more work would follow, with construction of the watch towers, converting buildings along the route to be used as barracks, and adding additional layers of defence.

The entire area behind the wall had been cleared and patrols were now rechecking everywhere as planned. We asked if they needed our help again as the winter weather was curtailing a lot of our usual activities, but a trip down the motorway was something we could manage should they need us. They appreciated the offer, but decided they had sufficient personnel to conduct the operations and didn't want to burden us with another long trip down to the southernmost tip of the mainland.

As in times gone by when winter shut down regular activities, the community sheltered inside the warmer rooms of the castle and spent time together. We came up with tasks and projects that would keep us busy. We held regular quiz nights and talent shows, which more often than not were raucously funny, lack-of-talent shows, with the volunteers not minding making a fool of themselves in order to entertain everyone else. All these activities and more kept the community bonded and kept cabin fever at bay.

When winter finally relinquished its icy grip on us we knew we'd all be busy again, so we enjoyed the time to rest in preparation for the coming spring. The only work outside the walls we undertook was patrolling the local area just to keep an eye on it, and the regular runs between us and the Brough's which also ensured the road remained open.

Fort Bristol still conducted their regular weekly run up to us with supplies and for personnel changes which kept that route passable as well.

Life started to become, if not mundane, then comfortably secure. We had a splendid roof over our heads which was warm, but most of all provided us with security, and we had enough supplies to last us for a long time.

February was as cold as any of us could remember. Heavy falls of snow lay in deep drifts against the castle walls and even stopped the regular runs between the bases for over a week as it was deemed unsafe to travel. The few crisp, clear, sunny days in between storms were magical as with nothing at all to do they were declared 'snow days' where absolutely no non-vital work was completed.

Playing with the children, building snowmen, holding community snowball fights and even making a sledging run down the mound. The banked sides on it enabling you to steer a sledge through the turns we'd made gave the children and adults alike a thrilling experience as it weaved down the steep bank.

By the end of February winter began to loosen its hold upon the land and spring preparations began in earnest.

CHAPTER FIFTEEN

In dark basements and other hidden sheltered spaces, the coming of spring caused a change to the countless masses of those that, by some unseen and unheard signal, had consolidated together to survive the winter. A fog of steam from condensing exhaled breaths hung over these groups like a warning cloud of impending doom.

Their hibernating state was disturbed only when one of the group moved into the centre of the mass to be consumed as the only way to sustain the others throughout the cold months.

Each sacrifice was consumed to the bone to help fuel the changes the virus needed to make, and as the temperature rose the mass of bodies on the outer edges were no longer needed to stop the inner rank from freezing. Instead it created a rising bloom of heat that radiated inwards, superheating the thousands of zombies. This heat was the catalyst the virus needed to make its final changes to the bodies of the infected, and as spring loomed the mutation was near perfect.

In blissful ignorance the survivors prepared for the coming spring as millions of zombies, still hidden from searching eyes, waited until the virus knew they were ready to be unleashed.

As March nudged February aside the last of the snows on the high ground surrounding Warwick eventually melted and the floods caused by the inundated streams and rivers slowly subsided.

After a few forays to inspect the surrounding area we decided to begin scavenging and searching for survivors in earnest again. The groups would be smaller as many in the castle were needed to prepare and plant the acres of ground set aside for cultivation, but the experienced and well-armed expeditions would continue to expand the areas we'd searched for everything of value.

The greenhouses and our newly erected poly tunnels would increase our growing capacity by a factor of many, and we were already seeing signs of growth. We knew we wouldn't be able to plant the acreage needed to feed ourselves entirely straight away, but the vegetables and other crops growing, along with our ever-expanding chicken population, would provide a good portion of what we needed to get us closer to self-sufficiency.

For the first few days of spring the castle seemed a lot emptier than it had during the winter months, where there had always been someone to bump into and talk with but now everybody had jobs to do, either outside the walls or in the castle and grounds. This meant that it was only mealtimes that the community got together, and morale was good as we shook off the inactivity of winter and looked forward to achieving the goals we'd set.

A radio call came in from Fort Bristol asking if we could deliver to them some more armoured cars from those we had stored in the castle grounds. They were all still being serviced and moved regularly by a crew of mechanics to keep them in prime operational condition, so were ready to simply fire up and drive off.

Now the bulk of the work on the wall was nearing completion and the area behind it had been swept many times for any errant zombies, The command on the Scilly Isles decided to release more personnel to help them at Bristol.

This may change when they started to move people from the Scillies to the mainland, but until then it had been deemed that their efforts would be more usefully spent at Bristol. To enable the influx of personnel to be effectively deployed they needed additional armoured cars to escort the daily scavenging and search parties deployed.

They could easily have sent a detachment of drivers up to drive them back themselves, but Walker-Jones had requested that we organise the expedition as he was due to arrive in Bristol in a few days' time for an inspection. His packed itinerary allowed no time to visit us at the castle but he thought a meetup to discuss a few items would be a good idea, hence two birds were killed with one stone, and we agreed to transport the vehicles to Bristol.

Escorted by a tractor and trailer and one of our own armoured cars we would drive a convoy of vehicles down the motorway, spend the night at Bristol, meet with the admiral, and return the next day.

The mission had very few working parts to figure out, so we got it planned and got it done.

As the day was clear and sunny I chose to ride in the trailer towed behind Shawn's tractor, with Louise by his side as usual. The misery of cold, wet winter journeys hunkered down in the trailer from the worst of the weather became a distant memory as the sun shone on an unseasonably warm day. Looking around me I saw I wasn't the only one looking to soak up some sunshine, as others basked in the small but welcome warmth the bright day offered.

The mood was as good as the weather, so we kept watch and chatted between ourselves as we journeyed on the familiar road. We didn't expect to encounter any issues on such a well-travelled route, at the completion of which we anticipated the added bonus of spending a pleasant evening amongst people we knew well before returning the following day. All in all, the day felt like a bit of a jolly, even though the mission was a serious one.

Making good time we stopped at Daniel's place, his final resting place on the side of the motorway. We tidied up his grave and the area around it where the winter gales had blown over or damaged some of the eclectic range of tables and chairs, all of which had been left at the site to make it a more comfortable resting place. It had become a well-used and welcome resting place when journeying along the route and we always made a point of stopping there, to not only have a break, but to honour one of our own.

Fort Bristol had the air of a small, bustling town when we arrived. Many more people now called the place home than we had housed at the castle. It was a hive of activity with vehicles and people, on their own or in groups, all moving around with purpose and discipline.

"Not used to seeing this many people about," I said to Ian, who leaned against the side of the trailer beside me.

"Yeah," he replied, pointing to a group of Marines marching across the concrete dock being chivvied along by a sergeant. "At least we don't have any of that shit to deal with…not sure if we ran it that way we'd be as content as we are. Rather them than me."

I smiled in reply. It was to be expected I suppose, it was a base run by the military and so was run on a more rigid disciplinarian style than the mainly civilian population of the castle were used to. But then again, we had Maud, who probably wielded more power in her little finger in her own unique way than the base commander could.

Once parked we headed up the gangplank of the ship moored alongside the dock to meet Walker-Jones who we'd been told had arrived that morning. We were directed to the officers' mess where the admiral was waiting for us to begin the meal.

We soon discovered that the meeting he had requested was not really a meeting at all, but more of an informal social event under the guise of business. The Islanders had formed a few social groups where those with skills or the willingness to learn a new one got together to practice their chosen craft and to help pass the long winter nights. One of those groups had made a large quantity of baby clothes and toys for baby Hope, and Walker-Jones had wanted to present them to us personally rather than simply having them shipped on the next supply run. He was apologetic that he didn't have the time to deliver them in person to Chris and Nicky, as managing the wall's construction and preparing to inhabit the newly reclaimed land occupied most of his time.

The items were beautifully made, and we were touched by their thoughtfulness. We were sure Nicky would be over the moon with them, so with genuine appreciation we accepted the gifts.

One of the admiral's staff officers gave a presentation on the wall's progress using photographs taken both from on the ground and in the air. We learned that the main berm had been completed, and the photographs displayed on a large screen attached to a wall gave us our first view of it since we had left over a month earlier.

Since Hadrian's Wall was built by the Romans in the second century AD to protect Rome's northernmost border from the Picts, and many centuries later King Offa of the Mercia's erected another wall to protect his kingdom from the Welsh, no other defensive structure of this scale had been built on the British mainland. The bank was over twenty metres high with a deep, wide ditch in front for added protection.

The ditch had already flooded in some places as watercourses were dammed by the dyke, turning long stretches into moats. The double layer of strong fencing topped with razor wire running along the top of the whole structure created what looked to be an impassable barrier. Guard towers, all within line of sight of each other, enabled the entire length to be under constant surveillance and protection.

Walker-Jones interrupted his officer, most likely I assumed to get the meeting moving onwards, and not for us to just see pictures and plans of what a good job they'd done.

"It's all very impressive, but the work doesn't stop there as it'll need full-time team of engineers to maintain and improve it constantly. The first trailblazers have already been selected to begin populating and working the land once spring arrives. We'll start small at first with no expectation of self-sufficiency at all, but as our confidence grows through trial, error and hard work, these pioneers will pave the way for others to follow."

Having seen the wall in construction and already knowing it to be a remarkable achievement, it was good to see it nearing completion and the plans for populating the safe area behind it were progressing.

We knew there was far too much land for the few survivors we had. Great swathes of it most probably would be left for years, possibly decades, before the population grew enough to warrant it being used, but it would be there and that was the point. Without the wall nobody could safely live there until the last of the zombies had been eradicated. That sent my mind off on a tangent, having been reminded that only the ancient, high walls of our adopted home separated us from annihilation.

Once the presentation ended we spent some time touring the ever-expanding base of Fort Bristol. The original ring of containers was still in place providing a well-protected inner bastion housing the accommodation and administration blocks, but other layers, made up from more of the abundant containers, had spread across the vast dockside area as if they'd been breeding.

Linell, the same engineer who gave us our first tour of the facility when we'd delivered the initial convoy of supplies, was still in charge and gave us another tour.

"After meeting with you and your comments about how it was, to all attempts and purposes, a castle I was building…well it got me thinking," he told us as we followed him across the dockside after walking down the gang plank to meet him.

"I did a tally of how many containers I could utilise and—" he turned and smiled at us conspiratorially, like a schoolboy caught mid misdemeanour. "I went for it! You see, my parents always took me to castles when I was a young boy and the most impressive ones always had multiple layers of defence that got taller the closer to the keep they were…It was just that I never had enough Lego blocks to build one when I got home and that always frustrated me."

I laughed good naturedly at him.

"Don't tell me, your parents always knew you were going to be an engineer?"

He blinked in surprise at me before replying.

"They always joked I was born to be one. Why do you ask?"

"Oh no reason," I said, waving to the stacked containers around us. "Just the image of you in short trousers building a castle out of Lego. What's changed? Oh yes, the blocks have just got bigger, and now your toy box has an unlimited supply of them!"

"You know what? I've never made that connection before…"

He laughed, going red with embarrassment as the image of him playing at grown up, huge scale Castle building. Once he had collected himself he continued, directing us through the gateway.

"The outer layer is only one container high with few guard posts, and those are mainly centred around the gate. It is more of a perimeter fence to demark our safe area."

He led us back through the gateway and pointed to the next ring of containers.

"The next ring is double-stacked and more heavily defended as you can see."

This layer of defence we could see was much more heavily defended with multiple machine gun nests lining its top, but he didn't stop to let us admire it as he indicated for us to follow him through the gate towards the last ring of containers. It was as if he was in a rush and wanted to show us his prized collection of Star Wars figures or something. We followed him through a doorway cut into a container and up a few flights of stairs until we emerged on top of the triple-stacked inner ring of defence. The height enabled me to see over the top of the other two rings of containers.

"Have you added more staircases?" I asked Linnell as I admired the view.

"Yes, with multiple access points, and you can see from here that I adopted your idea of using extra containers as gun positions. Thank you for that…really solved a problem I was having," he replied, pointing to the containers stacked even higher at regular intervals around the walls.

They did give the impression of crenelations where defenders of old could fire their arrows and projectiles down at attackers before hiding from incoming missiles behind the merlons between them, much as our own castle had.

We inspected the nearest container. It was unmanned as only the outer cordon was defended when the base was not on alert, but it held a mounted machine gun which pointed out over the walls through the hole cut in its outer face, with plenty of ammunition stacked ready for reloads.

The field of fire from the top of the inner wall enabled it to fire over the top of the outer layers. If Fort Bristol was attacked it could lay down a ferocious three-layered barrage which would surely enable it to fight off any attack, from either the living or the dead.

Linell patted the machine gun subconsciously as he joined us enjoying the view.

"Drills have reduced the time from alarm to fully manned in just under five minutes, and we're working on improving that by making a few structural changes to ease a few congestion points."

Fort Bristol was the perfect example of a concentric castle design adapted to the modern age. It boasted multi-layered defences, each one stronger the close to the centre you got, with the failsafe of a navy ship tied alongside the dock for evacuation if the defenders were overwhelmed. Something none of us imagined would be possible.

When the tour was complete we spent some time checking over our vehicles and loaded our gifts for Hope, along with a few other supplies they had for us so we could get an early start the following morning. A weather front had disappointingly arrived during the day and a cold rain started falling, promising us an uncomfortable return journey in the trailer.

We decided to draw lots that evening to choose who would ride in the warm, dry armoured car if, when we woke in the morning, the weather continued to promise misery.

We spent a pleasant evening enjoying a meal and a few drinks before turning in sooner than we wanted to, ready for an early start in the morning.

CHAPTER SIXTEEN

The Brough's Farm

"Still bloody freezing," Kip Ferris complained as he hunkered down trying to shelter against the rain that sheeted down.

"Oh for the love of…will you stop moaning for one day? Just one day? It's not that fucking cold anymore, the snow's all gone, we're just bloody soaked," Stu Marks groaned, sick of the constant stream of pessimism from the man he had been partnered with to watch the walls of the Brough's farm.

"Well, what are we even doing out in this anyway?" Ferris went on, undeterred by the anger in Marks' tone. "When was the last time you even bleedin' saw a zombie, eh? Tell me that."

"How about I break your ankle and toss you over the wall? See if that attracts one?" Marks growled with a smirk on his face in an attempt to diffuse the situation.

Ferris watched him warily, unsure if the threat was genuine or not. He knew he was getting on the older man's nerves, but it wasn't in his nature to let grievances go unaired, so he doubled down in a vain attempt to make his point despite the olive branch thrown in his direction.

"Months, mate. It's been months. Not even the road crews reported seeing any, so I reckon the cold's done for 'em."

Marks said nothing, holding his tongue lest he lose control with the whining man beside him, but his silence was taken as a piqued interest.

"They've all froze, right? Must have. All we had to do was make it to winter and poof! No more zombies. It's meant to be spring now despite this bloody weather, I bet we won't see a single one of the ba—"

"Will you, for the love of everything holy, shut the f—" Marks snapped with real venom in his voice for the first time.

"Movement!"

The shout from far to their left ended the argument before it could take hold, snapping both men's attention to the empty ground ahead of them.

"Lights!" came the next order, and Marks fumbled with cold hands to work the large spotlight attached to the wall of their post and activate it.

In an instant the dull grey of predawn was banished by the harsh beam of bright white light cutting swathes over the flat ground surrounding the farm's walls. He scanned it left and right, tried to maintain a methodical pace but fought the urge to whip it around in a desperate search for what had caused the alarm. They didn't possess night vision optics, they were told it was because the batteries for them were a finite resource so only the watch commanders were given them, but Marks knew it was more likely that idiots like Ferris would mess around with them probably dropping and breaking them in the process, so like all the good toys, they'd been taken away and kept under lock and key.

"Where?" Marks called out as his nerve broke.

"Your eleven o'clock, two hundred metres," came the shouted reply.

Marks turned the light to the right direction and lifted it slowly, estimating where the beam would land on the right distance to hold it steady.

Nothing. Nothing moved and nothing stood there, waiting for a sniff of them to animate it into moaning and shambling in a futile bid to eat them.

Marks relaxed, sagging with relief.

"Probably a fox," Ferris grumbled.

"Stand down. Probably a fox," came the orders in a voice that sounded almost disappointed.

"Told you," Ferris said smugly. "And it's still bloody freezing."

But Stu Marks didn't hear Ferris renewed complaint. As he killed the powerful beam of light, he had seen a glimpse of something that his brain failed to register. His eyes sent the images, but they hadn't been interpreted correctly, at least that was what his first conscious thought had been, because there was no way what he thought he'd seen could be real.

He switched the light back on and jerked the beam over the area he'd recently lit up, only to invite an angry question yelled at him.

"Bloody hell what are you playin' at? I said stand down!"

Marks froze at a scratching noise and a low, rhythmic panting like that of an animal. His eyes locked onto Ferris' in the weak light cast by a sun not yet peeking the horizon. Before either man could think sufficiently to make words the noises from below them, from outside the walls, turned both of their heads down in time to see a pale-faced body leaping high like no human had the ability to do so.

Both men screamed.

Both screams were cut off by wet, sinewy rips, and the pre-dawn became a nightmare for the living.

~

Sargeant Gallon was woken by the first flurry of shots that cracked around the farm's courtyard. Instantly alert, he rammed his feet into his boots, grabbed his rifle and webbing, and ran outside into utter chaos.

Searchlights shone from all the towers, slashing their beams of light towards whatever was out there beyond the high walls. Every gun from the watch towers fired, tracer rounds from the machine guns sending their laser-like streaks of light outwards.

"What the fuck is going on?" Gallon screamed, unheard as his voice was drowned out by the cacophony.

The courtyard was in darkness lit only by muzzle flashes. Needing to see what was going on, he ran to the main power switch that activated the external lighting normally switched off during the hours of darkness. That was their standard operating procedure both to preserve the night vision of the sentries and to avoid having the generator running overnight, wasting valuable fuel and attracting possible unwanted attention.

It took a few seconds for the generator to start before the lights flickered a few times before fully lighting up to turn the dull pre-dawn into yellow-hued daytime.

As Gallon looked around, everyone who had been sleeping mere seconds before ran out in various stages of undress, all carrying their personal weapon and shouting in confusion.

He needed to know what was going on. It was chaotic and order needed to be restored.

He screamed at the soldiers who were still emerging from their quarters.

"Get to the fucking walls!" he bawled, running with them.

He skidded to a halt when a group of soldiers to his left let loose a torrent of automatic fire at one of the sentry platforms. Changing his own direction, he ran to see what the hell they were firing at.

"Fucking zombies!" someone screamed.

Whatever had been on the platform was now bullet riddled and dead but Gallon stared at the two other bodies lying on the platform.

Bodies wearing camouflage.

Without hesitation he leapt at the steps leading to the platform, and on reaching the top one glance confirmed that two of his men were dead. Both had had their throats ripped out as if savaged by a wild animal. Their uniforms torn from their bodies covered in deep gashes told him they had died horribly in a vicious, unrelenting assault.

Turning his head to stare at the culprit he saw a creature unlike any zombie he had seen before, and he had seen and killed countless undead since it all began.

Zombies were slow, shambling, rotting shells of the person they had once been. They didn't look like this one, with its pale, naked body muscled like an athlete. It looked like a hunter. Like some kind of evolved predator that terrified him.

Gallon glanced up. Only thirty seconds had passed since being woken by the first shots and the yard was still full of shouts, swearing and the signs of total confusion. The shooting had died down as at least some of the training the soldiers had kicked in, reminding them to only shoot at a target they could see and not blaze away at shadows like frightened amateurs.

He cursed at himself as his own shock subsided. He was in command, and he had to lead. He'd wasted valuable seconds allowing confusion to reign.

But what the fuck had happened?

The lights illuminated the ground fifty yards beyond the walls. He stared out and into the darkness beyond but apart from smoke rising from where thousands of bullets had ripped up the fields making them appear freshly ploughed, he saw nothing.

His voice, trained by years of service boomed, above the sporadic firing.

"Cease fire, cease fire!"

The firing petered out as the order filtered through panicked ears.

Ignoring the dead bodies at his feet that he could do nothing about, he angled the searchlight that had been uselessly pointing downwards and swept it across the perimeter. As the bright light penetrated the darkness beyond the fixed lamps, his heart stopped.

The beam lit up a mass of bodies standing just outside the ring of illumination, highlighting pale, expressionless faces and muscled bodies.

His heart thumping in his chest like a bass drum, he swept the beam around more, stopping when he noticed one that seemed taller than the rest. Gallon fixed it in the bright beam, and even from the distance that separated them the look of pure evil glaring back sent a shudder of fear through his bones.

They locked eyes for a few seconds, as if they were two opposing commanders on a battlefield. That this abnormal zombie was the enemy leader wasn't in doubt, but he could think of no logical reason explaining why or how he knew it. Of the massed ranks of undead assaulters, only this one stared directly at him, assessing him, seeming to figure out his intentions and imagine tactics to counter.

He broke eye contact with the enemy commander, ending the spell of ominous silence and tension between them. He looked around the fully lit yard, seeing every firing step and tower manned by confused and frightened soldiers who all saw what he did.

A shout from below made him turn. Stuart Brough was at the bottom of the steps, wearing a dressing gown and wellington boots on with a rifle in his hands.

"What's going on?" he asked.

His voice was calm and quiet, as if being woken in the middle of a night by a barrage of gunfire was an everyday occurrence.

"Something ripped two of my lads apart," Gallon responded, looking back over the wall to confirm his mind wasn't playing tricks on him. "And there's hundreds more of the bastards out there."

Stuart swiftly climbed the ladder to stare outwards and lock onto the anomalous leader.

"Jesus!" he uttered in disbelief.

The enemy leader was still lit by the beam, and they watched as it moved its head to inspect the troops surrounding it before staring very deliberately back at Gallon.

Gallon, unaware of precisely what was about to happen knew in his very bones that it was going to be nothing good.

"Oh fu—" he started saying.

The lead zombie opened its mouth to let out a loud, blood-curdling roar that washed over the defenders like a precursor of doom.

As one the massed ranks bent forwards and ran at them, a tsunami of flesh with only one intention: to kill.

Gallon didn't need to give the order to open fire as every gun opened up. The crack of rifles and the deeper, chattering boom of heavy machine guns performed a symphony of defiance with the kerchunk-kerchunk of grenade machine guns adding percussion.

Gallon raised his rifle and fired at the solid mass of advancing flesh where no individual target could be seen for long. Firing in short bursts he emptied his magazine, risking a glance around as his hands moved automatically to seat a fresh one.

The continuous fire ripped mercilessly through the ranks of rapidly advancing undead, but they pushed through the deadly storm of hot lead and high explosives, enraged, undeterred and unafraid.

Bodies disappeared in mists of red spray as large calibre bullets vapourised them, but each dropping body was replaced by another that leapt through clouds of blood spraying in gory remains to drive their assault home.

The front rank of enemy reached the ditch on his left and leapt at it with inhuman agility.

Rifles angled downwards as the desperate defenders fought to stop the front ranks getting closer, but they kept coming. The wire fence above the ditch slowed their advance, the lead ranks rebounding off the taught strands of barbed wire until it was flattened by the weight of numbers running at it.

The forest of sharpened spikes lining the ditch impaled the frontrunners running blindly into them. The wooden tips speared through bodies driving clean through and out of their backs for another to impale itself on it, forming gory kebabs of still-thrashing undead flesh.

More leapt over those now smothering the last line of defence before the wall, as sheer numbers rendered the defence inert.

Gallon's eyes widened as they leapt at the tower to his left, its defenders blazing away wildly on full-auto, throwing back bodies that clawed and scrambled up the walls he had once thought unassailable. With rising dread and horror, he watched as four zombies reached the platform and swarmed the three soldiers who went down kicking and screaming as they resorted to using empty rifles as clubs in a desperate last bid to live.

Gallon raised his own rifle with tears of anger and fear running down his face to empty the weapon at the platform, briefly sweeping it clear of the undead until it clicked empty once again and more undead leapt up to replace their fallen.

CHAPTER SEVENTEEN

Gallon didn't reload. He gazed dumbstruck around the yard as all around him the defences and walls were flooding with pale bodies that clawed and tore at his people.

"We can't hold them," he muttered to himself.

"What?" Stuart screamed beside him as he fumbled to reload his weapon.

"We can't hold them," Gallon said again, louder this time as his body began to reboot and catch up with his mind. "Back to the farmhouse!"

Gallon turned for the ladder, roaring his order over and over in the hope that others would hear it and pass it on.

"Retreat! Back to the farmhouse! Back! Baaaack!"

Remembering the proper protocol and fumbling with adrenaline, his shaking hands grabbed the whistle from a pocket on his uniform. He put it to his lips and blew on it to give their retreat signal; one that had been practiced many times but never imagined having to ever use.

The slow, shambling zombies they were accustomed to would never have been able to breach their heavily fortified compound after all, but contingencies always had to be catered for.

Pulling the whistle from his lips he screamed at the top of his lungs; his sergeant's voice cutting through the cacophony of firing, of screams of terror and pain echoing everywhere as desperate men and women fought for their lives.

"RETREAT, RETREAT, RETREAT!" he bellowed.

Stuart still emptied magazine after magazine at the advancing wall of undead, so Gallon grabbed him by the shoulder to propel him down the ladder. Illuminated by the bright lights, more soldiers leapt from the firing steps and towers, risking injury over death as clawing hands and leaping bodies threatened to engulf their positions.

A moment of pride flashed across Gallon's racing brain at the discipline the survivors still retained. Instead of turning and running, something every fibre of his own body wanted to do, they still faced their enemy. Instinctively gravitating together as individuals joined others to form rally squares that, even though virtually running backwards, maintained a storm of gunfire aimed at the walls which swarmed with an ever-growing number of zombies.

Zombies were thrown back from the walls or fell to the yard, their smoking bodies riddled with bullets, but for each body that fell yet more leapt over it and advanced, their twisted faces showing nothing but rage and a hunger for human flesh.

Gallon watched with horror as those not quick enough to respond to his desperate command fell under the waves of bodies leaping from the walls and advancing towards them across the yard.

Zombies threw themselves recklessly at soldiers struggling to reload weapons with panicked hands. Their screams of agony as teeth ripped into their flesh burned into his soul as the dread of failure and imminent death rose within him.

Hope rose when his mind registered the deep and steady booming of heavy calibre machine guns firing from somewhere over his head behind him. The heavy bullets held the advancing undead back as fat bullets tore through soft flesh and bone, slicing swathes of destruction through the tide of approaching death.

Explosions began ripping through the horde as the familiar crack and boom of exploding grenades blew gaps and holes among the masses, sending body parts flying upwards and outwards with each detonation that tore through them.

The brief respite created by the heavy bullets and grenades provided just enough time the retreating defenders needed to reach the house.

"Get inside!" Gallon screamed at the few survivors around him.

The door was now only a few metres behind him and, still stumbling backwards and firing, they rushed to it. Rapid glances around him observed his people as they threw themselves inside, though each one that reached the perceived safety inside decreased the amount of outgoing lead.

Despite the devastating volume of fire coming from the windows over his head and the explosions of grenades, the enemy's advance gathered a momentum that spelled disaster.

Seconds seemed to turn into hours as he inched backwards, sensing more than seeing his people reach the door just as his rifle clicked empty. With no time to reload he dropped it on its sling and drew his sidearm, standing his ground with the sole intention to kill as many as he could to give his people time to get inside.

He was prepared to make his last stand protecting those he was responsible for, snapping off single shots at heads when his back hit the door frame.

He was going to die, and he didn't care.

Rage replaced fear as he thought of the friends he would never see again.

"Shut the door!" he screamed.

He was alone facing hundreds of them, and he was going to die.

He screamed blue murder at them, every shot shattering brains out of the back of the skulls closest to him.

Gallon was prepared to meet his maker, but he was going to make the bastards pay for it first. Performing a fast reload he raised the pistol again at heads only a few paces away.

"Come on, you fuckers! Come and—"

A hand grabbed the back of his shirt and dragged him backwards, causing his last shot to go skywards. Yanked forcibly through the door and thrown to the floor he watched as hands slammed the door shut and leaned their weight against it. The door shook with the impact of the attackers charging against it, and it took a few seconds for the locking bars to be dropped into place to secure it.

Gallon looked around, shocked at the realisation that he still lived. He was glad, he found, despite his willingness to go down fighting, and swore to himself that for however long he remained so, he would fight as hard as he could to make it even longer.

It was chaos as everyone else ran around grabbing whatever they could to barricade and strengthen every door and window on the ground floor of the farmhouse.

Gallon got to his feet and shook himself like a dog to clear his head and get his emotions back in order before taking command again.

The doors and windows he could see were holding. They shook in their frames and plaster fell from the edges, but he knew they were strong and would work for now. Gallon had to check everywhere.

"Barricade every door and window down here!" he screamed.

People were already doing it anyway, and he knew the command was more to get himself back into the fight.

He ran upstairs to find the Brough's still manning the guns they had dragged into position. Two fifty-cal machine guns pointed out of the windows and a half empty box of grenades lay open. Their rate of fire had decreased since the survivors had reached the safety of the farmhouse, but they were still firing the occasional burst and lobbing grenades out of the window.

"Not too close to the building," Gallon warned, envisioning a stray grenade undoing their hard work in securing the house.

The firing stopped when he spoke, and he approached to look out of a window to see the yard teeming with a seething mass of zombies pushing against one another as they tried to reach the walls of the farmhouse. He watched in shock as those nearer the back leapt over those in front to scramble desperately forwards over the mass of bodies like crowd surfers at a rock concert.

This was the first chance Gallon had to study them properly, and even though his mind had registered their difference in the desperate fight of a few minutes before, his wildly racing theories now came into focus.

He studied one among the masses, picking it out for no reason other than it still wore the shredded remains of a t shirt that somehow clung to its body. The red fabric made it stand out from the rest so he wouldn't lose it in the writhing mass of dead flesh below.

Instead of shambling, rotting former shells of what they had once been, shuffling along on uncoordinated limbs in search of their next meal of live flesh with dull, dead eyes these creatures were something else entirely.

Once the human survivors had learnt how to avoid and kill the ungainly enemy, their only strength lay in them gathering together in innumerable hordes to create an unstoppable wave, but those people had also learnt and adapted and now lived behind high, unassailable walls the masses could only wash harmlessly against. Those walls were also lined with enough firepower to destroy everything the living might face, but this new iteration filling the yard were unlike anything he had seen.

Their bodies had changed; heavily muscled and looking to be at the peak of physical fitness.

Their once dead, black eyes now shone brightly as they searched hungrily for prey with an eagerness Gallon had not witnessed before.

Only one description came to his mind was the one he had had when he had briefly glanced at the one that had been shot on the walls.

They were hunters, and deadly ones at that.

His blood chilled and an involuntary shudder swept over him as he stared at the horde below until movement on the walls grabbed his attention.

The one he had seen, larger than the rest who appeared to have given the order to attack, stood in isolation on a firing step against the walls with tattered scraps of what was once a white shirt clinging to a body that seemed to have expanded over the shredded material, trapping the few pieces of cloth in its skin.

The menace exuding from it as it glowered across the yard dropped Gallon's body temperature even further as he stood transfixed by the sight of pure evil that opened its mouth and roared.

Every undead head in the yard turned to stare at their leader before another roar from its lips split the air, and it waved its arm as if issuing orders.

Gallon jolted at his own stupidity. It had all the appearance of their commander and there it was standing on the walls, lit clearly by the lights and promising to be an easy kill. He grabbed for his rifle hanging by its sling and raised it to his shoulder to line up the sights on its head.

As if knowing what was about to happen the monster stared back at Gallon in the split second before he pulled the trigger. It scowled scorn and derision at him. It dared him. Dared him to try and kill it.

Click.

The firing pin fell on an empty chamber. He hadn't reloaded his weapon in the panicked retreat.

Cursing in anger and frustration he couldn't force himself to break eye contact with it. He could have pushed Brough's son off the machine gun and fired, but something stopped him. The thing on the walls roared again and pointed at Gallon before giving what could only be described as a dismissive gesture, and in a single leap jumped over the wall and out of sight.

In less than a minute the yard emptied as all the other zombies turned and leapt nimbly at the walls to disappear from view, leaving only the shattered bodies of the dead behind littering the yard.

The silence, once all the rasping and roaring throats had departed, was deafening. Gallon stood for a full ten seconds staring at the empty yard trying to grasp what he had just witnessed. Whatever changes that had happened to the zombies over the winter, the main thing he realised was that they now were being led by one that displayed a level of intelligence never seen before. His mind raced as the thoughts racing around his head settled into a semblance of order until his eyes were drawn to the few scraps of camouflaged clothing that lay scattered between the still smoking bodies of the hundreds of dead zombies.

He'd lost men and women under his command, and at that moment he had no idea how many. A wave of furious filled guilt and self-loathing filled every fibre of his being as he physically jolted with shock. He had failed.

His command needed to take stock, mourn their dead and regroup, for he had no doubt that they would be back, and they needed to prepare. He needed to lead his shattered command to fight.

"I need an ammo and weapon count!" he roared.

His corporal ran up to him, his white, shock-filled face forced him to supress his own panicked thoughts; Gallon's people needed him now more than they ever had.

"Dean. Glad you made it," he said, lowering his voice. "I need a head count…need to know who's left."

The corporal nodded soberly and started to turn away to begin, but he turned back and grabbed Geoff's arm.

"Sar'nt, you need to radio this in as well," he whispered sharply knowing Gallon had forgotten.

"Fuck me, you're right, Dean," Gallon replied, cursing his own stupidity.

They weren't alone. He could call for the cavalry to arrive and save them. He turned and ran downstairs to the radio, on the way realising that this could be happening everywhere and if it hadn't, they needed warning.

CHAPTER EIGHTEEN

Fort Bristol

I woke to alarm bells ringing loudly throughout the ship and red lights flashing in the darkness.

"Action stations. Action stations," a surprisingly calm voice blared from the speakers of the ship's address system.

Bathed in the red glow I struggled to dress, my panicked hands having the opposite effect on the speed they were trying to achieve. I opened the door to the one bed officer's quarters I had been allocated to find the gangway filled with sailors and marines pulling on flash hoods and helmets as they rushed to their assigned stations. Shawn opened the door opposite mine with a terrified Louise standing beside him as we observed the ordered chaos.

"What's going on?" he asked.

I bit back the retort that it was a daft question as clearly he knew as much as I did.

"Don't know," I shouted to make my voice heard over the noise of the klaxon blaring and shouts of running sailors rushing by.

The commotion subsided within a minute as the well-drilled crew reached their action stations. I stepped into the now empty corridor looking around wondering what to do next when a sailor wearing a flash hood and helmet approached us briskly.

I didn't know who he was, but he clearly recognised me.

"Tom, Admiral Walker would like you to join him in the CIC. Follow me please."

He turned and started walking away as if expecting me to follow him, which I did with Shawn catching up to me.

"Bugger that, we're coming too," he said, gripping Louise's hand to follow close on my heels.

The CIC was packed with people all looking very serious and busy, with every station manned by sailors working with rigid concentration. The klaxon was muted behind the heavily armoured walls as this was the place where in battle the ship's combat and control systems could be operated even when the vessel had taken heavy damage.

Walker-Jones approached as soon as he saw us enter.

"The Brough's have been attacked. Your chap Gallon just radioed it in."

"What?! Did they get the bastards that did it? Was anyone hurt?" I blurted out, shocked at the news.

Walker-Jones eyed me with a grave expression.

"It wasn't people, Tom. They've been overrun by zombies. Half of his command is dead, and they've barricaded themselves in the farmhouse. He's asking for reinforcements or evacuation as he fears they won't be able to fight off another attack."

I started blurting out random questions as my mind tried to absorb the information.

"How the hell did they breach the walls? Did they leave the gate open? Surely, they've got enough firepower to defend themselves?"

The admiral shushed me with both hands in a calming gesture that didn't work.

"We're collating what we know so far," he said firmly. "We're still on the radio to him so if we wait we'll know more, and then we might be able to react accordingly. We don't know what we're facing so I called action stations just in case they attack here as well."

He my dawn of realisation and spoke quickly.

"Don't worry, my first action was to alert the castle, but Gallon had already told them as they're the nearest to the farm. All bases are on full alert, just in case."

A panicked look sprang across my face at the thought of not being at the castle to defend it and my family. Walker-Jones stopped me talking by placing a hand on my shoulder as he knew what I was about to say, because I needed to get home immediately.

"Tom, let's gather information first. Yes, you are going home soon, but we need to know what we're facing first."

He glanced over both shoulders and lowered his voice so only I could hear him.

"From what I've heard it doesn't look good, so there's no point going off half-cock. That's how people get killed."

He turned away before I could reply and went to stand behind the officer manning the radio. I watched, hardly able to breath in fear and anticipation as I saw the officer finish writing on a sheet of paper which he handed to the admiral.

Walker-Jones studied it for a while, his features creased in concentration before disbelief filled his eyes. He scanned the page again before looking up and barking orders.

"Watch commanders to my conference room!" he snapped, then looked at me. "Tom, your senior people too, if you please."

Five rushed minutes later I arrived slightly breathless at the ship's conference room with Hammond, Eddy, Ian, Jamie and Shane. I'd found them on deck watching the hive of activity that Fort Bristol had become as they went on full alert.

Ian and Jamie had donned their full armour as soon as the alarm sounded, and they clunked and rattled their way in behind me, again looking like a bad directors call on a movie set as he got the next scene wrong. Shawn and Louise were already in there.

Walker-Jones's usual air of unflappable calm looked disturbed, and his double take at seeing men in medieval plate armour onboard his ship made him shake his head as if resetting.

"No questions until I've finished," he said, glancing down at the sheet of paper in his hand. "At approximately oh-five-thirty a mass of zombies breached the walls at Brough's Farm. The defences were unable to hold them back, forcing them to retreat to the farmhouse and lock it down. Unfortunately, a sizeable portion of the garrison were killed in the attack."

His blunt words glossed over the obvious fact that they had died a terrifyingly painful death as their flesh was ripped from their bodies.

"The zombies have now left the compound and have gone to ground somewhere beyond the walls."

"They left?" I blurted out, shocked by the sudden change in behaviour.

The admiral held his hand up to stop any more interruptions.

"Sergeant Gallon reports that these zombies are unlike any we have seen before. He reports that they are..." He glanced down and read from the report in his hand. "More mobile, heavily muscled with far superior coordination, meaning they had the ability to climb the walls with ease."

He paused to deliver the most terrifying part.

"And they appear to be following orders from one individual described as a monster, in that it is much larger and appears to possess intelligence and the ability to communicate with the others. Gallon reports that it seemed to interact with him, when he tried and failed to shoot it."

The whole room stood in shocked silence as we all tried to make sense of what we'd just been told.

"We need to get home right now," I said.

"Yes, Tom, you do," the admiral replied. "But with this new information we need to plan. There appears to be a new enemy out there and given what just happened we must be prepared to meet them. If they breached the walls at the Brough's, are any of us truly safe? How high can they climb? Simply put, we don't know the physical or tactical limitations of this new enemy."

"That's why I need to get home now!" I replied firmly.

Eddy, who had remained quiet throughout the meeting spoke up.

"Tom, please listen. If they got over the walls at the Brough's despite all the defences and firepower they have in place, we need to stop and think. What if we meet them on the road? It sounds like they could easily overwhelm our trailer, so if we want to get home safe we need to work out how."

"How has this happened?" Shawn asked, addressing the elephant in the room. "Why has this happened? Are you saying they…they evolved over the winter or something? Is this why we found them huddling together in basements? Are they all going to be like this now? There could be millions of these bloody super zombies out there!"

"I still need to get home. Now!" I repeated with much more force in my voice.

"Tom, think for a moment please?" Walker-Jones replied with a kinder edge to his tone.

He knew what me and the others from the castle were going through. We had family out there, and we wanted to go and help protect them against whatever was coming.

The admiral summoned some senior officers for a hushed discussion in a corner before a few of them bustled from the room.

"Everyone's safety is my primary concern," Walker-Jones announced as the meeting got underway again.

He looked at me and raised his hand as if warning me to be quiet at what he was going to say next.

"I therefore cannot authorise any travel by road until we have a clearer picture of what's going on."

I jolted in anger but heeded his warning and waited for him to continue.

"I have just ordered the evacuation of all land behind the Corn Wall. Only the wall itself will be patrolled, its positions strengthened, and rapid evacuation procedures will be put in place.

He looked at the castle residents.

"I have also just ordered helicopters to prepare for take off and fly you immediately to the castle. Another helicopter is also preparing to leave to perform an immediate reconnaissance of the Brough's. It will be transporting additional troops who will be dropped off to reinforce the garrison until we can plan the evacuation…and before you say it, we haven't the lift capacity immediately available to take them all in one go. Our one remaining chinook is down for maintenance, but they are expediting the work and hope to get it in the air by tomorrow at the latest."

I clenched and re-clenched both fists to try and salve the pain of inaction.

"The helicopters taking you home will carry reinforcements to bolster your own defences. I am waiting to hear about capacity, range and endurance capabilities of the aircraft we have available…Anything else you can think of, please speak up now as understandably time is of the essence."

I was going home, and in a helicopter would be there in less than an hour, so I shook my head and looked at the others who all replied the same. The urgency to return home to our family, friends and loved ones was everyone's first and only thought.

"Get your gear together whilst we make the final arrangements," Walker-Jones said.

He turned to walk out the room without another word as there was no time for pleasantries when crisis mode was active and speed could save lives.

My kit was a small day sack holding a change of clothes and spare ammunition for my personal weapons, so I was back outside and heading for the dock in no time at all.

As we waited on the dockside for the helicopter Shawn voiced my own worries.

"I hope Geoff can hold the Brough's place until we can get our shit sorted."

CHAPTER NINETEEN

"They're sending a helicopter with reinforcements while they work out the best evac plan," Gallon told the room after removing the radio headset.

Stuart Brough and his family had gathered in a corner of the lounge, as all around the house barricades were checked and reinforced. Those apertures not firmly blocked were defended by multiple rifle barrels.

"They're offering you and your family a ride out when it gets here," Gallon told them, his tone portraying much more than that simple statement.

They were being offered life while those remaining would most likely die if a second attack came.

Stuart shook his head firmly.

"I'm not leaving until everyone else does. The rest of my family will though," he said, shaking with emotion. "Enough people have died now, and in the past, to protect us."

Gallon understood but he had no words. Stepping across the room he placed a hand on Stuart's shoulder.

"I cannot leave until everyone else does," Stuart insisted quietly.

A tear rolled down his cheek and his shoulders shook with the after-effects of too much adrenaline. As he tried to hold it in, his wife enveloped him in a consolatory hug.

Their eldest son stepped forward, "We're staying, dad. This is our home too. We can't let others fight for it and just…run away. besides, there's no way in hell we're leaving here without you."

Stuart raised his tear-streaked eyes to look at him and spoke sternly.

"No, son, you get your mother and everyone else to safety."

He looked at his grandchildren, who had been forced to grow up so much in the last months effectively robbing them of their childhood.

"I need you to protect my grandchildren. I've lived my life, but you have a chance if we get through this. You've got a chance to carry on the family name, and when this is all over you can return and continue what we created here."

"Dad, No, I—"

Stuart Brough straightened his back as his resolve built up to deliver his ultimatum.

"If you love me, get on the helicopter," he said firmly before turning and walking out of the room, allowing no argument or protest at his decision.

Gallon knew he needed to break the air of tension and despondency that had befallen the compound. A helicopter was inbound, probably within an hour or two, not only bringing reinforcements and resupply, but offering the civilian residents the chance of escape.

Those staying behind knew that unless the promised evacuation didn't happen soon, they likely wouldn't make it.

The super zombies hadn't broken into the farmhouse because, for some reason, the huge one that seemed to be commanding them inexplicably ordered them to withdraw. That was what bothered Gallon the most. A mindless horde was a known quantity, but when their enemy could think tactically, could plan, his hopes for survival plummeted.

As for the reinforcements, Gallon hoped they'd been made aware of the situation and they would all be volunteers, otherwise when they arrived he feared he might have a mutiny on his hands.

He stood, unable to just idly await death, knowing they had to do something to help themselves if only to keep their minds off the situation, and being busy was the best way he knew to do that.

He couldn't get involved in the Brough's agonising decision, but he needed to keep his people together. He wasn't going down without a fight, he'd made that fact clear during the attack, but they needed to give themselves at least a vague hope of survival. That needed to come from him, so he drew in a breath and prepared to play the role.

Time to inject a little spine, I think, he told himself.

"Okay, people. I want a weapon and ammo count now. Tell me what we've got left to fight those bastards with," he barked confidently, seeing the survivors of his garrison straighten up.

"After that, we're going to lock this place down tighter than my arse after a vindaloo!"

"I'm going to inspect the walls," he said, pointing at two of his men he knew were steady and reliable. "You two! On me!"

Gallon and his two men, who both held their weapons tightly in nervous hands, waited until the door was bolted and locked behind them before they picked their way across the gory remains covering the yard. Cautious to keep their distance, they stabbed at every skull displaying any vestige of life with fixed bayonets. A few twitched and emitted rasping breaths as their destroyed bodies rendered them immobile, but not one that was noticed was left to be a potential killer.

The sheer number of bodies shocked them. The yard was filled with hundreds, and as Gallon climbed the ladder to a tower to look beyond the walls, the view stunned him into momentary silence.

The open field was littered with hundreds more corpses, but the ditch, their first line of defence, was now redundant. Bodies filled it, making it virtually level with the surrounding land. The once warlike and imposing array of spikes that had seemed an impenetrable barrier still stuck up in places above the morass of death but were rendered useless.

Bodies filled the entire lengths of them, some still displaying signs of lethal animation.

"Fuuucck," he said, drawing out the word under his breath.

"Sar'nt?" one of his men asked, snapping back to the job at hand.

The walls could no longer be defended, not with their defences already overrun. He couldn't ask any of his people to stay and fight on them when their ineffectiveness had been proven during the attack.

He thought ruefully that they would most likely abandon their post at the first sight of another assault and truthfully, he couldn't guarantee he'd be able to stop himself running if they came again. He knew the walls held their heaviest weaponry in the mounted machine guns and grenade machine guns there, and if they were to stand a chance then they needed them.

"Let's get these back to the house," he said indicating the guns standing idly on their mounts with barrels pointing impotently skywards.

As he turned away movement across the field caught his eye, and he spun back to raise his rifle. Something was happening at the treeline, the edges had darkened as if the undergrowth that sprouted along its periphery had thickened, but it was too distant and the short-range scope on his weapon wasn't strong enough to make out details.

He grabbed some binoculars hanging from a hook and raised them to his eyes, discovering the edge of the woodland thick with them. Roving the binoculars he couldn't estimate the numbers emerging, but they had to be in their thousands.

And they all just stood stock still staring at the farm.

Another movement made him jerk the binoculars left, resting on the leader, if that was the best name to call it, pushing its way through the ranks to glare menacingly right at him.

"Get down!" he hissed as he dropped, not wanting to be seen or create any sort of response from them.

"Get the guns back," he ordered quietly. "I'll keep watch."

He estimated he'd have just enough time to reach the safety of the farmhouse if they attacked. Crouching against the wall he tried to keep as low a profile as possible with just the top of his head and binoculars peeping over.

The distance was too great to shoot anything with a degree of accuracy, so he didn't raise his rifle.

And besides, he thought, glancing down at the six magazines he carried. Wouldn't make a bloody dent anyway.

His job was to observe, gather any possible intelligence, and most of all give warning of the next attack.

Minutes passed and nothing moved as the uncountable mass of the undead just waited.

"Sar'nt?" came a quiet call from below.

Without diverting his eyes Gallon called back, his voice barely above a whisper.

"What? I thought I told you all to get inside. Now bloody do it."

"Do you want us to get some more ammunition from the barn? We need it."

Gallon thought for a few seconds, cursing himself for knowing it and not already ordering their own resupply.

He reached for the whistle that was on a lanyard around his neck and replied quietly.

"Yes, do it now, but if you hear my whistle you drop everything and get back inside pronto."

"What about you?"

Don't worry about me, I'll be right up your ass running like Usain Bolt with the shits."

The metallic sounds of guns being quietly dismounted from other positions served as confirmation of his orders, and he was as proud of those under his command then as he ever had been. The survivors had put away the grief of losing friends and were getting back to what they had been trained to do: soldiering.

Gallon watched but couldn't understand why they didn't attack. That question was answered when he realised more were adding to the enemy numbers stretching further back into the woods.

The shock of the situation hit him. The leader, or whoever he was, was waiting for more to arrive.

Where are they coming from? How the bloody hell do they know to come?

He knew that the numbers already facing them could engulf the farm, but if even more arrived it would put the matter beyond doubt. That they were showing tactical awareness and operating under orders scared the life out of him.

Not the mindless from before the winter anymore.

The minutes stretched out as he kept his lonely vigil on the gathering army of death.

Occasional noises from behind him didn't sway his concentration. Guesswork made him think they were reinforcing the farmhouse and dragging things around, but he dared not turn to look in case he missed them starting their second assault. He had seen the speed they could move at and knew it would take them no time to cross the field that separated them, so he kept his eyes glued to the enemy ranks to save those vital seconds until eventually a low voice called up to him.

"Sar'nt? Helicopter's ten minutes out. We've cleared a space in the yard for them to land and the Brough's are good to go."

Gallon looked back at the yard for the first time seeing an area had been cleared of bodies now carelessly stacked in a corner, allowing a small space for a helicopter to land. At the farmhouse, more boards had been fixed to the lower floor windows, reinforcing them further. More noises could be heard coming from within the building which told of yet more work underway.

"Good job, Corporal," he said cracking a smile for the first time since it began at the man below him. "I'll stay here and watch the bastards. Once the evac's gone I need to send a report off so I'll need someone here to replace me."

The corporal nodded, then turned to rush back to the farmhouse.

A few minutes later a faint whop-whop reached his ears. He knew it would be arriving from the south, so he kept lifting his eyes from the binoculars to try and spot it approaching.

The noise grew louder until a Merlin burst fast over the top of the trees directly over where the main mass of zombies centred around the leader and, as one, they craned their undead heads upwards as it flew over them.

This was the moment Gallon feared most.

They, or at least their leader, displayed a tactical understanding of the situation, waiting in sinister silence for more to arrive. Now that silence had been broken by the thudding of helicopter blades.

Gallon focused the binoculars on the leader as it stood and stared at the metal object that had appeared from nowhere to head for the farmhouse.

Distance and the roar of the aircraft drowned out its scream, but Gallon watched through binoculars as the mouth opened and the body jerked at the effort of emitting the command.

Arms that previously hung inanimately by its sides began whirling frantically to reinforce that command with a visual emphasis.

The dark mass against the treeline changed shape as the wall of undead flesh charged.

Gallon raised his whistle and blew on it hard, then turned and leapt from the tower's platform to roll like coming in to land from a parachute drop.

Up and running, he saw the door to the farmhouse open as those inside came out to greet the helicopter. All eyes were looking upwards and not at him until another blast on his whistle made them turn to see him running towards them.

Realisation dawned on them immediately at what was happening, and they turned and pushed against others still trying to come out, causing a brief commotion. Gallon careered through the door at full pelt, knocking a few people over and crashed into the hallway wall to crack the wood panelling lining it.

"Shut the fucking door!" he screamed causing hands to jump to the task of locking and barring it.

Picking himself up off the floor he ran up the stairs to one of the windows facing the yard, seeing the helicopter settle into a hover ready to land.

Gallon waved both arms like a madman, pointing in the direction of incoming enemy. He yelled fruitlessly, trying to warn them of the danger, when the helicopter rose sharply and its door gunners began firing above the walls.

"Sar'nt. Every window facing the yard is now a gun position," a corporal reported. "Everyone knows their place and we've got plenty of ammo ready to go."

Gallon nodded his thanks at the man who had organised everything while he kept watch, thinking that in a normal world he'd recommend the man for a sergeant's cadre, but now all he could hope for was to live to see tomorrow.

"Good work," he said, then cursed as he thought about the helicopter.

So near and yet so fucking far!

The promise of reinforcements and evacuation was all a pipe dream. A hope, not a reality.

Looking at the helicopter he judged from their angle of fire that the enemy had reached the walls.

"On your weapons!" he shouted needlessly as every machine gun or grenade machine gun had a team ready to fire and feed them when they ran out.

"Keep them on the walls, don't let them get in the yard. Don't wait for the order to fire! When you see the bastards, you let 'em fucking have it!" he bellowed, relying on his voice to reach those in the other rooms.

He wanted to man one of the guns personally so he could blow them apart himself, but he knew that command was more than that. It needed more from him than simply manning a position.

Stepping back, he went to each gun crew in the room and dipped into his vast stock of Sergeant's phrases to bolster the spirits of the defenders, repeating his instructions to try and keep them out of the yard again and again, he went to every other room that had been turned into a gun position.

He was looking out a window when the first zombie appeared on the walls, quickly followed by many more. Every gun opened up, causing the first wave to disappear in clouds of blood and gore as the world became a chaos of percussion, but more leapt over them to jump headlong into the deadly hail of lead and explosives.

Above and off to one side, the helicopter laid down a deadly barrage beyond the walls and Gallon could only imagine the destruction wrought.

A soldier ran up to him saying the helicopter pilot wanted to talk to him. He turned and ran to the radio.

It was hard to communicate over the booms and blasts that shook dust from every ceiling in the house and assailed every fibre of his being, but by shouting his words clearly and slowly, and holding the headphones tight against his ears to block out as much noise as possible, they managed.

Landing was clearly not an option. As soon as the helicopter descended, the guns from the farmhouse would have to cease firing and the yard would immediately flood with undead. They both agreed that the helicopter would stay overhead and provide support until the need to refuel or rearm forced their withdrawal, then they would fly to the castle to refuel and rearm, then return as soon as possible.

Luckily, foresight had led to the castle having a store of fuel for just such a contingency so the helicopter would have the capability to fly many missions until it was exhausted or the mission was abandoned if the farm became overrun and lost to the enemy.

"Distance to the castle?" the pilot asked.

Gallon didn't know the distance measured by crows, but he knew how long it should take by air.

"About twenty minutes flight time. How long can you stay on target?"

"Fuel isn't an issue, but ammunition will be soon."

"Any estimate of enemy numbers?" Gallon asked, enunciating each word carefully to be understood.

"Negative. Bad news is they're still coming from the woodland. Sorry, chap, but I'm seeing tens of thousands."

Gallon bit back the variety of offensive words he wanted to use and steadied himself for a second. Glaring at the soldier operating the radio he could tell by the man's expression that he'd heard the same estimate.

"Understood. Do what you can, out."

Gallon tossed the headset down and ran back upstairs to find every gun firing, sweeping everything that reached the top of the walls off them. They were holding them back for now, but it was taking everything they had. The floors of the rooms were full of spent casings making it treacherous underfoot, and the fumes from the relentless gunfire created a noxious fog that stung his eyes.

Looking out of a window he watched the helicopter hovering just beyond the walls. Every mounted machine gun fired downwards, soldiers filled the doorways to add the weight of their personal weapons to the fight, pouring thousands of rounds a minute into the unseen masses beyond the walls.

One of the soldiers threw an object from the doors which was followed seconds later by the crump of an explosion. Gallon realised with shock that they must be throwing grenades from the helicopter – something that went against just about every rule – as the risk of one being dropped and destroying the helicopter was too great to contemplate.

Safety rules be damned because their situation was dire.

Gallon moved through upstairs rooms keeping an eye on his command, seeing that everyone did their utmost to keep the guns firing. Large quantities of ammunition boxes for all weapons had been carried upstairs ready to use, but he could see from the empty boxes thrown into corners they were burning through it at a prodigious rate.

No one was idle in the house.

Stuart's wife was busy making piles of sandwiches and mugs of tea to keep the defenders sustained. No one had had any yet, but the need to keep her hands busy kept her going despite the ridiculousness of the act. The dust falling from the ceilings was coating everything she made with a fine layer of powder.

People hauled ammunition boxes from the makeshift magazine in the cellar to where they were needed. Gallon's corporal had told him that they'd managed to gather most of the excess ammunition stored in a barn which was good news, but whether it would last was another matter.

The call he dreaded came over the radio. The helicopter had fired everything it had and was flying to the castle to rearm and refuel. The pilot couldn't say how long it would take, but they'd do their best to return as quickly as possible.

"We'll inform them to be ready," Gallon reported, glancing at the radio operator and receiving a nod. "Just get back here soon as."

"Will do. Hold fast – more help is on the way. See you soon, out."

Gallon had questions but no time to ask them, as their true test was about to begin.

CHAPTER TWENTY

Fort Bristol

Our helicopter didn't hang around.

As soon as the last person was aboard and before the door was shut, the pilot applied power and lifted off to angle aggressively forwards and raced away from the base. Nervous glances were exchanged between the passengers not because of the flying, but because we were desperate to get home before anything happened.

Twisting in my seat I saw another helicopter following close behind. Walker-Jones had called for volunteers to fly to the base to help boost our forces, having to select the first fifteen and disappoint the multitude of others.

Some were squeezed in with us, but the rest travelled in the aircraft behind. The helicopter heading to the Brough's had left a few minutes before us as getting that one away had been the priority seeing as they were under attack and needed help urgently.

We hadn't received any updates on how they were doing in the rush to depart, but I trusted that if anything major happened we'd be informed. No news might be good news, but not knowing felt much worse to me.

I stared ahead, agonising over the possibilities as the land flew below us in a green blur. I could only imagine the desperate preparations going on at the castle after being woken by the news of the attack at the Brough's. I looked at the others, as if simply willing everything to be all right would be enough.

Get a grip, Tom! I told myself. We need to plan what to do, not pray for piña coladas.

Communicating through the headsets we wore, we discussed what defensive improvements could be made back at the castle. We knew the place well and had worked hard since moving in to make it not only a home, but a secure one where we could live safe in the knowledge that nothing could assail the walls.

Now we had reports of so-called super zombies with increased mobility and who knew what else, we might need to go back to the drawing board.

The image of a zombie film we'd watched where they had formed a human tower to assail walls far higher than ours couldn't be discounted as implausible until we knew what we were facing.

Improving firepower was an obvious idea. We had more than enough weapons in storage to add to the walls, but having weapons and having enough people to fire them was the issue. Also, with the sheer size of the castle, it took time to get from one end of the ramparts to the other through a maze of passages and internal and external staircases, some of them steep and precarious in places to negotiate.

If one area of the walls was threatened, we needed to come up with a plan to reinforce it quickly, and the best idea we came up with to solve that was to have a quick reaction force on standby somewhere central.

They were all ideas, but until we reached the castle nothing could be implemented. I felt better for planning even if nothing ever came of it, because the alternative was to sit in silence and contemplate all the ways things could go wrong

Flying over the countryside I saw no reference points as to where we were on the journey until I spotted the River Avon and the town of Stratford-upon-Avon zipping below us to tell me we were close. I started to pay attention to the ground below us, hoping not to see a mass of zombies heading for our home.

The plan was to land in the inner courtyard of the castle itself, and not on the lawns outside as we usually did, to protect the helicopters in case of attack and enable them to remain in use.

Before long the castle came into sight below. Relief flooded through me as it wasn't besieged by a mass of leaping, running figures as my deepest fears had imagined, but looked as normal and calm as it usually did from overhead.

Our helicopter hovered, descending gently before touching down. My urge was to leap from the helicopter as soon as it met solid ground but the pilot had warned us to stay onboard until the other helicopter had landed safely. While we waited I looked out the window, seeing that the scene of calm witnessed from above was a lie.

Outside, people rushed everywhere. From the shape and colour of what was being carried they looked mainly to be ammunition boxes being stacked in various places around the grounds. I saw Stanley and Eddie struggling to carry a green box between them up an external staircase to the ramparts where I could see many more had already been placed. They were preparing and I would soon find out what had been done in the few hours they'd had.

As soon as the other helicopter touched down I jumped out and ran to where I'd seen Becky and a few others waiting. She looked as nervous and fraught as I had seen her in ages. Waking up to the news of the attack had clearly affected her, and she wasn't the only one.

Hammond and Digby were also there, and as soon as I released Becky from the hug they asked me to accompany them to the command centre.

"This is a shit storm!" Digby spat as we rushed through the door.

"What's going on?" I asked stupidly, not engaging my brain.

The fact he didn't pull me up on it told me the stress everyone felt.

"Reports from the pilot overhead at the Brough's is not good, I'm afraid. The zombies attacked again before they could land, forcing the evac to be cancelled. They're now overhead providing fire support for as long as they can, but they've reported that thousands of the bastards are surrounding the place, and thousands more are apparently still coming."

A few seconds of silence hung heavily while my mouth hung open.

"Th...Thousands? We need to get them out of there, NOW!" I said, stating the obvious with no idea how such a simple goal could be achieved.

"Don't we know it," Digby replied to no one in particular. "We only received this update a few minutes ago. We're here to—"

The radio operator called out, interrupting him.

"Sir? The helicopter's on the way here now. They've run out of ammo and need a resupp—"

"You two," Clarke snapped, pointing at two soldiers passing by outside the door. "Get down to the courtyard on the double and tell them to be ready to resupply the helicopter with as much belted seven-six-two as they can carry. Go!"

The two soldiers ran as ordered, and Clarke turned back to the radio operator.

"Tell the pilots here that the first bird ready is to take off immediately. The farm has no air cover!"

With a determined nod the radio was worked and orders passed on.

"As I was saying," Digby continued. "We need ideas, and please bear in mind that time is of the essence. We need to prepare the castle, because I can't imagine what's happening there will be an isolated incident. I've already organised for additional weapons and ammunition to be placed on the walls, but much more still needs to be done."

Digby paused, swallowing hard.

"It looks as though the beast has awakened after a winter spent hibernating," he said ominously with a slight quiver in his voice.

He shook himself from his portent of doom mood and grimly looked around the table.

"Ideas, please. No matter how stupid they may sound."

We threw ideas on the table such as airlifting the defenders off the roof of the farmhouse by winch, only to discover the available helicopters weren't equipped with them.

"Besides, it would take too damn long to winch them up one by one," Digby said, shooting down the plan even if it wasn't viable.

Eventually, and with a looming dread rising in my gut, we decided that the only way to evacuate them was by road.

The one glimmer of hope we had was that we reckoned we could provide continuous overhead coverage with the additional helicopters now in play.

Those three vital assets were all we had, as the other three the country had were grounded for service and maintenance issues. Engineers on the Scillies were expediting the servicing, but helicopters were complicated beasts that took time to make airworthy.

The logistics of getting a convoy to the Brough's could be problematic if the reports of the zombies' new capabilities were correct.

If they could easily climb over the walls at the Broughs then the sides of a trailer, or an armoured car with its exposed gun positions on top, would pose no obstacle to them at all.

"I reckon I can codge up some cages to cover them," Shawn said excitedly.

Without waiting for a reply, he ran from the room. Both pilots also excused themselves as they, after a quick conversation between themselves, decided to see how quickly they could get more machine guns mounted on their helicopters.

"On that note, I suggest we get the hell on with it," Clarke said, hinting at the bloodlust rising in him.

Shawn and one of the pilots ran back as we were leaving the room to report that both ideas were workable. They were told to get on with it immediately.

My confidence that we could perform a miracle and evacuate the farm rose with every decision we made.

The helicopter refuelling and rearming system was going smoothly, with the fuel truck filled with avgas having been brought into the yard to connect to them directly with its onboard pump. It went against our rules to have a fuel lorry in the inner courtyard, but this was an emergency and red tape could cost lives.

The passenger seats and windows had been removed from the helicopters allowing more guns to be mounted and reducing their weight to allow for more ammunition to be loaded. Looking inside most of the deck space on both was taken up with ammunition boxes lashed down safely.

One of the helicopter's rotors began turning and the whine of the jet engines rose as more power was applied. I knew from previous experience that the take off routine took a few minutes of external walkarounds by a crew member and a long checklist for the pilot and copilot. This time, however, as soon as optimal power was reached the helicopter lurched into the sky and headed off low over the castle walls, such was the urgency of the situation.

"Why isn't the other one taking off?" I shouted in Clarke's ear over the receding roar of turboshaft engines.

"It will soon. There's no point them both being overhead at the same time as they'll have to return together for fuel or ammunition. If we delay its departure, we hope to soon be able to maintain a rotation of two overhead and one resupplying going forwards."

I nodded at the sense of the decision. The military minds around us were using their experience and practical knowledge to eke every advantage we could out of the situation.

In another corner of the courtyard the screeching sound of metal being cut and the flash of welding drew my attention. Shawn, with a few helpers, was working on the cages to surround the fighting vehicles and offer protection against leaping zombies. Metalworking and fabrication were most definitely not my area of skill, so I asked Clarke if there was anything else he needed me to do.

"I'd be happier if we had more ammunition within the walls and maybe a few more vehicles…We've got plenty of ammunition within easy reach, but my gut's telling me to get as much for ready use asap, along with every armoured car we can get inside and turn them into a mobile machine gun nest if the shit hits the fan in here."

Stunned by his ability to predict catastrophe I stared at him.

"Can you organise that please? Grab whoever you can, so long as they aren't tasked with something vital. I'll get the gates sorted to let you out."

CHAPTER TWENTY-ONE

I looked around. Everyone I could see was rushing around with purpose apart from the military personnel who'd rode the helicopters with us as they'd been ordered to man the extra guns being fitted in the helicopters. Those not assigned a gunner's seat were ferrying boxed ammunition to the waiting aircraft.

"Who's not going on the mission?" I shouted at them, ignoring the social niceties for three of them to raise their hands.

"Can you drive?" I demanded, feeling like the question was a stupid one, but not something I could simply assume.

Offended looks and nodding heads indicated they could.

"Good. Follow me," I ordered.

I told them to grab their weapons and follow me as I rushed over to the wall near where the armoured cars were parked.

Breathless from exertion I looked at the young eager faces staring at me. Sensing mixed trepidation and excitement, I opened the cupboard attached to the wall and grabbed a handful of keys.

The one issue with most armoured vehicles is that they didn't use keys to start them, relying on being guarded by armed soldiers to keep them safe.

Being unable to start one in an emergency, or indeed in most situations, if some unfortunate squaddie had misplaced them would spell a bad day out, so most operated on a simple button start and very little extra security apart from maybe a battery switch to isolate the electrics.

Most of the armoured cars and other military vehicles we had gathered were parked in an area of the grounds outside the walls and we'd decided early on that it wouldn't be helpful for them to be left like that. If some hostile group penetrated the castle grounds there would be nothing to stop them being stolen and used against us, so the mechanics sent to maintain the fleet in optimal condition had fitted a simple Lucas key system to all the ignitions, and even changed the keys on the non-military vehicles we'd collected as well to match.

Simply put, all our vehicles could be operated by the same key which we had plenty of.

I handed a handful of the keys to one of the soldiers and pointed to another.

"You're with me, you two are driving," I said, and started to turn away to head to an armoured car when a voice stopped me.

"Sorry fella…What are we doin' again?"

The soldier, who looked barely old enough to shave, spoke in such a thick, Liverpudlian accent it took me a few seconds to work out what he'd said before letting out a brief laugh at my mistake. In the rush to get going I'd forgotten to tell the soldiers I'd volunteered exactly what it was I'd volunteered them for.

"Sorry lads, my brain's moving faster than my mouth. We're going into the grounds to bring armoured cars and trucks loaded with ammo back…Shit…You know how to drive an armoured car?"

Luckily, they all confirmed they did.

"You're riding shotgun with me," I said to the soldier I'd told to stay with me. "You two work it out between yourselves. One driving, one shotgun. All keys are the same. We drive out, I drop you two off, and we all come back here where I'll pick you up and we repeat until we've got enough."

Nods of affirmation rippled around my new gang, so I pointed to the nearest armoured car and told them to get in.

We shot out through the gates as the need for haste made me throw caution to the wind. Deciding that ammunition must be the priority I headed for the area where I knew the most was stored. A lot of it was kept in containers, as they could each hold a large quantity in dry, secure conditions. We also had a lot of seven-and-a-half-tonne curtain-sided lorries fully loaded with ammunition, and usefully we'd spraypainted what they contained on the side of each.

We'd chosen these lorries as they could fit through the barbican entrance, so when we needed to replenish our armouries in the castle they could easily get to where they were needed.

I made a mental list with each run completed as I tried to get some of everything I knew we required. As we worked, the other helicopter took off, and a short while later another returned to refuel and rearm. I guessed they'd also be adding more machine guns and gunners as the one that just landed hadn't been worked on yet, so I knew the ammunition we were bringing in would soon be put to good use.

My team of borrowed soldiers were operating like a well-oiled machine now. I simply stopped beside the one we were taking next and the two men jumped out, started it, and followed me back to rinse and repeat.

The inner courtyard was rapidly becoming very congested due to the need to keep an area clear for the helicopters, but needs must, so we continued. Driving through the gate on my next return journey Clarke waved me down.

"That should be enough ammunition," he yelled over the courtyard's cacophony.

I gave him the thumbs up and sped off to start recovering armoured vehicles.

As the two soldiers scrambled into my armoured car for the next trip I said.

"Good job lads. Now for some armoured cars. How about you drive one each from now as once your inside you'll be protected and won't need one riding shotgun."

Grinning with the excitement at what we were doing they both agreed.

None of the armoured cars in storage had weapons mounted or carried any ammunition as that could be quickly and easily added when they were needed. The vehicle I drove was armed as it was kept within the castle walls and maintained for immediate use, so I kept my Liverpudlian gunner employed above me as the other two each drove a vehicle back under the cover of the turret gun.

We were almost back at the castle on our third run but out of sight of it, with the following vehicles a few hundred yards behind me when the sound of a gun firing made me slam on the brakes.

"Zombies, fuckin' loads of the bastards!" the soldier manning my vehicle's gun yelled.

He fired a long burst from the mounted machine gun. Instinctively I hauled on the wheel, carving great chunks of mud out of the grass to turn the vehicle around and see what was happening.

A swarming pack of about fifty zombies ran towards the armoured cars following us even as they raced in our direction as panic made the drivers put their foot to the floor. The soldier above me in the hatch fired in controlled, professional bursts dropping sections of the pack as bullets struck home.

"Shoot them!" I screamed, seeing they were gaining on the second vehicle even at the speed it was travelling.

My gunner ignored my helpful suggestion and carried on doing his job.

My mind registered in an instant that these zombies were unlike anything we'd faced before. They looked completely different and were keeping up with a speeding vehicle instead of shambling like drunks.

The machine gun above my head continued rattling away, the large calibre bullets ripping through the approaching mass as the leading ranks disappeared in clouds of body parts and blood, but those behind rushed onwards, running straight into the barrage of lead decimating their numbers.

"Bollocks to this," I growled, raising my voice to warn my gunner. "Hold tight!"

Flooring the throttle we zipped past the unarmed, fleeing vehicles and aimed straight at the centre of the pack.

The blade on the front carved through them, cutting a swathe through the heart of the mass. Foot to the floor I jammed the wheel over, and in a long power slide destroyed small trees and bushes as the heavy vehicle slid sideways across the wet grass. Still with my foot hard on the accelerator I carved more long furrows in the grass as I regained control and turned it round to face the enemy once more.

There was no time to think or contemplate what was happening. One second we were alone just trying to get the task completed as quickly as possible, and the next we were facing dozens of this terrifying new enemy.

We had to get back to the castle. My gunner fired as he blasted the ones that were now leaping onto the rearmost vehicle. Body parts flew into the air and destroyed carcasses fell from it as bullets sparked from its armoured sides. More still chased both cars and I kept my foot to the floor so I could close the distance to help my gunners aim.

We were almost up to them when the car in front swerved violently as zombies leapt at the cab.

Your safe my mind screamed just keep going. The panicking driver was oblivious to the fact that cocooned in the armour of the vehicle no zombie could reach him. My heart dropped as we saw his vehicle slam into something and lift up into the air savagely to drop down and remain motionless.

I realised he'd ran hard into a massive tree stump and stranded the vehicle. I fought with the controls to swing back and help him, catching sight of him throwing open the hatch and bring his rifle to bear on the remaining zombies swarming him.

Why didn't he stay inside? My brain raged as I saw him empty his magazine in seconds.

Unable to reload in time, he threw his rifle aside, drew his sidearm and began firing it. Only five were left but they leapt at the vehicle and clawed up its side. One fell from sight as it lost its grip with a nine-millimetre round smashing its brain.

Helplessly we watched, unable to fire in case we hit the soldier and too far away to use the vehicle as a weapon, the desperate struggle just ahead of my windscreen as I raced towards him.

Three were thrown off the vehicle as he shot them at brutally close quarters, but the fourth reached him. It grabbed him, and with more strength than a human had any right to possess, pulled him bodily from the open hatch.

Gripping him in its arms it bit deeply into his neck. I had barely registered this when, still holding the writhing body of the soldier in its mouth, it jumped from the vehicle straight into my path.

I had no time to react as they hit the ground metres in front of me. I closed my eyes in shock at what was about to happen as the plough smashed into both of them.

I knew nothing could survive that impact.

I knew I'd just killed one of our own.

A howl of anguish and rage erupted from me, the logical part of my brain unable to yet comprehend that the poor man was dead the moment that thing laid hands on him, and his quick end at my hands had probably been a mercy.

As far as I was aware we'd killed all of them, but we still needed to get back. I turned the vehicle savagely and picked up the radio knowing the gunfire would've been heard inside the walls.

"Open the gate NOW!" I shouted whilst I tried to control the speeding vehicle with only one hand on the wheel.

I threw the radio down, not wanting to engage in any more conversation until we were safely back behind the walls.

Skidding to a stop in the yard I leapt from my seat and ran to the other vehicle, pulling the passenger door open to find the driver sitting rigidly; white faced with hands still gripping the wheel and staring straight ahead with the engine running.

Everyone who had been busily working in the courtyard was rushing over to us to find out what the hell had happened with Clarke and Digby leading them. I reached over and patted the man on the leg in some vague display of support.

"What happened?" Clarke demanded as he reached me.

As I started to tell the short story Horace and Princess ran past me at full pelt, both with their hackles raised as they barked and growled at the armoured car. My brain, numbed by the events of the past few minutes, didn't register that the dogs were our early warning system, capable of detecting the undead long before we spotted them.

Over the long winter months they'd rarely barked, and only then to alert us of a returning patrol. Those barks were more of a friendly "welcome home" sound, but now their barks were loud and full of aggression as shouts of alarm came from the other side of the vehicle.

We rushed around the vehicle to find out what the hell was going on, seeing the dogs barking and snapping at the underside of the armoured car.

The driver, recovered from his temporary catatonic state at the sudden and recent death of his friend, wondered what the sudden commotion was about and jumped down to investigate.

A pale, blotchy, heavily muscled arm reached out from under the truck and grabbed his ankle.

He screamed in shock and pain as his legs were pulled from under him, ending the sound abruptly as his face smashed into the ground. With outstretched hands and fingers formed into claws that gouged deep trenches into the grass, he tried to resist as the arm pulled him beneath the vehicle. Shouts of alarm emitted from everyone's lips as those nearest grabbed his arms and attempted to pull him back out like a morbidly terrifying tug of war.

Man versus beast.

Dead versus alive.

A huge, armour-clad figure burst through the panicking crowd, smashing people out of the way like a strike from a bowling ball with an axe raised in preparation to swing. The power of the downward chop was so great the blade made a swooshing sound as it cut through the air, slicing straight through the outstretched arm severing it from whatever was under the vehicle to embed the blade deep in the ground.

Suddenly released, those pulling on the soldier tumbled backwards in a pile as he was yanked clear. A roar resonated from beneath the armoured car as a one-armed zombie rolled out and scrambled to its feet.

Muscles bulged as it opened its mouth and bellowed a challenge at those facing it, unconcerned at the thick, black blood spurting from its severed arm.

Everyone instinctively took a shocked step backwards as those of us who were armed grabbed for our weapons.

Ian, in an impressive display of strength and speed that went against the normal slow, lumbering man-mountain he liked to portray, didn't panic as the rest of us had.

He stepped lithely forward, heaved on the axe still embedded deep into the ground, and in one movement arced it upwards to remove the other arm outstretched in front of it as it reached for the closest prey.

Ian reversed his grip on the handle and, with a smooth, back-handed swing, cleaved the head from the snarling monster before any of us had raised a weapon.

The beheaded beast remained upright for a few seconds, more blood squirting from the stump of its neck until its legs gave way, and it collapsed to the ground.

In typical Ian style he looked at his handywork for one moment before shrugging to loosen his shoulders and inspect the blade of his axe.

"That's sorted that then," he said conversationally, pulling a rag from a pocket to clean the blood from the blade of his axe.

Whistling cheerfully, his usual daft expression returning to his face, he looked up at the shocked faces staring at him with a twinkle in his eye.

With nothing forthcoming from the shocked crowd, he nudged the body at his feet with an armoured toe, smirking as he was never able to keep the amusement of his own jokes from showing on his face.

"Come on…it's armless now."

Nobody was in the mood for comedy.

Ignoring Ian I studied the headless body lying on the ground. It was like nothing I'd seen before.

If I hadn't just witnessed how fast they moved, hadn't seen them outrun a speeding vehicle or display superhuman strength by lifting a fully grown man from the vehicle as though he weighed nothing, I wouldn't have admitted that we were looking at a zombie.

I realised nobody but the three of us knew what had happened yet. We didn't need to worry about the dead one in front of us, but what might be out there beyond our walls concerned me greatly.

Clarke and Digby stood close by, both with their weapons held ready as they stared dumbfoundedly at the headless horror. I explained as succinctly as I could what had happened, and why only three of us had returned.

I could tell that their first thought was the castle defence as they both involuntarily looked up at the surrounding high walls.

Our defences were already well-guarded as the castle had gone on full alert as soon as the news of the attack at the Broughs was received. If anything approached, they would be spotted.

Louise ran across the courtyard towards us shouting.

"Message on the radio. We need you, now!"

Not knowing who she was shouting at, me, Clarke, and Digby turned and followed her back to the command centre without hesitation.

CHAPTER TWENTY-TWO

The scene at the Brough's was chaotic. The instant the helicopter had been forced to depart when it ran out of ammunition and could no longer sweep the lead ranks from the walls, the massed zombies swarmed the walls and reached the yard.

"OPEN FIIIIIIRE!" Gallon roared, pouring his own rifle's power through a gap at a crowded window.

Firing everything they had, the defenders destroyed rank after rank but nothing could be done to stop them reaching the farmhouse itself. Bodies began piling against the walls causing the next surge to inch closer to the upper windows.

The Brough's grandchildren had been carrying ammunition like some modern iteration of powder monkeys aboard sail-powered warships, now threw grenade after grenade from the windows, such was the savage conclusion of their childhood.

Each explosion blasted holes in the advancing ranks.

Holes that were filled instantaneously by more scrambling, leaping attackers.

Panic once again rose in Gallon as he watched the inevitable outcome loom closer with every second. With every member of the undead army that leapt over the walls.

Determined never to give in, he yelled encouragement and cycled his rifle like there was no tomorrow.

Hope soared again, when over the continuous cacophony of gunfire and explosions, he heard the deeper noise of an approaching helicopter. The noise rose until it burst into sight, doors open and bristling with barrels that opened up to pour down death and destruction.

The continual assault faltered as the helicopter's guns devastated the hordes incessantly streaming across the fields, giving those in the farmhouse the opportunity to destroy those that had reached the yard.

Knowing they were not fighting this battle alone, that help had once again arrived, boosted the defender's diminishing morale. With whoops and yells of relief, everyone found that extra ounce of effort to pour fire down into the yard and sweep it clear.

The second he knew the situation was, if not under control, then slightly better than it had been, Gallon stepped away from his firing position to check the condition of the beleaguered farmhouse and his stalwart defenders.

Shocked and wide-eyed faces at the miracle of still being alive after such an onslaught greeted him as he moved from room to room, again drawing on his experience and using colourful insults to comfort and uplift spirits.

Running downstairs into the gloom only lit by a few lanterns as every door and window was firmly barricaded, he was momentarily confused as he found himself walking through thick, treacly oil that splashed and sucked on his boots with every step. Grabbing a lantern from a table he shone it downwards at his feet to find the floor awash with thick, black blood.

With shock he realised that the thousands of dead bodies the yard was piled high with had all bled creating a lake of blood that had found its way into the house under the doors.

Looking at the front door which had bookcases and other furniture stacked against it, a greasy tide of black sludge seeped into the room beneath it.

'For fuck's sake.' He muttered to himself in disgust. 'Are we going to drown instead?'

Stuarts's wife had donned a pair of wellington boots and was still in the kitchen making trays of tea and sandwiches.

He splashed up to her, her hands were shaking, and tears poured down her face at the terror of what she was enduring. He knew the huge pile of sandwiches she'd made was just her way of dealing with what was going on. She was the self-appointed cook for the whole garrison and worked tirelessly every day making sure all were fed and watered to her satisfaction. Now, to cope, she was blindly making more food than the survivors could or probably wanted to eat.

"Helen," he said softly, getting her attention and wanting to get her away from the deepening slick of blood. "Why don't you take some sandwiches and mugs of tea to everyone upstairs? I'm sure they'll appreciate it."

Her eyes jerked up wildly as she was shocked out of her almost catatonic state before she absorbed what he'd said and nodded.

"I just wanted to make sure no one went hungry," she said quietly, adding a weak shrug as if her behaviour needed an excuse. "Everyone's fighting to keep us alive, and I…I didn't know what else to do."

Her shoulders shook as she began crying. Gallon put his arms around her and gave her a comforting hug.

"You're doing the right thing. Now go and hand out those sandwiches so they don't go to waste," he whispered in her ear.

Struggling with a fully laden tray of dust-covered sandwiches and flasks of tea, she carefully made her way upstairs.

Sickened by what was happening but knowing there was nothing he could do about it and with continuous firing still coming from every window in the house, supplemented by the constant barrage from the helicopter outside, he splashed his way to the radio.

~

Warwick Castle

Clarke signed off from Gallon and turned to face everyone who had been listening in on their conversation.

"We have to go now. We have to get them the hell out of there," he said forcefully before deflating and staring at nothing with glassy eyes.

"They won't survive the night if we don't," he added in a far softer, almost bleak tone.

He rubbed his hands against his face as he made many internal decisions that would put more lives in jeopardy, but we all knew leaving them to die in defence of the Brough's Farm was not an option. He dropped his hands and looked at the faces staring at him.

"Right, this is a volunteer-only mission. I know Shawn's working on two armoured cars and two trailers. I'd like to take more but that's all we have, so let's get them loaded and ready to go. We should still have enough daylight to get there and back if we get a move on. This is going to be a smash and grab mission. In and out with no fucking about."

"But...Andy?" I asked. "If the yard's waist deep in zombies like Gallon's saying, how the hell are we going to push through that to get to the door?"

"Not a clue, Tom. Not one fucking clue. We'll just have to figure it out when we get there," Clarke replied with a shrug of his shoulders.

"What about a JCB?" Digby offered. "Or a tractor with a bucket on the front?"

"We don't have enough available that could either keep up with a convoy or with enough power to shift that amount of...shit...fast enough. Plus, and feel free to correct me if I'm wrong anybody, but I don't think we have any with sufficient added protection to get the job done?" Clarke answered after pondering his suggestions for a few seconds.

Nobody corrected him, but an idea came to me.

"Why don't we take the tank? It doesn't need any more protection added, and if the crew are all sealed up tight inside they should be safe from anything, right? And if that can't get through a yard piled high with bodies then nothing can."

"The term is 'closed down'," Clarke answered with peevish pointlessness, but he was nodding in agreement.

The tank was shut up tight, with padlocks securing extra locking bars welded to it and kept outside of the main walls but it was always fully armed, fuelled and ready to go. The lengthy process to arm it had made this decision logical if it was needed quickly, but it was lost on none of us that this was the first time it would be used in anger.

With no time to waste we rushed outside to get everything ready as Clarke radioed Gallon to tell him the plan.

~

The Brough's

The arrival of a second helicopter overhead made an immediate difference as the firepower doubled. Even fewer zombies made it through the cordon of red-hot, supersonic lead to reach the yard granting those inside continued respite.

Gallon, not knowing how long it would last, rotated his people off the firing line to give them all a break. He told them they'd done well, that he was proud of them. He told them to, even if they didn't want to, eat the trays of food Helen was fussing around with. Food was fuel and they all needed their tanks brimming if they were going to survive. He told them the news that a convoy was setting out from the castle to rescue them, giving them all the boost that hopefully their terrifying ordeal may soon be over.

He spoke as much to try and convince himself as he did those under his command.

Bergens were filled with ammunition and other useful items as they began preparing for evacuation, more to keep everyone busy and their minds away from the situation outside the thin protection of their walls.

~

Outside the walls, just within the cover provided by the trees on the edge of the field facing the farmhouse, the heavily muscled leader watched as wave after wave of those he had ordered to attack were destroyed. The woods behind him were filled with the sounds of thousands of feet slapping the earth, with rasping breaths and snarls, as more flocked to answer his call to arms. He had summoned these groups ranging in size from a few dozen to many thousands by an unheard command, for the first time operating with a plan to rid the Earth of their competition.

Each of these groups had also nurtured in the centre of the pack their own leader, who warmed to the highest temperatures by the bodies crowding around and feasting on the most flesh willingly given by those in the outer rings allowing the virus the perfect conditions to make its final changes.

These individual leaders willingly subjugated themselves to the one who had summoned them. Only one could lead, and they would follow his orders slavishly as these leaders became his lieutenants in the greater army of the undead.

He was the one chosen by the inexplicable twists of distorted nature.

He was the one who would lead their campaign and begin the new era.

The era of undead supremacy.

His thoughts did not need to be transmitted vocally, linked as they were by something science could not explain. They were connected as if by an organic extension of himself. If there was more than one leader, then the virus' efforts would be wasted as a Darwinian process would eventually select the best candidate through a process of elimination.

Either by a biological stroke of genius or a fatal flaw in the virus' makeup, that process of natural selection had been bypassed and simply chosen him to be the one.

If one led, then all others would follow.

His consciousness understood that the tactics used to overwhelm the farmhouse and eradicate this small pocket of humans was failing. The right time to succeed would come, but it was not now. Throwing more into the attack would only weaken his forces by reducing their numbers, and following the same tactics would lead to failure.

Messages also entered his awareness from other groups far away, transmitted in some cases over hundreds of miles to appear as knowledge in his mind, making him aware of other groups. Drawn by the smells emitted by humans they were heading towards other places. He sent these other leaders, these lieutenants that automatically became his subordinates, his own knowledge so they would not waste their numbers as he had by testing the defensive capabilities of the humans.

Shame of failure did not feature in the process. No pointless human emotions clouded judgement. No arrogance or anger affected the decision-making process.

The virus learned from every action, adapting and advancing to reach its ultimate goal, and he was the key to that learning process.

As he roared to those near him, his lieutenants repeated those orders in the forest behind and in the field before him. Once more they stopped and withdrew as one as bullets from the helicopters chased them across the open field until they vanished from sight under the cover of the trees.

Inside the farmhouse the sudden lack of fire from the farmhouse and the helicopters caused panic.

It was what was keeping them alive. What gave them respite from a desperate defence of a single building.

Shit, they've stopped firing, Gallon thought. Why have they stopped?

Running to a window he fully expected to see an unstoppable wave heading towards them across the corpse-littered yard. Instead he saw no movement at all. The helicopters were still there, still hovering over the field outside the walls, but every gun they carried was silent.

His ears rang even after the firing inside the house died away to nothing and the shouts to reload in preparation for the next wave resonated in his mind to accompany the high-pitched whine.

He ran to the radio needing to know what was going on. The blood seeping under the doors had been spread everywhere by so many boots trampling around the house. The upstairs carpets had become thick with it as it was carried on running boot soles.

The depth of the biohazard increased as more flowed inside despite attempts to stem the tide by jamming towels into gaps, slowing the incoming rate but not stopping it.

Splashing through the sticky, foul morass he picked up the handset and transmitted on the open channel asking for information.

The news from the pilots that the enemy had withdrawn was received warily because they'd done so before only to attack in even greater numbers, but a respite was a respite and knowing that a convoy was on the way to rescue them lifted their spirits. Not being attacked gained them precious minutes, turning the vague hope of survival into more than just an empty wish. The calm gave them time to prepare for whatever happened next, so he chivvied and urged everyone to keep going. All the time wishing for the clock to speed up so rescue would arrive sooner.

CHAPTER TWENTY-THREE

The tank, its huge engine roaring and black exhaust smoke billowing, led the convoy. The outer gates closed the second after we were clear, as the heavily armed team operating them rushed back to the perceived safety of the castle walls.

Even though everyone expected it, no more zombies had been spotted within the grounds. The fifty or so in the initial attack were all we had witnessed, but little did we know more were watching us; eyes staring from darkened buildings and from the gloom of the surrounding woods.

The bed of the trailer I was in was a mess of hastily thrown in ammunition boxes and extra weapons making it hard to maintain my footing as Shawn built up speed.

Shawn and his team had, in my opinion, done a brilliant job in the short time they'd had to reinforce the protection on the vehicles. Using steel posts scavenged and stored long ago should we need to replace any of our perimeter fencing, Shawn had fabricated cages to cover the trailers and armoured cars. They weren't neat or straight by any stretch of the imagination, showing the rush in which it was put together, but as I held on to it, I had faith it would work.

It felt sturdy enough to do the intended job of stopping a leaping zombie getting to the fresh meat, allowing us time to blow its brains out before the cage succumbed.

Once we'd gained our trailer legs most of us kept watch, manning the machine guns and grenade machine guns that lined the sides while others organised the huge amount of ammunition we had thrown on board into something resembling order, stacked against the bulkhead with the spare weapons.

Sergeant Dave Eddy was in the trailer beside me, his eyes wrinkled in concentration as he stared outwards. I slapped him on the back.

"Here we go again mate," I said in as cheerful a voice as my nerves could manage

His eyes pierced into me as he turned his head and spoke sombrely.

"I've got a bad feeling in my bones, Tom. These fuckers have got tactical awareness now. Before, they just mindlessly shambled towards us, easy prey for our guns and blades, only a danger if their numbers were too great…"

He let out a mirthless laugh.

"Tell me something…The last time you faced them, were you afraid?"

I shook my head automatically in response, then remembered the last time I'd faced them was in the hospital and the desperate fight we'd had to hold them back. He continued before I had time to correct him.

"No, exactly. You knew you'd be fine as we had the weapons and experience to kill all the bastards. Whereas six months before, you'd have shit your pants and run away."

Despite the tension in the air, I chuckled at the accuracy of his description.

"We were happy when they disappeared over the winter. We bloody celebrated, thinking that however many survived they would be easy to kill…But we didn't understand the clues."

He broke off, glaring intensely into my eyes.

"The groups we found in cellars and dark warm places and killed…We talked about it, we knew what they were doing, but not why. Only…only now I think I understand it."

He stopped talking as his eyes scanned the passing countryside, but I could tell he was still thinking and had more to say, so I waited for him to continue.

"An enemy can only defeat a superior force that has already won many battles by changing tactics and not by repeating the same mistakes," he said, making me feel like he was quoting something I was supposed to know.

His next statement sent a chill through my body as the truth of it hit home.

"We've not changed a bloody thing, Tom…but if my bones are right, they have. It's what they're capable of we don't fully understand. We know what we've built at the Brough's. Yes, the defences aren't as good as ours or those at Bristol, but before today we would've confidently said that they'd stand up to anything thrown at them. From what we know, they didn't stand a chance and were overwhelmed in seconds. Seconds! We know Gallon, he's among the best there is, and no way did he let his guard slip."

He dropped his gaze to his boots and spoke softly as if talking to himself.

"We haven't changed…but they have."

He ended the conversation by pulling on the charging handle of the machine gun he was manning, chambering a round, making it ready for immediate use.

My thoughts raced as I considered what he'd said. Wiping away those unwelcome ideas I followed Eddy's lead and charged my own weapon, imagining that every bend in the road, every tree or ditch hid a horde waiting to ambush us.

Knowing the route so well I ticked off the well-known landmarks along the route to track our progress. The huge tank roared and squealed at the head of our convoy, its size and power lending a brittle feeling of invincibility to our rescue plan.

Radio calls kept us updated. Since the last attack at the Brough's had ended, all had been quiet. One of the helicopters though had flown a wider circle around the area and reported seeing more zombies still swarming across the fields heading towards the farm. They engaged every group they spotted, killing as many as they could until they too went to ground as if avoiding contact with the living.

On hearing this Eddy snorted another dark bark of laughter.

"Told you. Tactical awareness."

He left the rest unsaid for my imagination to wreak havoc.

Tension mounted when we drew close to the farm. We all stood ready, weapons cocked and eyes searching as our convoy pulled off the main road and onto the track that led to the farm.

The moment we left the road I saw a brief movement in the distant tree line, but by the time I had swung my weapon around it had gone, so my attention returned to the once open fields surrounding the farm.

The entire area was a mass of bodies. In places the corpses were so thick I couldn't even begin to count how many lay on top of one another, and in some places the evidence of the desperate defence even obscured the track.

The tank led the way through the sea of death, its tracks crushing corpses to a gory gruel under its more than fifty tonnes of weight. The driver of the vehicle following had to gun his engine to push a plough through what the tank left in its wake.

No one spoke. The scene was too shocking to put into words as we stared out over the uncountable thousands of dead zombies. We'd heard the fight had been desperate, but now we witnessed what they'd faced it was impossible to imagine how they'd survived.

And these were just the ones the helicopters took out, I told myself.

The downwash from the aircraft above buffeted us as they drew lazy circles in the sky in search of targets.

Clarke, who had taken the commanders seat in the tank stood in the open hatch, his hands ready on the mounted machine gun.

"Everyone stay outside until I push through the gate and update," he broadcast tersely, leaving no reason for a reply.

Outside the bodies were piled up against the walls, forming a slope that reached its top and obscuring the structure completely, so only the guard towers showed above the disgusting scene of destruction.

I watched the tank slow as it hit the gate. The protruding barrel of the main gun punched easily through, but then it faltered.

Engine revving, the tracks ripped corpses apart to scatter their remains in red plumes of gore like confetti thrown at a wedding.

The front of the tank reared up as it struggled to push the gate fully open, and only then I saw what had almost stopped it.

The yard was filled feet deep with yet more piled-up corpses which had sealed the gate shut. Pushing through the bodies, the tank kept rising up until its weight crushed what was beneath its tracks to pulp, spewing that backwards in a red rooster tail as it pushed on.

"Good job someone thought to bring the tank," I said to nobody, feeling the self-congratulations to be more than a little hollow.

In the woods, the leader, his senses heightened to almost supernatural levels, heard the noise of the vehicles approaching long before they came into sight. His heightened senses detected the tantalising scent of what his instincts told him to attack, eat and destroy. From his darkened position his blackened eyes watched as they approached the farmhouse that had killed so many of his followers.

Growls of pure evil loathing emitted from his lips as he processed, planned and waited.

"There's no way they're getting out through the ground floor," Clarke radioed us. "They're going to have to climb down onto the tank from the upstairs windows, ride it out and transfer outside."

I glanced back at the woods where I thought I'd seen movement. Even with the barrier of so many dead clogging the ground between it and us, I'd seen how fast they could move, and knew they could be on us in no time at all.

If they attacked when the defenders were fully exposed, sitting on top of a tank, then it would be a massacre. But what other option did we have to get them out of there?

Also, until the tank pushed another pathway through the massed corpses – something our other vehicles lacked the power for – we were sitting ducks.

I gripped the handles of my machine gun and pointed it towards the woods ready to unleash a torrent of lead at the first thing that showed itself.

CHAPTER TWENTY-FOUR

Stuart Brough insisted on being the last one down the ladder despite Gallon's protests.

It was his house, and not unlike a captain of a ship he considered it his duty to be the last to step foot from it.

The Challenger tank was huge and had enough space for everyone to cram on top of it provided it didn't turn its turret, as if it did it would sweep most of the stranded defenders away. The tank's height almost allowed those inside to just step out onto the turret, but for ease a short ladder was wedged into position.

Stuart, before he climbed down, threw the last few bergens left in the room to the waiting arms not far below him.

"Hold tight everyone, this is going to be a bit bumpy," Clarke shouted as soon as he was onboard.

The tank lurched and the tracks spun as they sought grip among the squelching morass of former human remains, the metal blades ripping bodies apart like a food blender on max power until they found grip. The driver, as soon as he was clear of the farmhouse's walls, slewed the tracks to turn the tank on its axis.

Bodies built up against its sides, squashing more into unidentifiable chunks of blood and bone. Blood ran in thick, gloopy rivers in the cleared spaces caused by the churning tracks as the tank headed out through the gate, jolting and rocked over the dead, with the farm's occupants clinging on tightly.

My eyes kept flicking from the treeline to the gate as I could hear the tank's engine revving louder as it moved closer. The hastily built cage would make it slower for people to board the trailers as they couldn't just climb over the side, but we'd already discussed that on the way, deciding that we'd have to open the rear door to let them climb in. It wasn't harder, just slower.

And speed is the key to survival right now.

From the darkness of the treeline the leader growled with malevolent triumph as soon as he saw his enemy appear, sitting atop the roaring metal object. His level of comprehension didn't understand what it was, but this was the first time his enemy had been in the open since he'd ordered the initial attack when they were exposed on the walls.

He'd stood on those walls as he urged his followers to attack. He knew the human he'd locked gazes with during that first assault was dangerous. His predatory instincts told him this was their leader who must be destroyed if they were to overcome the nest of delicious smells his olfactory senses had drawn him to.

Now he saw him in the open. Now was the time.

In the pause since the last attack he'd gathered even greater numbers to call upon, as more had flocked from afar to his signal.

Drawing in a full breath he prepared to begin the new assault.

At the same time he broadcast his thoughts to his lieutenants, he roared his own verbal command to those gathered dumbly around him. As one, the surrounding masses emitted their own rasping, throaty roars of acknowledgment and obeisance. He stood tall as they streamed past him and once more went on the attack.

~

The tank was almost up to our trailer when the shape of the treeline changed as thousands of zombies swarmed from it. Every gun that could bear from the two helicopters overhead, every weapon in the trailers and armoured cars, opened fire at once.

The one tactic drilled into us by our military instructors was the effectiveness of overlapping or interlocking arcs of fire. It was a tactic developed and perfected in World War 1 where each machine gunner didn't act independently, spraying the attacking troops running in the open between trenches with random machine gun fire, but instead they fired at an angle across the path of the approaching enemy.

Other machine guns fired across that line of fire, interlocking with them to create a solid wall of lead that would cut any attack to pieces. The more machine guns interlocking fire, the more effective the deadly tactic became.

The helicopters firing down upon the field at an angle could not execute such tactics and simply maintained a constant rate of fire, thinning the advancing zombies by sheer weight of lead. Those in the trailers and armoured cars tried not to panic and do the logical but far less effective act of wildly firing a weapon. They did their best to maintain discipline despite the terror heading towards them. The grenade machine guns fired independently, lobbing their destruction into the thick swarm and blowing holes in it with each explosion.

Despite all that, the undead masses pushed through the lead-filled barriers of death and high explosives and kept advancing, causing the gunners to adjust their aim and break the interlocking arcs.

Tactics developed to create the carnal house of death epitomised in the horrendous casualty figures from World War 1 were being tested to the limits by an enemy who didn't flinch from the attack, no matter how many around them were being killed.

With so many people on top of the tank Clarke couldn't swing the main gun around to bring it to bear and fire its high explosive shells. The only weapon he could employ was the top-mounted commander's machine gun which he began firing even as the tank closed on our trailer.

Everyone on the tank needed to get into our trailer RIGHT NOW. Someone pulled on the locking bar and swung our rear door open as the tank slewed around to get as close to us as possible. The moment it was close enough those on top with arms reaching out for help were pulled onboard. We'd hoped to distribute the survivors between both trailers, but that was going to be impossible and everyone crammed onboard ours.

Only Stuart Brough, Sergeant Gallon and one of his soldiers were left on its top.

They stood heroically, giving everyone else the chance to reach safety. Standing shoulder to shoulder they fired their weapons, swapping magazines as fast as their experienced hands allowed.

To make matters worse the tank was so close it blocked our rear door from closing. Both helicopters directed all of their fire in front of the tank, making it a simple thing to work out that the zombies were now all concentrating on our exposed friends.

Pulling the last person onboard I looked up at the sharp crack of explosions. Gallon and Stuart had both dropped both their weapons on their slings and were throwing grenades out in front of them whilst the soldier still fired from one knee.

Clarke had his machine gun angled low, firing down to the sides of the tank. Through ears dulled by the firing I heard him scream at the three still on the tank to fall back.

Throwing one last grenade each they both turned and ran the few steps across the tank and dove into the trailer. The soldier seemed not to have heard or was determined to give them covering fire by emptying his magazine at the front runners of the approaching horde. As he turned to jump towards us a zombie leapt at him.

Grabbing him, it just threw him backwards into the masses as if he weighed nothing.

One second, he was there, and the next he was gone.

At the same time, Clarke dropped down into the tank and pulled the hatch closed just in time as zombies swarmed over it. Our problem was that, until the tank moved, we couldn't close the rear door. The back of the trailer was wide open, and even more zombies were now swarming over the tank less than a metre away from us.

Dave Eddy, quicker to react than anyone else, pulled one of the GPMG's from its mount and pushed past us swearing in anger at the death we'd just witnessed.

He stood with legs braced at the edge of the trailer and opened up, venting his rage with a barrage of bullets fired from the hip. He raked the gun from side to side, sweeping away dozens of zombies about to leap into the trailer from the tank.

Others, including me, lined up beside him with our personal weapons raised to form a rank alongside him, adding our own bullets to the outgoing barrage.

The tank bellowed black smoke as its driver applied power to pull away from us. Its turret spun and the coaxial machine gun began chattering away before the main gun fired with a sound like nothing I'd ever experienced.

I didn't see where the shot went, but I was momentarily stunned by the percussive force that washed over me. Fortunately the shockwave also disorientated the attacking zombies and stopped their relentless advance for a few precious seconds.

"Get another gun up here! Ammo's almost gone!" Eddy bellowed.

Gallon, now back on his feet and adapting to the situation, pulled another machine gun from its mount and joined his fellow sergeant and shoulder to shoulder they stood their ground and fired, both screaming incoherent roars of rage at the enemy.

It looked so incongruous and fake to me that it could've been a scene from a cheap action movie.

Two battle-scarred heroes defying the odds and saving the day by single-handedly killing everything before them.

But unlike those movies where bullets never run out, in real life they did.

As Eddy fired the last round from his gun he turned and grabbed another held ready for him.

The sheets of lead we were sending downrange blew anything near the open trailer into nothingness as every leaping, scrambling creature that climbed over the berm of bodies we were creating was hit multiple times by the close-range fire.

Eddy, sensing we had gained a brief advantage, raised his voice to give orders.

"On three, get that fucking door shut!"

We raised our smoking barrels in the air when his count reached three and the ropes that pulled the door closed were heaved on, slamming it with a reassuring metal clang.

A brief sense of relief washed over me at the feeling of safety the closed door gave me, until less than a second later reality slammed home as I looked outwards to see the desperate situation we were still in.

The main front of the attack, which had initially been on the tank before diverting to our trailer, now spread across our entire convoy as each vehicle became an island surrounded by a sea of attacking terror. The cages stopped them reaching us, as leaping bodies grabbed at the bars and pulled themselves up over the cage, clawing arms trying to grab those inside until they were blasted away by point blank fire.

I saw the complete situation in a flash. If we remained static the zombies would simply engulf us. If we were moving, we might just stand a chance.

"We need to move!" I bawled. "We need to move now!"

The leader prowled at the edge of the woods as more continually ran past him to join the attack, throwing their bodies mindlessly into the maelstrom of death the weapons created.

He could see once again that he had failed, and the massed attack had taken precisely one of them.

Rage, if the primitive force that coursed through his body could be called that, filled his being. He needed to change the tactics once more.

He sent his thoughts to his lieutenants and roared his own command for those in earshot to retreat to the woods.

As one, the plethora attacking us turned and ran, leaping and scrambling over the fields of destroyed bodies back towards the woods as our fire followed them until they disappeared from sight.

Bullets and grenades killed hundreds more until no targets remained and our guns fell silent, the metal of their barrels plinking as they cooled.

CHAPTER TWENTY-FIVE

Wide eyes flitted between other shocked gazes as we came to terms with the fact that we were still alive.

Everyone was too dumbfounded to say anything. Gallon, tears of grief running down his face at losing another of his command moved first, his anger driving him onwards as he snatched at his radio.

"Let's get the hell out of here."

"We'll plough a road for you to follow," Clarke responded immediately from inside the Challenger.

The tank revved and pushed ahead, mangling the piled-up corpses and creating a gore-filled road of broken and crushed body parts for us to follow.

The movement of the trailer snapped us all back into action as Shawn started driving, and both Eddy and Gallon refitted their borrowed guns back onto their mounts. With the farm's occupants – minus one – onboard the trailer was packed and hard to move around in. Empty and discarded ammunition boxes and magazines littered the floor as the sergeants started issuing orders, barking them out as rapidly as the machine guns they had been firing.

"Maintain grenade fire into the treeline!"

"Throw this shit overboard and clear some space!"

"Reload everything we have and get more ammo ready!"

The orders weren't aimed at any individuals, but the barrage of words broke our collective state of shock enough that we followed them. The grenade machine guns resumed their very unwarlike popping as they lobbed deadly orbs into the trees where explosions and flashes answered.

None of the enemy were in sight but as tree trunks exploded with a direct hit, the deadly shower of fragmented metal and wooden splinters each one caused would make the cover of the woodland a death zone.

Our trailer rocked as the tractor spun and slid its wheels through the road of pureed body parts left in the tanks wake, others in the trailer threw the dozens of empty ammunition boxes overboard or used them as scoops to collect the thousands of spent cases that rolled across the metal deck of the trailer making it treacherous underfoot.

Above, the helicopters lazily tracked our movement, circling around us as they searched for more targets. Eddy and Gallon kept up their urgent pressure, allocating the new arrivals a fighting spot on the vehicle or making them porters, ready to maintain a steady flow of ammunition going to the guns when we next saw action.

None of us were in doubt we would be attacked again, it was just a matter of when, where and by how many so we needed to prepare in order to survive the onslaught. Eventually with much slipping, sliding and wheel spinning we reached the road, and a hopeful feeling of relief washed over us as the convoy built up speed.

We were on the way home, but would we make it?

From the cover of the trees the leader watched the convoy drive away. He strode out into the field, carelessly stepping over the thousands of destroyed bodies of his followers.

The death toll meant nothing to him. They were a means to an end, and the end was to kill every last one of the living. Two of his lieutenants were guarding the body of the soldier pulled from the tank. The second he had seen the man hauled down his thoughts sent a message to keep him alive. He needed to satiate his personal need for fresh flesh that filled every fibre of his being.

He was the leader, and the freshest meat was his by right.

The soldier lay petrified on the ground. Claws had ripped his uniform to shreds, and his body bled all over from superficial wounds. Frozen by fear, only his eyes moved as they locked upon the larger, muscled zombie heading towards him through the surrounding throng that parted respectfully to let him through.

At a guttural command the lieutenants dragged him up from the ground and held him by his arms. His legs, unable to support him, collapsed but they easily held him upright in the shape of a crucifix. The soldier stiffened at the approach of his impending death, and his senses that had fled in terror returned in force.

His fate was sealed, but he had no intention of going quietly. The leader drew closer until his face was inches from the now defiantly kicking, swearing, screaming man. The soldier spat in his face and tried to lunge forwards to use his own teeth as a weapon, but the leader ignored the kicks as irrelevant. He ignored the verbal abuse and globs of spit covering his face and simply stared, glowering a maliciously evil intent.

He sniffed the air, his nostrils filling with the delicious aroma of the living. Moving as quick as a striking cobra his mouth opened, and he bit deeply into the man's neck to turn the screams into a gurgling moan. Drinking deeply from the blood still pumping through his body, he felt the man's strength passing on to him. The blood, much richer than the near-rotten, nutrient-poor flesh that had sustained him during the winter's hibernation sent a jolt of power through his body as if he had been injected with adrenaline. He continued sucking the lifeblood from the still-living man whose struggles grew weaker with every ounce drawn from his body. As the last vestiges of life faded from the man's eyes the leader pulled away with a gasp, drew back his right arm, and rammed the sharpened claws of his fingers into his chest.

Wet, sucking noises sounded over the cracking of bones as the soldier jerked like he was being electrocuted, before going instantly limp when the leader ripped his heart out.

The leader ignored the lifeless body as it contained nothing of use to him now. Holding the bloody, still pulsing heart in the air as if it was a trophy before biting deeply into it.

His eyes closed with ecstasy as he chewed and swallowed. Feeling more invigorated and powerful than ever he tossed the remainder of the heart away for it to be fought over like stray dogs competing for scraps. Turning away, the mob descended on the corpse to tear it apart in a feeding frenzy.

His force still grew as thousands more streamed to his beacon, replacing those already killed by a factor of many. The infusion of nutrients from the blood and heart he had just consumed had boosted all his powers. The thoughts that entered his head as other leaders hundreds of miles away broadcast their own messages took on an almost picture-like clarity.

Through their eyes he could see a wall of metal boxes on a flat, grey area with larger metal objects behind it on a gently rippling surface.

He also saw high walls of dark stone with towers reaching to the sky.

He saw a high wall of brown earth topped with towers.

All these visions flooded his taste receptors with the deliciously sweet tang of living blood and flesh he knew was hiding behind their walls. His heightened powers already granted him dominion over other leaders who gathered their forces where the smell of humans was the greatest. He was the only one to have attacked in force, and his failures had taught him what not to do.

Now, as his body absorbed and reacted to the burst of energy, his mental clarity improved. He had to decide what to do to overwhelm these puny, fragile beings that had defied all his efforts so far.

He sent out the command for everyone to hold their positions as he planned the next move.

At the castle, Fort Bristol and the Corn Wall, frantic preparations were underway. Every able-bodied person available was either on lookout or preparing for an attack which had yet to come. Extra guns had been mounted on every wall, and mountains of ammunition had been stacked ready for use. Behind the Corn Wall the evacuation was well underway, and every nonfighting person waited at Newlyn docks to be transported to a waiting ship by an armada of small boats.

Since the news of the attack was broadcast, apart from the rescue mission, all patrols and expeditions had been cancelled or recalled. This meant every available person was ready to defend the walls, but it blinded those defenders as to what was going on beyond their compounds.

They didn't see the distant, hidden eyes watching them. Eyes that had a much wider reach than anyone could know.

CHAPTER TWENTY-SIX

On the trailer a sense of managed panic reigned as we sped along the road. Travelling bumper to bumper we followed the tank as it roared and squealed its way along the tarmac road.

Eddy was organising for the right ammunition to be stacked near the guns that could fire it. As he carried a linked ammunition belt to hang from a hook near a machine gun, he turned to face me.

"We've already burned through about half of what we brought with us. I hate to say it, but if we get into contact again, we're gonna have to conserve the bloody stuff," he said with undisguised concern.

I stared back in shock. The only thing that had kept us alive was continually firing everything we had until the barrels glowed red, only now he was saying we needed to conserve ammunition!

"You can't be serious?" I replied.

He stopped and put a hand on my shoulder.

"We have to take it into account. If it runs out before we get back, then we are truly fucked."

Soberly I stared ahead, willing the next well-known landmark on the much-travelled road to come into sight, as its passing meant we were a few miles closer to home and my family.

Through the eyes of others, the leader watched the helicopters come and go from a place with high walls and towers. From the time it took one to leave overhead to reappear in another's vision, his brain which was now operating at a much higher level of cognitive ability than before, knew the other place wasn't far away.

The things in the sky had devastated his army more so than the puny defenders in their moving metal boxes. He knew the other two places had none of those flying contraptions ready to spit death and destruction, and that without them he would have overcome those he was trying to destroy.

The other groups were gathered and ready for his order to commit them to the fray.

His brain didn't think, he simply acted on instinct and transmitted his will to be followed. There were no options to weigh up and consider. If there were no flying things at the other places, then if those sub-leaders launched their assault it told him that they would fly away to where they were most needed, meaning less of them over each place which would make overrunning them easier.

It was time to test the instinct of spreading his enemy's forces thinly.

The defenders on the Corn Wall and Fort Bristol one moment peered outwards with nervous determination at nothing, before suddenly being faced with thousands pouring from where they had been hiding and heading straight for them.

Fingers already hovering near triggers moved into position and added the required amount of pressure to start sending lead and high explosives outwards along with very loud calls for reinforcements.

The received calls for reinforcements placed command in a quandary. With only three helicopters flightworthy and available, and with all three currently supporting the castle's rescue convoy, the hard but logical choice was to allocate one helicopter to each location.

Both Bristol and Cornwall had the capability to rearm and refuel them but when that was being done, they would lose the cover they provided.

It was also known that the main factor that had kept people alive so far was the cover provided by the three of them working together. An impossible choice, but one that had to be made.

"Provide a fighting chance for all three bastions and risk being overrun, or abandon land we fought hard for?" Admiral Walker-Jones asked darkly. "Gentlemen, I see no upside to abandoning any stronghold we possess…divide our air cover accordingly, please."

His orders were acknowledged with a curt nod as one of his senior aides stepped away to make it happen.

Walker-Jones leaned over the table where the map of operations lay, letting out a heavy sigh before adding more words for his benefit alone.

"And may God help us."

"Fuck, fuck, fuck!" Eddy shouted as he threw the handset away in disgust following the radio call he had just received from Clarke in the tank.

"They're attacking at the Corn Wall and Fort Bristol now. Command has no choice but to divert a helicopter to both those locations," he called out loudly so everyone in the trailer could hear.

Even as he spoke one of the two helicopters overhead peeled away. Lowering its nose, it sped off in the direction of the castle. Eddy pointed upwards

"That one'll stay with us. The other two are refuelling and rearming... the one already at the castle better get his skates on if he's going to be any bloody use down south!"

As my mind reeled from the news, I soon realised that it was really the only option. We currently weren't under attack and every second of travel was taking us closer to the safety of the castle. Yes, the helicopters had helped to keep us alive, but the other places were under attack and needed their help too.

Another thought struck me then, a thought that gave me hope.

"So, the castle isn't under attack yet?" I called out.

Eddy looked at me as the awareness dawned on him too and he grabbed the radio handset from where he had left it dangling. He spoke into it for a few seconds before I heard what he did over the speaker.

No, the castle had, as yet, not seen any aside from the pack that had attacked us as we gathered the vehicles and ammunition hours ago.

I sighed with relief at the only good news I seemed to have heard that day.

We were only about an hour from the castle, and I prayed we would get there in time.

At both Fort Bristol and The Corn Wall, a desperate fight for survival raged.

The outer ring of containers at Bristol had never been designed as its main defensive wall, and it fell quickly against the multitudes that leapt up and over the single line of containers, overwhelming the unfortunate sentries who mostly died screaming their rage and desperation, swinging empty weapons like clubs as they futilely fought to hold them back.

A few survived, who when seeing their fellow defenders being overrun realised that running was really the only way to stay alive. They abandoned their positions and fell back to the next defensive ring as defenders fired over their heads trying to kill the zombies chasing at their heels.

Most didn't make it. Some survived, gratefully scrambling up the ladders hastily lowered to them.

The next ring of containers fell as the zombies surged through a deadly hail of fire and explosives, leaving thousands dead in their wake, to pour over the double-stack of containers like a breaking wave hitting a sea wall in a storm. They ripped apart any living person without the wit to realise that their position was untenable. A few brave defenders, unable to retreat, formed small islands of defiance as their sandbagged positions became their desperate last stand against impossible odds.

They did not sell their lives cheaply, holding the attackers back for long enough to allow more to retreat to their last line of defence of triple-stacked containers.

As those last positions went silent apart from the sounds of flesh being ripped from recently dead corpses, the mortar positions in the inner ring began firing without fear of hitting any of their comrades.

Firing at their minimum range they lobbed their bombs high into the air for them to fall vertically onto the now abandoned ground outside their last layer of protection.

Containers blew apart and deep holes were gouged from the concrete yard, but the high explosives ripped great swathes through the attacking hordes creating enough gaps for the concentrated fire from the multiple guns lining the walls to, for the moment, stall the attack.

Giving them time to regroup after a hellish ten minutes of desperate fighting which had killed many and reduced their three-layered defences to a single line which had to be held at all costs.

The mortars fell silent as the helicopter burst overhead and added its reign of death to the swarms below.

It seemed that the arrival of the helicopter was the signal for the attackers to go to ground. As suddenly as they'd arrived, they turned and fled, chased by the bullets from overhead until they all disappeared into the myriad of buildings centred around the docks.

~

At the Corn Wall the single layer of defences, designed to protect humans from the zombies they knew from old, fared far worse.

"We're spread too bloody thin," the captain in command of the wall muttered to himself as he stood on one of the towers built to defend the gate blocking the A30.

Not knowing where the attack would come from, he'd been forced to spread his forces along the whole five-and-a-half mile stretch of the wall. He had QRF forces waiting in lorries and armoured cars at strategic places ready to reinforce any area screaming for help.

The attack, when it came, concentrated on the point where the main road met the wall near Hayle. The captain watched with dread as no matter how many were blown to smithereens by the ferocity of the defence, the waves of attackers kept forcing through the hail of bullets and explosions to reach the wall and flow over it.

Pausing to look around as he slammed another magazine into his rifle, he knew he was trapped by the seething mass leaping at the tower he was on. He watched as no matter how ferociously his people fought, they were being overwhelmed by the sheer number of attackers.

It was over, he saw that, so he issued the only order he could.

"Retreat, retreat, retreat!" he screamed into his radio.

The only satisfaction he felt as a zombie ripped his throat out as he swung his empty rifle at it, was that he could hear his order being repeated and whistles blowing to reinforce his last command.

The helicopter arrived just in time to offer its help as armoured cars sped from tower to tower along its length to evacuate everyone. As the zombies surged down the road sometimes only yards from the last vehicle in the speeding convoy, the helicopter fired everything it had to hold them back as it desperately tried to buy time for the erstwhile defenders.

When they reached Newlyn docks the chasers were so close that the occupants of the last few armoured cars were forced to abandon everything they had with them and just leap into the water to be picked up by the launches heading in to pick them up.

Here a valuable lesson was learnt, as even though the last few unfortunate escapees who had leapt into the water were pounced on by their chasers, those who desperately clawed their way beyond jumping reach found themselves unexpectedly safe.

Seemingly the one thing the new super zombies couldn't do, was swim.

Running zombies leapt headlong into the cold waters of the dock, only to sink like stones with only a line of bubbles marking their plunge to the depths of the harbour.

Some clung to a living person struggling desperately as they sank. For those treading water awaiting a rescue boat the scene would have been laughable if it wasn't so terrifying.

Reeling and shocked from the narrow escape, the guns on the rescue boats swept the docks of the undead until they turned and disappeared into the houses and streets of Newlyn and Penzance as if recalled by some unheard signal, chased by the helicopter spitting fire at them all the way.

~

The leader sensed all these events at the distant locations and knew his tactics would succeed.

Knew that soon they would all be feasting on live flesh.

It was just a matter of timing. He sent a command to his lieutenants who were spread among the tens of thousands gathered around him, and roared his own orders to those nearby.

He sent the command to the ones near the high stone walls and turrets to attack.

Running and leaping at the front he led his immeasurable multitudes as they raced after the convoy forming a dark, spreading smudge on the landscape as they advanced.

CHAPTER TWENTY-SEVEN

At the castle, the same scene as in Cornwall and Bristol played out.

One second nothing was in sight and the next the grounds surrounding the castle were thick with advancing death. Attacked from all points the defenders opened up, sending sheets of lead and explosives into the leading ranks. The mortars – already set up and ranged on preset target areas – began lobbing their bombs into the masses, blowing red mist filled gaps in the solid mass running and leaping towards them as directed by the spotters giving fire missions via radio.

Castles, by their very nature, were designed to withstand attacks from without, and their high walls could not be surmounted by a single leap. Castle designs had also evolved over the centuries when they were the primary defensive concept, built to protect and project power over the surrounding area. Its towers, curving outwards from the walls, where once arrows, rocks, boiling tar, or water had been the main weapons employed to kill any attackers seeking shelter against its high walls, now modern weapons of war issued death.

Pouring fire down on them, the living defenders were just as desperate and willing to destroy anyone attacking them as those from a millennium before.

Machine guns spat their bullets at the thousands streaming towards the walls and futilely clawing at the ancient high stones stretching into the sky above them. Bodies piled as the undead leapt over re killed ones to themselves be destroyed by bullets, for their own bodies to add to the growing butcher's mound; each body slowly raising the ramp of corpses creeping inexorably higher up the walls.

Everyone at the castle not tasked with protecting those too young or infirm to fight were either on the walls, part of the reserve force, firing the mortars, or hauling more ammunition to where it was needed.

Maud sat stoically by the radio, fielding calls from the defenders as the intensity of the attack grew. She had her small team of brave runners ready to relay messages radio could not reach, and while inside her fear grew to palpable levels her face remained impassive.

~

"Fuck!" Eddy shouted, throwing the handset down again.

It seemed to be his favourite word at the moment. I hadn't heard the call over the noise of the tractor, so I looked at him with a 'what now?' expression on my face.

"The castle is under attack."

That was all he needed to say to make my stress levels go through the roof. I wasn't there and my family needed me. Hell, everybody there needed us right now!

Above our heads the helicopter peeled away and powered off towards the castle.

"Clarke's ordered the helicopter to assist," Eddy shouted, making me feel slightly better.

Ahead the tank roared as its driver tried to eke every last ounce of power out of the engine in an attempt to make it go even faster. Our speed increased by probably a mile or two an hour, but whatever happened, nothing would make us go as fast as I wanted to.

Woody ran from position to position along the walls assessing the situation. Digby was in overall command, but he was acting as his eyes on the wall so Digby could supervise the mortars, and the defenders tasked with maintaining a flow of fresh ammunition to where it was needed. He also kept a small reserve force back so they could reinforce any areas needing additional help.

It was killing Digby not being on the walls firing a weapon, but someone had to be in command, to take in the whole situation and not just one area.

Below the walls all the fences and other defensive structures they had built to keep any wandering zombies back had been completely engulfed, rendering them useless. The only thing keeping them safe were the very walls the defenders stood on, but still he was worried.

Every fighter fired down upon the uncountable thousands surging against those walls. The mortars didn't need to be aimed as the orders relayed through Woody positioned high on the ramparts simply indicated they switch from one preset firing point to the next, raining bombs down on the castle grounds and carving great holes in the masses.

Holes that were immediately filled by the next successive wave.

As Woody looked outwards there was no end in sight to the horde heading for them, but what worried him most were the bodies piling up against the walls.

The stacks weren't yet high enough to be dangerous, but every zombie killed as it leapt raised the ramp of bodies and his anxiety along with it a little more.

It wasn't an impossible notion that eventually they would build a slope with which they could reach the top and breach the defences. It had happened in one of the zombie films they'd watched as part of their training programme. That particular scene had resulted in a whole city being lost in a matter of minutes, but that was Hollywood where no one really died but they did make for dramatic and exciting watching. Now it was real world life and death. After watching these movies, they did discuss, mainly over a few drinks similar to a stupid pub conversation, what they would do if one of the many situations portrayed in them happened to them.

"It's like that fucking movie we watched...but there ain't gonna be an airplane to save us," he radioed Digby.

"Repeat your last?"

"Diggers...They're piling up against the bloody walls and the piles are getting higher! We're going to have to come up with something."

The thought went out of his head as the helicopter roared in low over the trees and added its weight of fire to the fray. He needed to concentrate on the right now and not the maybes of the future.

Diggers stopped and stared at the walls after the radio call with Woody, his mind imagining thousands of zombies sweeping over their top to fall to the castle's courtyard. He shook his head in despair as no solution came to mind other than keeping up the barrage of mortar fire and praying for a miracle.

As the leader ran at the head of the pack, he knew the helicopter wouldn't return to the convoy soon as he has sensed its arrival at the castle.

He also knew they didn't need to simply jump on the cages surrounding the vehicles, but rip them apart to allow his legions to reach the living inside the protection they provided. If some of the force attacking the castle joined with him, then combined they would engulf all the moving objects together, giving them no chance to repel them again. He sent out his instructions as he closed in on the convoy still out of sight.

Unseen by those on the castle walls, zombies began to stream away from the castle as they answered their leaders call leaving half of their undead colleagues to keep attacking it.

"Die you heathenish disciples of Beelzebub!" Charles the vicar screamed.

He fired his weapon, leaning over the parapet to shoot as many as he could before they reached the walls. Surrounded by empty magazines for his gun he deftly slammed a fresh one home displaying some very un-vicar-like skills.

When the firing pin clicked on an empty chamber, he ejected that magazine and let it drop to the floor, grabbing another from an open box of fresh reloads by his side to repeat the process.

Charles began singing his favourite hymn, Onward Christian Soldiers, as he emptied yet another magazine into the attacking masses below.

Woody stopped as he passed him, momentarily distracted as always by the sight of a cassock-draped man wearing surplus webbing over it. He glitched as the vicar let out the strongest expletives Woody had ever heard him say, then singing a stirring hymn as he fired a weapon which in another life he wouldn't have countenanced touching.

And also, the sergeant in him was impressed by how competent he looked, cycling the rifle like a seasoned soldier, calm under fire. He shook his head in wonder at the sight before getting his attention by tapping him on his shoulder.

Charles turned and Woody winced at the heat of the barrel that he pushed away before it could be inadvertently pointed at him.

Woody chided him with a smile and raised his voice to be heard.

"Remember, Vicar, pointy end towards the enemy!"

"I am so sorry my son," Charles replied, shouting above the roar of weapons still being fired. "I momentarily forgot your most excellent training in all the kerfuffle going on."

Woody laughed out loud in the first moment of levity he'd had since the alarm was raised first thing in the morning, at having what was going on being described as a mere 'kerfuffle'.

Woody looked out over the walls, seeing the ground before them thick with piled corpses being scrambled over by thousands who ran straight into and through the devastating maelstrom of bullets and explosives being laid down by the defenders.

Twice-dead bodies jerked and twitched as volleys of bullets slammed into them, giving the impression they still lived and weren't some horrendous, nightmarish reincarnation of what were once their slow and shambling enemy.

The grenade machine guns and mortars concentrated their massed fire further out, laying down a deadly barrage which the approaching zombies had to run through to then be faced with the guns of the helicopter which circled overhead adding its fire where the pilot decided the most help was needed.

After that cordon of death dozens of mounted machine guns and rifles fired from the walls sheeted the ground with their bullets.

Despite this incredible defence hundreds still reached the walls where they scrambled up the ever-growing slope of corpses.

It was the same situation on every wall of the castle. Zombies flooded forwards from all directions, running a relentless, macabre race between themselves and the bullets and bombs which fought to hold them back like a tide fight on a beach.

The problem with that thought was that Woody knew both the castles and walls of sand children built on the beach never won against the tide, which inevitably washed them away despite the builders best and final frantic efforts to hold it back.

Inevitable, he thought, sending a cold chill through his veins.

Charles peered into the distance where they kept emerging from the now-cratered and smoking treeline.

"I think fewer are coming now," he said pointing at the distant trees to reinforce his belief after a few seconds of careful study.

Woody followed the direction of his outstretched arm, hoping it was indeed true.

Zombies still streamed from the woods, but unless his own eyes were deceiving him as well, there just didn't seem to be as many. He clapped Charles on the back as he turned away.

"We might just win this one yet, Vicar," Woody said as he rushed off to check if the same thing was happening on the other walls before he could let his hopes by one single degree.

It was.

They still streamed forwards, most to be killed before they reached the walls, but less were now making it through and leaping up the ramp of dead.

There's definitely less of the bastards, Woody assured himself.

He ran down the nearest steps and sprinted to Digby who was taking ammunition boxes off the children who were ferrying the endless supply from the armoury.

"They're running out of reinforcements, there's less coming at us," Woody declared confidently.

Digby thought for a few seconds.

Every gun on the walls still fired, but from down in the courtyard the volume seemed to have slacked off. He trusted Woody implicitly so acted on the news.

"Okay, we seem to be having a bit of a lull right now. Let's rotate people off the line and give them a breather. If we can give everyone the chance to take a break down here and get some scram and fluids in them, it won't do them any harm."

He knew that despite the fight only lasting for about thirty minutes so far, firing a weapon continuously for that length of time is an exhausting thing. Everyone needed to be on their top game and giving people even a ten-minute break away from the action would restore them and stop sloppy mistakes being made.

Digby turned to the reserves.

"Grab an ammo box each and replace every other person on that wall there," he said pointing to a section. "Tell the others their turn will come."

Pondering his next move carefully he reached his decision and turned to the children who looked exhausted but still eager. Their reddened sweat covered faces showing how hard they had been working.

"Right, my bloodthirsty little devils," he said with a genuine smile of affection. "Do you want to grab your weapons and have a stint on the walls?"

Faces that seconds ago looked worn and tired, perked up immediately and looked at him eagerly. They had been quietly nagging him to let them fight ever since the attack began. Until now he had good naturedly refused their requests as he knew they would be more useful hauling ammunition which would enable more adults to be on the firing line. As the immediate danger seemed to be reducing, now was the right time to let them get their way.

Also, most of them only carried the small calibre rimfire rifles. They had all fired at and killed zombies in the past and carried them with pride when on sentry duty. But even the zombies of old needed a headshot from the small bullets they fired to kill them. With the much faster and aggressive ones attacking them now it would take a very accurate shot, or a very lucky one, to take a zombie down.

A few of the bigger children had been deemed strong enough to use a larger calibre weapon and had undergone very carefully supervised training from one of the sergeants before they were trusted to carry one when on sentry duty.

But he needed to give the adults on the walls a chance for a break and if three or four children replaced one adult where if they worked together they possibly stood a chance of killing some, it would allow a few more to grab a quick rest.

It went against their ethos of 'protecting the children at all costs', but he justified it to himself by reasoning that no more harm could come to them on the walls if they weren't about to be breached than in the courtyard? He had to work with what he had, and he made the decision.

He pointed to a section of the walls that was nearest to where he was and had a staircase close by in case they needed to get off the walls quickly in an emergency and sent them on their way. With a newfound energy, they grabbed their weapons and bags of ammunition and ran off. He gave his nephew Eddie a quick hug as he passed and ruffled the hair of those kids who got close enough to him in encouragement.

He looked at Woody, exasperation clear on his face.

"Fucking child soldiers Woody. What are we doing to them?"

Woody came to attention and replied in his best sergeant's voice.

"Keeping the little buggers alive sir, and making sure they'll survive in the fucked-up world we're living in."

He slumped as he continued in a quieter, more tender tone.

"What other option do we have? They've seen and done things no child – or adult for that matter – should ever do or witness. In my opinion they're doing just fine, better than us adults in fact…gotta cope with the present and we'll deal with the future when that arrives."

Digby pondered his words and replied sadly.

"Yes Sar'nt. I suppose we will."

He snapped back in to work mode. Even that brief respite thinking about the children had revived him. He needed to get back to being in command.

"Sar'nt, report from the walls if you can please. I want to know if now is a good time to resupply the helicopter. They must be getting low on ammo by now."

With a "right you are" Woody headed back to the walls, passing the first defenders coming for a break on the way.

CHAPTER TWENTY-EIGHT

In the convoy the tension was palpable. Our home, our friends and families, were under attack and we weren't there.

I felt so guilty. I'd volunteered to go on the mission to the Broughs without a second thought, believing there was no way the zombies would or even could threaten our home after we'd destroyed the first pack to attack.

If I'd known what was going to happen countrywide there was no way in hell I would've gone, yet here I was! Standing in a trailer looking across empty countryside, while my wife and children fought for their lives.

We'd rescued the Brough's garrison, but I felt like shit as I willed the castle to come into sight. I hadn't even thought how we'd fight through the thousands attacking them to get inside. My mind raced too fast to think straight. All I wanted to do was open up with everything we had and blast a hole straight through the middle of them and bugger the consequences.

Yeah, great tactic, right?

That all changed in a second.

The tank fired its main gun, causing us to jump and crouch down from not only the noise, but the shock wave that washed over us which again momentarily disorientated everyone.

Through dulled ears I heard both Gallon and Eddy screaming for us all to stand-to, as they both began firing their weapons.

As I stood up I was faced with a wall of super zombies leaping at us from the hedgerows. Grabbing the machine gun in front of me I put the stock into my shoulder and opened up at point blank range. The gun bucked violently against my shoulder as I strafed the barrel from side to side, my bullets blowing bodies apart and throwing them backwards into others leaping to take their place in the front row of death.

We couldn't get them all, and those that made it through our barrage leapt onto the cage. I could do nothing about them as my sole aim was to kill everything trying to get to us, so I had to trust in others to deal with them.

My entire world shrank to the few yards in front of me and to both sides as I swung my gun, pouring lead into writhing, leaping flesh.

The gun was suddenly pulled from my shoulder as a hand grabbed the barrel and twisted it powerfully to one side. Shocked, I grabbed the stock and tried to wrest control of it back, but the zombie grabbing it was far stronger than me. Acting without thought I pulled my sidearm from my leg holster and wildly aimed at the creature who had both feet planted on the sides of the trailer as it seemingly tried to pull the gun from its mount.

I kept pulling the trigger of my pistol until I hit it in the head by pure accident. It went rigid and I felt the barrel of the machine gun come back under my control as it fell from sight.

Screaming with both fear and rage, I rammed the pistol back into its holster and leaned into the gun to hold the trigger down, aiming at the snarling, raging faces looming in my vision.

My mind was only just beginning to comprehend what the zombie had tried to do. Booms of shotguns and rapid, automatic fire sounded all around me as everyone in the packed trailer fought with everything they had. Blood and gore blown from bodies spattered all over me as mine and other bullets disintegrated bodies at touching distance, causing great gouts of thick blood and gore to spray everywhere in a dark red mist.

It was trying to get the gun! my mind screamed at me as another grabbed for the barrel.

Time slowed for me. I watched smoke curl away from its hands as skin fried against hot barrel, the smell of burning flesh as it held on making me gag.

Better prepared this time, I kept my finger on the machine gun's trigger, still sending bullets outwards where they couldn't fail to strike a target as so many crowded around the trailer. I raised my pistol again and emptied the magazine until the pressure on the barrel was released, the skull of my attacker pulverised into an unrecognisable mess by my bullets.

Then the last of the linked ammunition fed through the breech and my gun fell silent.

For the first time I had a chance to look around the trailer as I reached for a reload. The cage was covered with zombies, most dead, but some still pulled and heaved on the bars until killed from the blast of a shotgun or a volley of rifle fire.

As I watched, transfixed, holding a fresh ammunition box I had picked up, a solitary zombie began dragging its dead comrades clear, throwing them one-handed off the trailer as if they weighed nothing. As soon as a space was made it pulled on the bars, flexing the metal against the welds holding them in place.

Stuart pushed a shotgun through a gap and fired. The heavy cartridge he'd loaded instantly turned the head into a liquefied mush that sprayed upwards before the headless corpse was thrown back by the force of the shot to fall from view.

Everyone else in the trailer not manning one of the mounted guns either fired a weapon or reloaded for someone else as the bed of the trailer once more became a mess of spent brass and discarded magazines.

I looked at the guns lining the sides. Everyone experienced the same problem I'd had; they were fighting to control the guns against the hands that tried to wrest them from their grip.

Those manning the grenade machine guns had resorted to their personal weapons which were thrust backwards and forwards between the cages bars as they tried to avoid those being grabbed as well.

The training we had been given on the grenade machine guns flashed through my mind. The grenades they fired only armed themselves when they were a certain distance from the weapon, basically to stop one blowing up in your face. The zombies surrounding us and climbing all over the trailer were within touching distance, meaning that any grenade fired wouldn't be armed, and even though it would punch into then with massive force, most likely killing them if they were human and not some mindless zombie that didn't feel pain, it wouldn't explode.

Which is probably a good thing, I thought, as we're all within the blast radius!

This meant that an important part of our defence was rendered no more useful than scrap metal.

I took in all this in only a few seconds before turning back to reload my machine gun which proved impossible, as clawing hands reaching through the cage scrabbling for anything to grip on to, made it too dangerous to put my hands anywhere near the breech for fear of being grabbed.

Unwelcome images of my screaming body being pulled through the mesh like some macabre food processor flooded my thoughts.

In frustration I grabbed my rifle from behind my back and was just about to fire when the bracket that fixed the machine gun to the side of the trailer couldn't withstand the force it was under.

With a crack audible over the maelstrom of battle it snapped, and my gun vanished as it was yanked away.

Shocked, I raised my rifle and emptied the magazine through the gap where the machine gun had been only seconds before. My rifle threw bodies back in sprays of blood but it could never compensate for the loss of such a valuable weapon.

We needed to make sure we didn't lose another one.

I turned to Eddy beside me, still firing his machine gun in short, controlled bursts.

I screamed the bad news in his ear, reinforcing my words by indicating the gap in our defences where my gun had been only moments before. He shouted that he understood, and to tell everyone else as he hooked his left elbow under the weapon, pulled it from its mount, took a step back so the barrel wasn't protruding as far out from the side of the trailer, and resumed firing as his loud voice boomed over the trailer.

"Control your fire or you'll cook your barrels!"

The temptation to keep your finger on the trigger and send as many bullets outwards as possible was strong given the state of panic, but that was only viable for a short time.

All guns heated up when fired, but the danger was when the barrels became too hot and distorted, as even a small change in shape rendered them useless and ran the risk of a bullet exploding before it left the muzzle.

I wasn't sure if anyone paid attention to him as the volume of fire didn't seem to decrease, but it only took a glance to understand why.

The whole trailer was chaos as everyone onboard fought with a desperate determination, and the only positive was that we were still moving. Looking ahead at the tractor pulling us along, it was no surprise that it too was covered with bodies that pulled and clawed at the cage protecting it.

Louise fired a shotgun from the window and Shawn used a pistol one-handed as he fought to keep the tractor as close as he could to the armoured car ahead.

The tank fired its main gun as fast as it could be reloaded, using massive 120mm high-explosive shells to blast a path through the massed enemy ahead.

The trailer lurched as it rode over the bodies crushed by tank, armoured car, and tractor wheels, telling me that we must be killing hundreds simply by running them over, but thousands more still attacked from all sides.

The cage rattled and creaked alarmingly, both from the weight of bodies sprawled over it and from the animated corpses grabbing and pulling on the bars. Some onboard the trailer had dropped their weapons and wielded the shorter boar spears to stab and push bodies off the cage.

A shout of alarm from the rear of the trailer caught my attention. I turned to see the armoured car behind in trouble. The soldiers onboard, standing in the hatches, were firing either the mounted machine guns or their personal weapons frantically at the zombies climbing all over their protective cage.

Then I noticed why they were acting so desperately. The zombies were concentrating their efforts on a part of the cage where a weld had given way under the relentless attacks, and every zombie that reached the cage bent the loose bar a little further outwards before they were blasted away.

Those at the rear of the trailer adjusted their aim and added their weight of lead to offer what help they could, heeding Gallon's roars of warning not to fire on their own people.

I ran to the rear to add my own weapons bullets to help, but the end was inevitable. A zombie reached the cage through the hail of fire to brace both legs against the side of the armoured car and heave to bend the metal free, its grey, pallid body bulging with overdeveloped muscles as it applied inhuman strength. A bullet obliterated its face, and as it fell from view the bar still gripped in dead hands, ripped off along its length creating a gap in the cage large enough to let a body in.

The leader, watching from a low rise of the field overlooking the road jolted as a surge of emotion a human would describe as victorious shot through his body. He sent out his next command. The zombies surrounding all the vehicles turned as one and surged towards the armoured car to engulf it.

Our bullets killed those on the outer edges, but their bodies protected others deeper in the morass preventing us from stopping the inevitable.

Our firing petered out as we watched with dread, unable to do anything but witness the tragedy playing out before us.

The armoured car swerved off the road as the driver lost control, sending it through a hedgerow to pitch its nose into the ditch beyond. So many surrounded the beleaguered car we couldn't see what was happening beneath the cage, but they still fought going by the muffled sounds of gunfire. The sound absorbed by the weight of packed bodies.

We kept on moving as we knew to stop was to die. Unable to do anything to help, it killed us to keep going, but what could we do other than to die alongside them? Some screamed, some demanded we stop and help, but sane heads prevailed.

I watched silently until the firing stopped to be followed by the muted thumps of explosions. The only possible conclusion was that being knowing that all was lost, whoever was left alive inside the vehicle had pulled the pins on grenades which, in the reinforced body of the armoured car, would mean their certain death. A certain death that saved them from being ripped to shreds while they yet lived, which was a choice I hoped I would be brave enough to make if it ever came to it.

Gallon screamed, snapping us out of frozen inactivity.

"They're far enough away now, get those fucking GMGs going!"

People had just died in the most tragic way possible, right before our eyes. People we knew. Our friends, but we had to keep going to make sure it didn't happen to us as well.

There was no time for tears, those could come later if we lived long enough. We jumped back to the guns and opened up, grenades bursting among the crowds still tearing at the armoured car while a hailstorm of bullets tore through flesh and bone turning the area around it into a red-misted zone of death.

We kept up the barrage, the satisfaction of killing hundreds of them not making up for our losses but paying a small deposit against the debt they owed us.

Rounding a corner the stranded car fell from sight and our guns went silent as, for the moment, we had nothing to fire at. The tractor and trailer which had been at the rear of the convoy closed the gap, filling the space where the armoured car had been, and was now tight up to our rear. I could see the terrified concentration on the driver's face as he stuck as close to us as possible.

The tractor blocked most of my view of the trailer. They had less people onboard as we had taken on all the survivors from the Brough's, but I could imagine the frantic preparations taking place, as was the case with us, to ready themselves for the next attack which must be coming soon.

We passed a building which told me we were about thirty minutes from the castle.

Close…but not close enough, I thought as the anxiety of inactivity rose in me again.

CHAPTER TWENTY-NINE

The leader's tactics of committing all his forces to attack just one vehicle had worked.

The myriad sacrificed, using their bodies as shields to absorb the bullets from the other vehicles, had enabled those nearest to break through the cage surrounding the armoured car and crack it open.

The tactic had worked once so logically it would work again, if the bulk of his forces attacked the last vehicle in the line while the rest maintained the assault on the others, then they would be unable to support them.

"That was bloody deliberate!" Eddy spat savagely.

"What?" I asked, unsure if he was talking to me.

Eddy turned, seeming surprised that either I'd heard him or that he'd even spoken out loud.

"I said that was bloody deliberate," he repeated angrily. "The whole bloody lot of them targeted that one vehicle after they found a weak spot. They used themselves as human shields!"

He was so angry, so animated that my urge to point out they weren't exactly human shields had to be ignored.

I was about to offer an opinion when movement flashed ahead of me.

"Here they come again!" I yelled before depressing the trigger on my rifle.

Once more my world shrank to the area directly in front of me as I poured fire into the fresh attack.

The spare magazines in my assault vest replenished during the brief lull were quickly expended so I began using a box by my feet to reload, dropping the empty one on the floor with a press of a button and flick of my wrist before grabbing a fresh reload. I had a spare rifle leaning against the side of the trailer and when I remembered, I kept changing over to allow the other to cool down. The trailer was a chaotic scene of shouting and screaming men and women, all working together to get through the hell we were suffering.

The tractor behind began blasting on his horn, and a quick glance realised my fears. The tractor itself was completely covered with bodies as the driver, unable to see ahead, had slowed down, increasing his distance from us as he attempted to keep his vehicle on the road.

I knew the mesh cage surrounding the tractor itself was strong, the design having been worked on over the months when those in the trailers were considered to be protected enough by their high sides, leaving the driver and the one riding shotgun more exposed.

Surrounded by a solid cage which was encased in bolted-on mesh, it should stand up to the punishment it was being put under. Both the driver and his passenger fired their weapons, blowing corpses off their cage in a desperate attempt to enable them to see where they were going.

Unfortunately, communication with them was impossible as nobody could hear anything through the radios with all the noise but I could see the hastily built cage protecting the trailer was covered in more bodies. I couldn't see what they were doing, but it wasn't hard to imagine. A desperate fight must be taking place, and we could do nothing to help as we were in the same situation.

The gunfire from that trailer increased to a crescendo, and I even heard desperate screams of fear and defiance over the firing before slowly the level reduced to nothing.

That could mean only one thing, and my entire being surged with rage, grief and fear.

Captain Hammond had been in charge of the trailer, and it was manned by some of his men and the reinforcements who had arrived by helicopter which was why it had been positioned at the rear of the convoy. The realisation that Hammond was most likely dead chilled me to the core.

Captain Hammond, or Steve as he was mainly called given how rank and position seemed less important in the new world, and his men, had been with us since our arrival at Warwick Castle. Our first chance meeting as we headed north on the motorway while they were heading south started a chain of events that led them to follow us to our new home with Willie in tow.

Quickly merging with our group, he'd been instrumental in our success at establishing the castle as a viable place to live, where his personality and willingness to get his hands dirty with all the hard work we had to do made him a popular character.

Gallon, his sergeant who was in the trailer with us, let out a roar of primal anguish. His affections for the young captain went far beyond the respect for rank that were ingrained into his soul. They had shared so much together, and he had been proud to see his young officer grow into the role and position fate had gifted him. Gallon thought of him as the son he'd never had, and therefore warranted his close attention and loyalty so he could use his experience to guide him to be the very best version of himself.

Blind with grief, Gallon roared his name and tried to open the rear of the trailer but Eddy dropped his weapon and tackled him to the ground before he could release the catch. Smothering him in a bear hug while the battle raged around them, Eddy held him tightly and whispered fiercely in his ear as tears of grief streamed down his face.

Eventually the fog lifted and Gallon responded to whatever Eddy had told him. Releasing him, Eddy helped Gallon to stand and he locked eyes with his fellow sergeant and nodded to convey much more than words ever could.

It said he knew, that he understood, and that he was back in the fight.

The tractor behind us swerved as the panicking driver tried to keep his vehicle on the road with virtually no visibility. I wasn't sure if he knew what had happened behind him, but it was hard to imagine he didn't.

The zombies then turned their attention on us. We were now one of only two vehicles left in the open, as the tank's occupants were sealed up tight with no chance of the zombies getting to them but it was still covered in bodies that ineffectively clawed at the armoured steel trying to scratch their way in.

It still fired its main gun and coaxial chain gun which swept the road ahead, but it couldn't directly offer us any assistance aside from crushing and pulverising bodies beneath its tracks and clearing the way to enable us to keep moving. The surviving armoured car, even though every hatch along its length sported a mounted machine gun or grenade gun, couldn't pour out as much fire as our packed trailer could, so we became the main target of their attack.

A wave of zombies washed over our trailer making the inside go dark as the light was blocked out. Fear disappeared as it became a brutal battle for survival. We all looked as if we had been bathing in blood, we were covered in it, and each close-range blast from a gun misted the air with a thickening cloud to coat us with yet more. Blood, guts, chunks of flesh and bone dropped all over us from the bodies lying over the cage.

If hell had a physical manifestation, we were in it.

Time had no meaning as we fought with everything we had and more. Fire, reload, fire reload...I had no idea how many times I had done it. I was blinded by smoke and deafened by sustained gunfire. It could have been hours or just minutes.

Reaching into the box at my feet my hands felt for another magazine but came up empty. I turned to the head of the trailer where the ammunition was stacked to grab another box and was shocked to see so little there. We'd set out with a mountain of the stuff piled in the back, more than we had ever carried before, and at the time it had been inconceivable to think we might use so much, but we had it available so we loaded it.

The pitiful pile I looked on now made me recall Eddy's warning of the need to conserve ammunition.

How the hell were we meant to do that though? The only thing keeping us alive where others were tragically dying around us was to expend all the ammunition we had!

I grabbed one of the last few full boxes of magazines, reloaded and carried on shooting. Through a gap my firing blasted in the blanket of undead meat covering us I recognised the motorway junction we passed over on the outskirts of Warwick.

We were getting close.

Others were taking magazines from the box at my feet which told me our reserves must be getting desperately low. Looking around, more people had reverted to using spears as their main weapons were discarded after firing their last round, thrusting them at anything that grabbed hold of the cage.

Eddy held his radio tight to his ear before letting out another long string of expletives.

"Fucking cage broke on the armoured car. They closed down before anyone got killed but they're out of the fight now!" he screamed at me.

There was no blame on them after what had happened to the other car. To stay in the open would mean death, so closing their hatches was all they could've done as soon as their protective cage failed.

The bars surrounding us were also feeling the punishment. Every time a strong hand grabbed one and pulled on it, they flexed and bent more and more. None of the welds holding them in place had broken yet, but it must be only a matter of time before one gave way.

Firing the last bullet from my rifle I threw it aside and pulled my pistol from its holster and started firing that. In no time the slide locked back on an empty chamber as I emptied my final magazine, while beside me Eddy angrily holstered his own pistol as he too fired his last bullet.

We locked eyes, sharing a moment of silent despair at the hopelessness of our situation.

A look of sad remembrance crossed his face as he reached into his top pocket and removed the solitary shotgun cartridge he always carried with him.

My eyes widened as I remembered the conversation we'd had all those months ago when staying at the farmhouse outside Cheltenham following our unsuccessful attempt to find Louise's parents. Clearing out the gun safe, Eddy had found the cartridge on the floor where it had been dropped and forgotten in the farmers haste to leave. He'd said at the time when he put it in his pocket that if he ever found himself reaching for it, then we were well and truly fucked.

The prophecy of his comment as we stood there, eyes locked, in a trailer completely covered with a carpet of zombies all trying to break through our protective cage almost overwhelmed me with the fatigue of despair.

We were trapped, and we were going to die.

Anger surged inside me as I fought the weak sentiment, hating myself for being ready to give up. I looked around the trailer, seeing a few people still with ammunition firing their weapons while everyone else fought with spears, screaming and shouting their defiance as they gave their all to the battle.

No, I am NOT going to die, my mind screamed at me. I'm going to make it back to my family.

Determination filled my body as I took the cartridge from Eddy's hand and pushed it back into his pocket.

"Not yet, Dave. We can fucking do this!"

I grabbed a spear from the rack and held it out to him, knowing that if he took it he was agreeing not to give up. His eyes lost their glazed, defeated look as my words sunk in. Glancing at the spear his face tightened with fury. Grabbing it, he screamed a savage war cry and turned to thrust it through the eye of a zombie trying to bite its way through the bars before moving on to kill the next, and the next, like some crazed bayonet master at work.

As the last gun fell silent I pulled a spear from the rack and joined him.

CHAPTER THIRTY

Digby was not happy, but he was satisfied that the defences were holding for now. Mortar bombs still fell as directed by Woody, and the ammunition supply was keeping up with the demand from the walls. The numbers attacking were still less than the initial crazed assault therefore he was still systematically rotating the defenders off the walls for short breaks, where even ten minutes sitting, having a mug of tea, a chocolate bar, or a smoke for those that did, seemed to be all everyone needed before they wanted to climb the stairs and rejoin the fray.

Most of the zombies charging the walls were re-killed before reaching the walls, but still the slopes building up on all sides of the castle grew with every animated corpse to reach that far before being ripped apart by concentrated gunfire.

The grenade machine guns were having some success in reducing these when fired at the outer edges of the slopes, disintegrating enough bodies to destabilise the piles causing them to collapse back on themselves like scree rolling down a steep mountain side.

The news received from both Cornwall and Fort Bristol was not good.

Cornwall had been abandoned entirely, and the survivors were watching the masses flooding the land from the safety of an armada of boats which had surged landward to rescue them. Many lives had been lost during the desperate escape, but quick thinking and acts of bravery had helped to rescue most.

St Michael's Mount had also been evacuated. Luckily the tide was in when the wall fell which saved it from being overrun and enabled the occupants to escape to sea, leaving Cornwall now once more under the sway of the undead.

At Bristol a more orderly evacuation had been ordered. Understanding that their final ring of containers would be vulnerable to a determined attack, Walker-Jones had ordered everyone to evacuate to the ships moored alongside the quay when the attackers had gone to ground, and those ships had cast their mooring lines to push off and hold position in the waters off the quay ready to unleash their guns should the enemy reappear.

Warwick Castle, as it had been from the very start, was now the only place on the mainland United Kingdom occupied by the living.

Walker-Jones ordered the helicopters to be refuelled, rearmed and sent back to Warwick.

Digby's tactical radio bleeped in his ear to tell him a call was incoming. He'd received the occasional update from Clarke in the tank via their main radio, but this was the first time he'd made direct contact, and the news they had lost both an armoured car and a trailer to the zombies sickened him.

From the little Clarke could see out of the viewing ports of the tank, the occupants of the armoured car had closed their hatches and were sheltering. Also, judging from the lack of gunfire from the tractor, he reckoned they were out of ammunition.

"Diggers, we're about ten – one-zero – minutes out. What's our chances of breaking through?"

Digby had no real idea if it was possible, but inaction was unforgiveable.

"Working on that, you just keep coming."

"Diggers, be honest with me now…if it isn't an option we'll have to stay outside. We can't risk them getting in just for the few of us out here."

Digby opened his mouth to respond but faltered, releasing the press-to-talk button on his radio.

Can I make that call? he asked himself, knowing that the answer was yes.

Yes, he could absolutely make the call to sacrifice twenty for the sake of all others. He could make it, but he might not be able to live with it afterwards.

This was a problem Digby had been musing over for some time, and he hadn't yet come up with a satisfactory solution that wouldn't guarantee to get more people killed.

They had to do something, though, and looking at his reserve force he decided the time for prudence was over. None of those reserves seemed grateful not to be in the fight, and something about that made him feel challenged.

"Right! Everyone to the walls," Digby said, trying to sound positive. "The convoy's close and we need to work out a way to get them safely back inside."

Ian threw away the mug of tea he'd been drinking lumbered to his feet.

"Sounds like a job for the knights if you ask me," he said, casually stretching off his back as if gearing up for some heavy work.

"The main gates open inwards, right? So if you concentrate the fire from the barbican and the walls surrounding it, we'll open the portcullis and the gates and hold back whichever of the bastards get through the barrage, then just shut the gate as we retreat back... Sound simple enough?" he finished with a shrug that clanked armour plates together.

"You can't go out there, Ian!" Digby protested. "You'll be facing too much risk...I won't allow it."

Ian hefted his axe to rest it on his shoulder and, raising his fingers to his lips, emitted a loud, shrill, two-tone whistle that cut through the noise of battle raging all around them.

On the walls his fellow knights knew what the whistle meant, and they started to leave their posts and make their way to him.

"To be fair, Darren. It's our lives we're risking so it's up to us...Unless you have a better idea, that is?"

Digby did not, nor did he have the luxury of time to imagine one. The simple fact was that if they wanted the survivors of the convoy to get inside the walls, someone had to open the gate and defend it for long enough.

Within a minute Ian's knights had gathered and he told them what they were going to do, and not one of them baulked at the terrifying position they were about to put themselves in.

They'd spent the last hours fighting them from the walls and so knew full well what the enemy was capable of. With faces grim with determination, they adjusted their armour so it was cinched up tight and checked each other's to make sure no gaps were showing.

Digby had quickly wrapped his head round the fact that the knights were going outside no matter what, and worked with the plan. He radioed Woody who began organising for every other person on the walls to head to the barbican and the curtain walls either side of it, ordering more ammunition and grenades to those locations.

Connecting with the helicopter pilot he told her what was about to happen, explaining that the action might leave everywhere else poorly defended, even though it was highly likely that in a few minutes every zombie in the grounds would be concentrating on the convoy. He tasked the helicopter crew with monitoring the perimeter from their elevated position to make sure they weren't blindsided during the gate action, while hovering off to one side of the gates, away from the dangers of incoming mortar rounds where they could still add a significant amount of lead to the fray.

To cover the danger of zombies making it through the gate he ordered the rest of the reserves around him who had not left yet to not head to the walls to concentrate at the gate.

Orders were relayed to the mortar teams to saturate the area directly in front of and either side of the gate with as much ordnance delivered as fast as humanly possible right up until Woody, monitoring the situation from the ramparts, ordered a halt. Digby gave him firm instructions to cut it as close as he dared to give the incoming convoy as much time under cover of their heavy, indirect fire weapons before he switched their target coordinates.

Pulling yet more defenders from the ramparts Digby ordered the two armoured cars parked in the courtyard to be manned and act as a rearguard for the ones gathering by the barbican.

It was hastily planned, but Digby felt they were covering the bases. The gates were going to be the weak point, so he left Woody in nominal charge of the walls while he would command at the gates.

Outgoing fired slacked off as everyone got into position and prepared themselves while Digby's radio beeped again.

"Two minutes out...shall we abort? We can try and lure some of them away if—" Clarke asked.

"Negative, it's all in hand. Approach the main gate under mortar cover."

"Confirm we enter grounds though the main gate and head for the barbican?"

"Affirmative."

"And confirm outer gate is undefended?"

"Affirmative. Outer gate is undefended...If we pull this off, you and your boys might have to foot the bar bill for the knights in perpetuity. Good luck."

~

Eddy ended the radio call and got everyone's attention in the trailer.

"Okay, that was Clarke...The plan is we drive straight through the outside gates and head to the barbican. They're concentrating our forces there with the helicopter overhead."

"Is that it?" I asked with undisguised incredulity. "They're just going to…open the gates and we'll just…drive straight in? How are they going to stop them getting in?"

I had a vision of hordes of zombies streaming after us as we drove into the courtyard to engulf everything inside under a mass of biting, grabbing flesh.

"No. No!" I said, shaking my head. "We need to go around and find another way in, somewhere the zombies aren't attacking, we—"

"I know mate," Eddy responded firmly, shutting me up before I went into a full meltdown. "He says the knights are going to do something stupid, but I haven't got a clue what he meant by that. Look, I think as we are in the position we're in we've just got to trust them." Eddy pointed upwards while still staring right into my wide eyes. "And to kill every last one of the fuckers clinging to us like shit on a sheep's back legs"

It took me a moment to visualise his comment which, even in our current situation, prompted an unbidden smile from me and chuckles from a few others too before we resumed our relentless work with the spears.

We must be close but as I couldn't see anything beyond the zombies crawling all over us, I just kept destroying brains and using brute force, push them off where another replaced it grabbing the bars and pulling on them before it must have even hit the ground.

The battle had so many moving parts, so many players involved making key decisions, but right then I was reduced to perforating zombie heads because that was all my tiny portion of the world permitted me.

So I did, with everything I had left.

CHAPTER THIRTY-ONE

Loping behind the main force following the vehicles, the leader sent instructions to his legions. While he had won some small victories by breaking through a few vehicles' defences to get at the bodies inside and tear them apart, the final victory eluded him and now they drew closer to the high walls that had also defied his efforts. Those walls had extracted an uncountable toll on his forces, but there was still time for one final effort. Still a chance to destroy the living and hunt them through their stone walled home until they were eradicated.

Broadcasting his intent to his lieutenants, he roared his commands again to those around him.

~

The main gate which we had strengthened, raised and kept locked as our first line of defence was no match for the tank which, unchecked, destroyed it as it drove over the leaf's, crushing the zombies that were leaping over it.

Overhead the helicopter's guns opened up as it peeled away from the castle walls and hovered off to one side of the convoy, pouring lead down on their pursuers as they drove through the corpse-littered, bomb-cratered grounds of the castle.

As the convoy came into sight of the walls every gun poured lead and explosives onto the throng surging around it. Mortars landed left and right of their approach as well as further ahead until Woody gave the order not to fire in their path again.

The zombies that had been attacking the walls all turned as one and ran towards the vehicles as if receiving a command, forming a dark, seething mass of bodies that merged into one biological glut of flowing, flesh-eating death.

As soon as the zombies moved, Woody knew that the main battle was going to be at the barbican entrance, so he ordered more of the walls defenders to join the forces already amassing there.

Ian stood at the head of the knights within the dark confines of the barbican entrance.

The palisade gate had already been raised, and only the final crossbar on the main gate secured it against the terror outside.

"We've trained for this!" Ian yelled, whipping himself and his friends into the frenzy they needed to survive what they were about to do.

They had their shields slung across their backs and long pikes in hand. Hand weapons adorned their armour, each one individually placed depending on the weapon or personal preference. Gathered in the gloom they could have been a flashback to ancient times where beleaguered defenders prepared for a foray to fight a besieging enemy, and the only historical errors were the handguns everyone carried in holsters strapped to their armour.

"Our friends need us, and we're the only fuckers crazy enough to do this!" Ian continued.

They could now hear the roar of the approaching engines over the continuous firing from the walls.

Ian, shoulders heaving with the effort of breathing fast, turned to face the gate and lowered his helmet into place.

It was time.

Resting his pike against himself, he used his free hand to push the final locking bar out from its brackets.

"Knights! With meeeeee!"

His battle cry echoed along the passage as he and Jamie pulled the gates open, and they stepped out into hell.

Clarke stared through the viewing ports of the tank, being afforded a clear view thanks to the firing from the walls which had swept most of the bodies from its armoured sides. It was a strange occurrence knowing that the bullets pinging and ricocheting off the metal were being fired by their own side, but safely cocooned inside the heavily armoured beast he was unconcerned about that particular danger.

Weirdly, a quote from the famous wartime leader Winston Churchill sprang to mind, causing a flicker of amusement to transform his expression.

Nothing in life is so exhilarating as to be shot at without result.

He had been shot at many times during his career – friendly fire or 'blue-on-blue' incidents included – but this was the first time without fear of being hit.

As the castle loomed into sight another thought shot into his head, and he swore loudly before speaking on the internal comms to the rest of crew.

"Now, chaps…someone correct me if I'm wrong, but I'm not entirely convinced we'll fit through the gates."

The silence he received was an answer in itself. That they were potentially so close to safety but potentially doomed by being stuck outside the walls, unable to leave the cocoon of armour surrounding them felt like a cruel irony.

His next thought was that if they became jammed in the gateway, he'd cause the others following to be just as dead as they could be.

He sighed sadly, thinking of his family now only a few yards away from him, but beyond reach. Closing his eyes as the reality of their situation hit home, the only option he had left became the plan.

They had one last act they could do to help more of their friends survive.

"Fuck it. Lads? Who's up for a glorious last stand?"

Grim, determined responses came back to him before he gave his orders.

"Driver, get ready to pull out of the way once we've cleared the path for the others, then we'll give those undead bastards a goodbye for the history books," he said with a bloodthirsty finality.

Clarke privately wiped away a tear that ran down his cheek as he picked up the radio handset to send his final instructions to the convoy.

"Don't be fucking stupid, Andy," Digby responded immediately. "Dump the tank and get in here as soon as you've stopped!"

Through the viewing port he could see the sea of bodies surrounding them and knew they wouldn't make it.

"Not this time pal," Clarke responded quietly but firmly. "Do me a favour though? Tell Tan and Emily…" his voice cracked and he couldn't continue, as the idea of never seeing them again rendered him incapable of speech.

"Will do, mate. Will do," Digby responded, his own voice cracking.

As the gates swung open, the knights stepped out with their pikes held ready, forming a defensive cordon that bristled with sharpened steel. The ground in front of and across the bridge was littered with unmoving bodies as the onslaught of continuous fire from above had pushed the massed ranks of living zombies away from the bridge that spanned the moat leaving it covered in corpses.

Ian stopped the front rank and ordered those behind to take their pikes as they drew hand weapons to thrust and swung them at skulls as they stepped over the piled bodies as they crossed the bridge and reformed their ranks.

The bullets and grenades from above were keeping them safe for now, but as the convoy approached their fire would have to be directed away from the vehicles to avoid any friendly fire incidents, leaving the knights exposed and vulnerable.

For now, amidst the maelstrom of battle, their blades and muscles were redundant as they waited in two ranks either side of the bridge.

But not for long.

Ian saw the tank approaching, its metal sides sparking as bullets struck it, blasting any zombie that leapt at it away. He flexed his shoulders, staring at the approaching tank and fast-closing hordes. He drew in a great breath and hollered.

"Knights! Prepare to kill!" His voice huge and commanding over the maelstrom of battle

Pikes lowered to be at the horizontal, held in strong hands by resolute knights.

Everyone in the ranks shouted, screaming their battle cries as they prepared for the coming onslaught.

The tank, engine roaring sped through the two ranks of knights locked a track and spun ninety degrees as the driver expertly guided it on to the bridge, crushing corpses lying to red gore as inches from the entrance it stopped.

With tracks spinning as it fought for grip amongst the carnage it had created, it reversed and cleared the bridge, spinning to face the zombies as soon as it was clear. The turret rotated as its main gun searched for the biggest mass.

The coaxial chain gun hammered rapid rounds into the mass before the weapon went silent for want of ammunition.

Ears, dulled by the continuous battle raging all around, were still shocked by the percussive wave that blasted over the area at the main gun firing, causing a momentary lull in the battle before senses were regained and fingers found triggers again.

The tanks hatches flew open and the occupants rose out, raising their weapons to bring fire to bear from a different angle. Clarke hauled back on the cocking handle of the top-mounted GPMG and opened up instantly, sending a torrent of bullets into the zombies leaping at both the armoured car and the trailer.

Zombies ran past the convoy, heading straight for the knights who had closed ranks to form a solid line protecting the bridge. Those on the walls altered their aim at the new threat, thinning the numbers running towards their friends.

The front ranks of undead ran straight into the pikes, devoid of awareness or their own mortality to impale themselves on the long, sharp blades. The knights braced themselves, straining against the forces trying to push them back. For a few moments they held the line as the shooters on the walls took advantage of the suddenly stationary targets, devastating the first few ranks being held back.

As the first zombies leapt over the blockage, Ian took another huge breath in, preparing to unleash his massive voice.

"Shieeeeeeeelds!" he bellowed at the top of his lungs, drawing the word out to become a battle cry of its own.

In one disciplined, practised manoeuvre the knights released their iron grip on the pikes and stepped swiftly back, causing the front ranks still pushing against them to fall over. They grabbed their shields from their backs and drew their hand weapons. The zombies leaping over the barricade of pike-perforated undead lacked the momentum and coordination to jump again, and they crashed into the shield wall where axes, maces and swords met them to thrust, stab and smash skulls.

Unbelievably the line held.

"They're bloody holding," Woody muttered to himself, taking his eye away from aiming to marvel briefly at the mighty display.

Firing his rifle from the walls, he ranged between all the places that could bring fire to bear on the gates. Having already ordered more defenders from other places around the castle to his position, given that the concentration of enemy assault meant they had nothing to shoot at, Woody turned to see panting, sweating people join them on the ramparts.

"Where do you need us?" someone yelled over the cacophony.

"Anywhere you can find a gap!" Woody yelled back, returning to the task of sending as much lead at the enemy as possible.

As he watched the remaining vehicles draw closer to the gates, a chilling realisation dawned on him.

Everything had been planned in such a rush that exactly how they would let the vehicles through had not been thought out at all. Ian, who was not actually the lumbering oaf he portrayed himself as, had, even amongst the desperate fight they were enduring, been thinking of how to extricate themselves from the situation he had volunteered them for.

Watching through the gaps in the shield wall as the vehicles drew closer, he ordered his riskiest command to date.

"Knights!" Ian screamed. "On my command, fall back from the centre and line the bridge to let the vehicles through. As soon as they're past, form line again."

The knights, high from battle fever, didn't question and just roared an acknowledgment.

Ian knew the vehicles that passed would be covered in a thick layer of zombies. If they could just stop more following them and retreat to the gates, could just get them closed and secure, then any that got inside should be caught in an enfilade by those in the courtyard and on the walls.

Then Ian remembered the tank that was guarding their flank. The moment they began to withdraw Clarke and his men would be isolated, a lone island of defiance surrounded by waves of the undead. He turned towards the tank and bellowed again.

"Clarky! If you're going to join us, now's the bloody time!"

~

Clarke swore with frustration as the last bullet from the belt fed into the breech and his GPMG fell silent. Knowing that the masses would be upon him before he could load another he resigned himself to his fate and was reaching for his rifle when he heard Ian's voice.

Myriad thoughts flashed through his mind as he looked at the zombies covering the ground that separated them.

Could they make it? Would he be able to hold his wife and daughter in his arms again? How many of them might die trying?

Twisting his features into a snarl he cursed himself for the momentary weakness, knowing that there was no decision to make.

They were being given a chance to live, and they would grasp it or die trying.

"You heard the man!" he yelled at his crew. "Come with me if you want to live!"

On the walls, Clarke's wife Tan watched in horror as her husband halted the tank and rose into the open to fire the mounted machine gun. A sixth sense told her what he was planning as soon as he hadn't taken the opportunity to make a break for safety the moment the tank had pulled clear.

Shouting and screaming in rage at his cursed heroism, and with mind-numbing dread at the fear of losing him, she had tried desperately to call out to him but her voice had been lost, drowned out by the storm of battle.

Altering her aim she directed her fire solely on keeping zombies away from her husband, determined to do everything she could to save him even when he didn't plan on saving himself. It was a hopeless task, as no matter how many her bullets killed two more took the place of the twice-dead who moved inexorably closer to the tank. She slammed magazine after magazine into her weapon as she muttered threats and curses at her husband's suicidal bravery.

So much happened at once that nobody could keep track of every facet of the desperate fight, but everyone tried their utmost to either survive or do their damnedest to make sure their friends and family did.

CHAPTER THIRTY-TWO

Everyone in the trailer looked as if we'd taken a swim in an abattoir's slurry tank as blood and body parts ripped off by spear thrusts coated us all from head to foot.

Our eyes, wide with stress and terror, were the only clean parts of our faces due to the constant blinking and wiping done to keep our vision clear. Despite muscles working well beyond normal expectations and energy reserves well past depleted, we still fought like maniacs.

Our ammunition long since expended, it was pure brute strength and determination that was keeping us alive.

Thrust, push, clear a space that was immediately filled by another clawing, snapping and snarling beast, and repeat. If it wasn't a literal matter of life and death our activities could've been described as monotonous.

I had no clue where we were as we were covered in a blanket of undead robbing me of the ability to track our progress. Time stood still as we fought side by side. It could have been five minutes or five hours since Eddy had told us we were getting close after the last radio broadcast was received, and I simply had no idea how much longer we were going to have to endure whichever layer of hell we'd reached.

"Now!"

I heard the muffled command roared by a voice I instantly recognised, feeling the first burst of relief for as long as I could recall.

~

The knights swung their weapons wildly at any head within range, keeping their shields locked together as they stepped back to line the bridge's sides and allow the three zombie-strewn vehicles to pass by.

Clarke and his crew didn't need Ian's shout to tell them the time was now, as they had to cross the few yards of zombie filled roadway instantly or die at the teeth and claws of the attacking horde.

Tossing primed grenades to clear a path, shrapnel and shockwaves punched past them before they threw themselves off the tank and into the carnage-strewn corridor cleared by the blasts. Guns blazing as they fired from the hip, they threw themselves headlong for the safety of the shield wall that was already closing.

Bringing up the rear, Clarke fired his weapon blindly behind them. This time his life really didn't depend on conserving his ammunition, on counting his shots to not run out, but instead speed and savagery were the only solution.

The only hope for a tomorrow.

The man in front of him let out a scream as an arm from the crowd grabbed him and yanked him into the throng. There was nothing Clarke could do about it, nothing he could do, it had happened so fast nobody had any time to react. If any of them had stopped to try and save him there would be two more names on the butcher's bill instead of one, so he kept firing, swinging the barrel around to his front as the masses began to close and cut off their only hope of escape.

His rifle issued an ominous click – the Dead Man's Click – that went unheard amid the chaos. As his last bullet blew a zombie's head apart with the barrel touching the snarling beast's forehead, he dropped it on its sling and drew his pistol.

With only seventeen shots left to his name as a reload would be impossible, Clarke aimed on instinct as his pistol became an extension of his arm. The hundreds of hours training spent on the range and in Hereford's infamous Killing House kicked in.

With it's barrel touching heads or fired upwards through the chin, brains and blood sprayed over him with every shot as he fought towards the knights.

Screaming in incoherent rage Clarke thrust his pistol at the next head that came into his vision's periphery before instinct and cognitive thought returned him to sanity. His finger slackened off the trigger as his brain registered it was not a zombie, but a living human.

Ian, wide eyed with the nearness of his own demise, simply grabbed him and hauled him bodily through the last gap in the shield wall.

"Protect our backs!" Ian roared as he focused again on killing instead of rescuing. "And retreat!"

"Here they come!" Digby shouted as the armoured car and both tractors sped into the courtyard.

Fire from all angles shredded the zombies clinging to the armoured car, its occupants safely cocooned inside the bulletproof interior as rounds sparked and pinged off its sides, re-killing them all in a few seconds.

The tractor and trailers were a different matter. Any fire from above could hit those protected only by a cage, meaning that the job had to be done at close range with well-aimed fire, and nobody inside the castle walls knew that one trailer contained only the shredded remnants of their former friends.

The zombies clinging all over the cabs and trailers released their grip and leapt to the ground as closer and easier to reach targets were now in sight.

Advancing in a line, Digby and the men and women with him fired carefully aimed single shots at every head that showed in their sights.

Quickly, the rapidly advancing targets became harder to kill cleanly and thumbs moved fire selectors to automatic as the battle plan began to lose cohesion. Zombies ran in all directions at whatever target they had noticed first, threatening the beginning of chaos within the walls while the fight still raged outside.

The knights, fighting desperately as they backed over the bridge one disciplined pace at a time to reach the gates. Ian didn't need to tell his knights to hold the line, to stay in formation and not give in to the urge to save themselves and run. They knew that to break formation would be to sing the death warrants for everyone, so they held their line, marching one stoic step backwards in time to Ian's command.

Fire from the walls was decimating the undead assaulters, but still they leapt, clawed and sprang at the shield wall which only through the knight's adrenaline-fuelled strength did not buckle and collapse. Clarke and his two surviving comrades now with reloaded rifles tracked their pace as they faced into the barbican at their rear, shooting any zombie that turned away from the courtyard towards them.

There was no way they could push the gate closed with so many bodies lying on the ground, so the portcullis was their only chance to stop them.

"BACK…BACK…" Ian called out their retreat.

"Jamie!" he gasped through lungs straining for oxygen. "BACK…Go and get ready to cut the rope on my shout mate. BACK…"

Jamie knew immediately what he planned and waited until the pressure on the shield wall lifted slightly before pulling back from the line. He ran to the door that opened onto the winch room, using his axe to slash through the few zombies that stood in his way.

Now in the confines of the barbican, more fire could be aimed from directly overhead where a parapet overlooked the space between the main gate and the portcullis, proving that the ancient's castles design was still perfect for today's world.

Lining the parapets on all sides, the new attack angle combined with the heavy fire still destroying the ranks outside stopped their advance dead.

Judging his moment carefully, Ian held the shout in his lungs until he knew they were all clear.

"Jamie, NOW!"

Jamie swung his axe against the taught rope that bore the weight of the heavy portcullis. The blade sliced through the rope, raising a shower of sparks from old stones. With the pressure released the portcullis crashed down, its frame recessed into the walls keeping it running true. The spikes fixed to the bottom crushed bodies mercilessly until they slotted into the holes in the floor designed to receive them as once more the castle was sealed against invaders.

A moment's silence reigned as the knights barely believed they had just survived what they had been through, until gunshots and sounds from the fight still coming from the courtyard reminded them that their day's work wasn't done.

Hefting their weapons they turned as one and ran towards the sounds of battle once more.

Not wasting time by pausing and assessing the situation, they emerged from the gloom of the barbican with blades swinging to hack down the zombies careering around their small corner of the courtyard.

Ian planted his feet to judge the swing of his axe perfectly, taking a zombie fixed on a target to his right high in the chest as it ran past him. The blow crushed sternum and ribs, folding the zombie around the blade to fall in a crumpled heap at his feet.

Looking down Ian still saw the flicker of recognition in its dead eyes as cracked lips drew back from blackened teeth.

Lifting an armoured boot heel Ian stomped down to crack the skull against ancient cobblestones before he filled his lungs to let out another mighty roar.

"Kill 'em allllll!"

The arrival of the knights turned the tide of the battle inside the courtyard and made victory certain as they carved through the enemy without mercy.

Digby searched for more targets, watching in horror as one of the last ones left mobile defied the odds and dodged every bullet aimed at it to leap over their crude, hastily built barrier and head deeper into the courtyard, straight for the doors to the Great Hall.

Only Nicky, Maud and the babies were in there and images of them being torn apart before anyone of them could get there in time flashed through his mind.

As it reached the steps, the main door swung open and Maud stepped out, shotgun in hand, to decapitate it with a single shot and a spray of bone and gore.

The now headless zombies skidded to a stop a few feet from her. Looking sternly across the courtyard she pumped another cartridge into the gun and held it ready, standing guard as if she couldn't trust anyone except her to do the job right.

Digby couldn't hold back a smile and a chuckle at the sight, knowing they'd all get into trouble later for allowing danger to get close to her charges. A danger which she easily, without hesitation, dealt with herself.

Digby knew that whatever deeds of bravery and heroism had happened and were still likely to happen in the future, the story of Maud, shotgun in hand, defending the steps of her home would probably trump every one of them.

His smile faded as shouts of shock and alarm came from the vehicles.

Exhausted I unlatched the rear door of the trailer and climbed down to stand swaying as my legs barely held me upright. Looking around I saw I wasn't the only one so afflicted, as some people collapsed to the ground to lay as if dead as soon as their feet touched solid ground; chests heaving with exertion and tears of relief washing clean rivulets through their blood-soaked faces.

Digby ran over to the trailer and skidded to a stop, raising his weapon as he saw the swaying, gore-soaked occupants standing or lying by it.

"My God…Everyone's turned!" he cried out, preparing to shoot me.

"No!" I screamed, raising my arms in the air automatically in the hopeless attempt to prevent a barrage of bullets.

Digby kept the rifle to his shoulder but moved his finger away from the trigger on hearing me speak.

I shouted at him. "Diggers! What the fuck are you doing?"

"Tom?" Diggers asked incredulously, lowering his rifle a fraction as he recognised my voice. "Is that you?"

"No, it's Father Fucking Christmas! Sorry I'm a bit late!" I spat back sarcastically as the adrenaline surge threatened to take my knees out.

Diggers laughed, which annoyed me beyond belief.

"You see anything funny around here?" I demanded.

"No, but…look, with how insane today's been zombies learning to speak isn't exactly beyond the imagination," he said apologetically, letting the rifle hang to point safely away from me.

"But they definitely wouldn't make bad dad jokes," he added, allowing the inane grin to crease his features again.

I looked at the others from my trailer as we swayed on exhausted legs or lay collapsed on the ground, thinking it was little wonder Digby couldn't recognise any of us, covered from head to toe in gore as we were.

Ian and the knights accompanied by Clarke and his two surviving crew and the soldiers from the armoured car had been checking that all the zombie corpses now lying around the castle grounds were dead. Satisfied that the job was done they joined us, reacting with shock at the sight of the trailer occupants.

Clarke took charge as no one else seemed to know what to do at that moment.

"Diggers, where do you want us?" he asked.

The sounds of all guns firing from the walls jolted Digby back to the present and he told him, waving his arm to explain his order.

"Go find Woody on the walls, he'll put you where you're needed most. Ian? You take your mad bastards as well. We just have to make sure we keep those undead fuckers on the outside."

Diggers watched them go and turned a sceptical eye back to me.

"How are you feeling? You all look done in if I'm being honest. Why don't you get some of that shit you're covered with off you? When you're ready you can rotate back on to the walls if you're up for it."

I watched as Clarke and his men filled their ammo pouches with more magazines from the open crates stacked on the grass. Ian and the knights also slung their blood-coated weapons, swung their shields over their backs and picked up rifles and ammo bags before heading to the walls. I tried to speak but somehow the signal between brain and mouth got lost along the way, wandering off to rock in a corner somewhere.

Unable to respond I simply nodded and walked away, stopping only when someone went to the other trailer and hammered a fist on the metal.

"It's safe!" he yelled. "You lot coming out or staying in there?"

Finally the words made it to my mouth.

"Leave it closed," I said firmly.

The man turned to look at me, incomprehension written all over his face before the expression fell into horrified shock. Digby joined me, having heard the exchange and figuring it out quickly.

"You're certain?" he asked me quietly, earning a sad but firm nod of affirmation.

"You three!" Digby barked, pointing at some defenders caught taking a breather. "Surround this trailer and shoot anything that tries to get out," he ordered before turning a sideways glance in my direction.

"Unless it can talk, that is," he added, giving me a nod and turning away to get back in the fight.

CHAPTER THIRTY-THREE

Still staggering and struggling to comprehend we'd survived, I led a shuffling procession over to the tanks we'd built to hold water pumped from the river. It was cold, but the shock brought us round more as we poured buckets of it over each other. The run-off water ran deep red which puddled on the grass, diluting with each successive bucket as we used our hands to scrub and rub the worst off us.

Maud, from her new position guarding the main doors, saw the state of us and quickly ordered piles of fresh clothing gathered and brought out to us. The garments were mainly military surplus items scavenged from various places and kept in a storeroom, along with flasks of strong, sweetened tea.

Modesty was abandoned as we stripped and discarded our ruined clothing to sort through the pile for items that vaguely fit us. Dressed but still shivering from the cold water, we warmed ourselves on the mugs of tea until, feeling vaguely human again, I looked around the castle.

The firing from the walls was continuous and loud from every quarter of the castle showing that we were still under heavy attack. Mortars cracked as they lobbed their explosives in a high arc over the walls and the helicopter ranged outside firing all its guns into the masses still attacking.

Guilt washed over me that I was enjoying a mug of tea while my family and friends still fought for our survival.

Grabbing a spare rifle as mine was still in the back of the trailer and would likely need a cleansing by fire before being used again, I headed to the walls to find my family. I gave no orders, had no expectations of anyone else given what we'd been through, but our entire crew followed my lead.

Crossing the yard Digby yelled at me to take an ammunition crate if I was going up, so lifting a crate of .556 magazines I began forcing my tired body up the stone stairs.

Becky, Stanley, Daisy with Princess by her side and young Eddie stood together, firing their weapons amidst a pile of expended magazines and empty bullet casings that made walking the ramparts treacherous.

They stopped shooting when they noticed me, Becky letting out a yelp of shock when she first saw me. I'd washed a lot of the blood off me, but my exposed skin and hair was still stained and encrusted with a layer of it. Once she'd recovered from the shock and realised I was not in fact some ghoulish apparition from the afterlife, we spent a blissful few seconds hugging but when I went to kiss Becky, she squirmed away.

"Sorry," I said, having become so wrapped up in our reunion that I'd forgotten about the state I was in.

Not knowing if I had survived as they'd received reports that the convoy had suffered many losses, their emotions were raw and heartfelt as copious tears of relief flowed at seeing me appear by their side.

Releasing them from my encompassing embrace, I charged my rifle and joined my family on the firing steps. As we stood in line shooting over the walls, I couldn't help but keep glancing across at them, relishing the sight of us being together again even though the new family bonding time seemed to be shooting zombies and not something more traditional, like a visit to a zoo or a bike ride.

This was my first time looking out over the walls during the fight and even though I knew many thousands were attacking us and still streaming towards the castle, the sight shocked me. The grounds as far as I could see were packed with approaching zombies, leaping and scrambling over each other in their mindless determination to get us. Bullets of all calibres fired from rifles or machine guns tore through them, cutting swathes of them down as grenades and mortars blew great holes in their ranks.

Yet still they advanced relentlessly into the maelstrom of lead and explosions.

As I raised my rifle to fire, a shape swooped over the castle spitting fire as another helicopter joined in the battle. I was mesmerised for a few seconds, watching the tracer rounds guide my gaze to distant bodies being thrown down.

It was from either Bristol or Cornwall – Bristol if I was alert enough to guess given the shorter distance - but I didn't care which because its arrival meant much more than the weight of fire it added to our defences.

It meant we weren't alone, and others were still sending help.

Soon the other helicopter arrived, and together they poured an incomprehensible weight of firepower into the enemy.

Time lost meaning as the day wore on in the constant fear-filled monotony of battle as we pushed ourselves beyond normal endurance until I felt a deep vibration throughout my body. I was looking around in confusion, wondering what on earth was happening.

Spikes of fear shot adrenaline through my body as I imagined that somehow the walls were collapsing when, with a roar of turbofan engines, a chinook swept in low and fast over the castle walls and immediately descended down to land.

"About bloody time they got that bastard fixed!" Eddy shouted on seeing the twin-rotored behemoth land.

As soon as its wheels touched the ground it disgorged dozens of soldiers who headed to Diggers waiting for them by the ramp, then ran off to wherever he sent them on the walls.

For the first time that day my hopes lifted, knowing that the helicopters and reinforcements would make an enormous difference to our defences.

As soon as the last soldier left the ramp its engines increased power, and it lifted off. With its nose lowered it sped away, disappearing from view long before the telltale whop-whop-whop noise did.

"Dad? Where are they going? Aren't they staying to help?" Stanley asked in a worried voice as it disappeared.

I too had felt a pang of disappointment when it went, but quickly realised why.

"It's going to get more reinforcements, son," I said, clapping him on the back with excitement at the knowledge that every delivery from it would help us see another dawn.

Woody came up to me and slapped me on my shoulder to get my attention.

"Meeting now!" was all he said before walking off to find his next victim.

After a quick hug with Becky and the kids, I turned and followed.

We gathered in the meeting room where the gunfire was muted by the thick castle walls. The crump of explosions rattled the mugs on the table and caused dust to drop from the ceiling, coating everywhere with a thickening layer of white powder. With faces dirtied by blood, dust, cordite and streaked with sweat we stared at each other for many seconds, unable to verbalise the day we had had so far.

Digby, who had been on the radio, took the lead.

"Right. I'll be brief. Now Bristol and Cornwall have been completely evacuated the admiral is directing all efforts on us. The chinook will keep ferrying troops and materiel here. It has night flying capabilities so the airlift will be continuous. The other helicopters will not be able to fly at night as the risk of collision and friendly fire incidents will ground them for pure safety reasons. Also—"

"Hold up," Clarke interrupted. "Why can't we rotate them so only one's in the air at a time? Seems stupid to ground all of them."

"Also," Digby went on, clearly annoyed at the interruption, "there isn't enough room in the courtyard for all three, so one will have to return to the ships anchored at Bristol and return at first light…but I'll talk to the crews and see if we can rotate the other two. Remember those pilots have been in the air non-stop for hours. We can't afford costly mistakes."

Clarke nodded, accepting the compromise but offering no apology.

"We've done well so far…" Digby said, stopped when he saw the grief-filled expressions of pain on our faces.

Letting his head droop towards the table he said quietly, his voice cracking.

"Yes, we've lost many – too many – but for now we have to keep going for the sake of everyone else. We'll grieve them later."

His voice regained its composure as he continued.

"Are we missing anything? Our ammo reserves are still in good shape, we have enough fuel for at least another day for the helicopters and more of that can be brought in by chinook if we get desperate. Is there anything we can do differently?"

Silence reigned over the table until Gallon spoke.

"We need to take their leader out, Sir."

His statement caused a shocked ripple of questions to flow around the room.

We all wanted to know what he knew, and the bombardment of consuming questions rendered him unable to speak at first.

Retelling the story of seeing the larger zombie on the walls of the farm that seemed to be directing the hordes, and his failure to kill it due to having an empty rifle. Gallon assured us that he believed what he was telling us.

It did make sense, as much as the concept horrified me. The zombies did react as if they were being commanded, those of us in the convoy and on the walls had all seen attacks by them change direction without reason to exploit a situation, such as the convoy arriving, or more heartbreakingly the cages around the armoured car and other trailer being pulled apart.

"We don't understand currently, and probably never will work out their command and control structure," Clarke said carefully. "But I think from what we've seen and from Geoff's report, if we assume they have one, then we must try and disrupt or eliminate it. It could give us another edge over them."

Silence fell across the table again as we mulled it over until Gallon said.

"Why don't we place dedicated snipers on the walls whose role is to take out any that seem to be behaving differently?" he suggested with a shrug. "They'll still be killing the Z's, but we may get lucky."

It was a good idea, so we left it to the sergeants to choose their sharpshooters. Another problem we had yet to solve was what to do about the ramps of bodies that were slowly creeping up the walls in a few places, and it was no stretch of the imagination at all to foresee them becoming places where our defences could be breached.

Firing the grenade machine guns to cause them to collapse back on themselves was slowing their inexorable rise, but we could not for the life of us think of a better solution to the problem. We discussed dousing them with petrol and setting them on fire, but weren't sure if that would cause structural damage to the walls by drying out the ancient mortar or using grappling hooks to try and dislodge more bodies, but that was decided the effort to reward basis made that impracticable.

In the end the only choice we decided we had was to keep blasting them with the grenade machine guns and hope for the best.

Clarke ended the quick meeting by picking his rifle up from the table and with a quiet but firm voice that conveyed the desperateness of our situation.

"Gentlemen, shall we? Once more unto the breach and all that."

CHAPTER THIRTY-FOUR

The leader prowled at the edges of the woods surrounding the castle as more zombies continually streamed past him into the fray. Through the eyes of others he could sense that there were no humans left at the other locations he had ordered to be attacked. The failure to kill those the virus running through his blackened veins drove him mercilessly to destroy, burned rage through his body.

Deciding that it was time to try a new tactic, he sent out the command for all to gather to his position.

In the area around Bristol and all across Cornwall where legions of zombies ranged in their hunt for human flesh, the masses turned and headed towards the signal. All over the country, groups of zombies that had emerged to search for victims received the unconscious signal and obeyed it unquestioningly.

They had found a few isolated communities and overrun them all with ease to feast on the flesh of those unfortunate survivors. Their senses were tuned to the delicious smells humans emitted, and no matter how carefully concealed or well protected their compounds were, none withstood the onslaught.

He grabbed one of the bodies that streamed past him. Unresistingly it allowed him to bite deeply into its neck and tear flesh from it. He chewed and swallowed the meat, taking bite after bite before dropping the unmoving, ravaged carcass to the floor. Even though this was the flesh that had sustained him and provided the sustenance for his body to change to what it was now during the long winter, he grimaced at the foul, rotting taste. It wasn't enough to satiate his needs.

His body told him he needed to feed to survive, and the rank meat from one of his own kind did that to an extent, but he had tasted the sweet, rich flesh of a living human and it was now like a drug to him. He needed it, his whole being craved it, and the only known source of it left was defying all his efforts to reach it.

~

Before darkness fell the chinook had dropped off another two loads of reinforcements with more promised throughout the night.

On each arrival it first lowered a net slung beneath it full of extra weapons and ammunition for its passengers before disgorging its full complement of fighting men and women. Our own ammunition stores, even though we had burned through an incalculable amount, were still sufficient to continue the fight for a long time. We hadn't requested additional supplies, but delivering more was never a bad idea.

Shawn turned on the lights he had installed when the night started to creep up on us. Connected to the generator, he'd fixed a ring of floodlights around the castle walls for such an event. The powerful lights turned the coming night back into day, flooding the grounds with bright, white light. Their use had always been intended to enhance our defensive capabilities at night, but the reasoning behind them had been to light up the fields of fire from the walls and to blind any attackers so they would be unable to snipe at the defenders hidden in the darkness behind them. We weren't concerned about being fired at now, just happy that night didn't affect our ability to defend ourselves.

With so many people now on the walls a proper rota was organised to give everyone more time off the frontline. Despite the continuous firing and explosions coming from the walls, the rooms of the castle contained an ever-changing gathering of people either sleeping, eating or just having a quiet moment to themselves before once more facing the enemy.

The one constant was that no one was ever far from their weapon or slept with their boots off. Extra flight crews for the helicopters had also arrived with the chinooks solving the problem Digby had raised. These crews allowed one Merlin to maintain its position overhead all night as it roved around the perimeter pouring fire onto the attackers until its ammunition was expended to be replaced by its fully fuelled and fully armed replacement.

~

The leader, knowing somehow that the darkness protected him, stood just outside the ring of light and watched the guns rip his forces apart. He'd been watching and learning throughout the day, heedless to how many he lost, he was now committing less of his still gathering forces despite still attacking on all fronts. Hidden by the night, Warwick was filling with countless thousands more as they flocked from all areas of the country, beckoned by his signal. A solid mass of them coalesced together in the roads and streets of the town awaiting their next order.

He just needed to wait until he deemed the time was right.

~

The lightening of the eastern sky signalled the end of a long, exhausting night of continual action even though the intensity of the assault seemed to slacken off when night fell.

We hadn't taken comfort from that, as the zombies had continually surged forwards in enough numbers for the walls to be needed to be fully manned by every fighter rotating on and off duty, as all tried to grab a few moments of much-needed sleep. Despite the longer rest breaks and snatched sleep, the general feeling was of exhausted determination.

Minds spun with tiredness. Shoulders and bodies bruised from the recoil of firing stood their posts on the walls and looked across the zombie-filled fields of carnage, weapons held in resolute hands and sighted on the next zombie to kill.

When the light was good enough the chosen snipers positioned themselves around the castle walls with their weapon and a bag full of ammunition by their sides, they started sniping at any zombie that just looked and acted a bit different to the others. Roving the grounds with their telescopic sights the regular deeper boom of their weapons mixing with the clatter of automatic rifles and machine guns became another sound in the symphony of noises we created as we fought to stay alive.

I could almost set my clock by the regular arrival of the Chinook bringing more personnel and equipment for us to throw against our enemy. I had no time to think about it, but the organisation of maintaining such a regular drop to us must have been a mammoth task of improvisation and logistical skill in itself. We now had so many people within the castle that the defenders virtually stood shoulder to shoulder along every aspect of our walls, pouring fire down on to our attackers. Porters laboured continually to haul ammunition to where it was needed to feed the guns, while others rested or worked at the hastily erected outside canteen area providing the fuel of the calorific type to feed the people operating them. From a small community of friends and family we'd changed into a small city of people all working together for a common aim, but I couldn't shake the feeling that Warwick Castle was becoming our Alamo.

From the gloom of the woods the leader growled as he paced, his eyes fixed upon the walls. Every time the huge metal thing with two spinning blades on top of it appeared and descended from view behind the walls, more delicious-smelling humans lined the walls. Each one would provide the nourishment his people needed to fulfil the virus's goal; to be the dominant entity across the globe.

Victory was certain, he just needed to judge the right time.

At the other places the humans had mainly evaded the attack by taking to the blue and grey thing that swallowed his followers whole. The castle had a similar ribbon of moving, swirling non-supporting thing behind it which he had ordered his followers not to enter, and which the humans could not reach from within the walls giving them no such escape route.

They were trapped, and soon, when he judged the time was right, he would launch his final assault, committing all of his forces in one unstoppable wave.

For his plan to succeed he needed to keep sacrificing his followers against the walls so the humans remained spread out along their length, and didn't concentrate at any one point.

He paced as he calculated and waited, anticipating that the right time was fast approaching.

CHAPTER THIRTY-FIVE

Piloting the Chinook was normally a dull routine of being steady and cautious. The huge machine was a gentle giant to fly and was a great craft to command cruising at its recommended best economic speed as you carried whatever cargo – human or otherwise – to wherever it was needed before gently setting it down to avoid damaging either the machine or whatever you were transporting.

Not so much now.

Flying the helicopter on non-stop laps at above and beyond its normal operating parameters was both tiring and exhilarating. The pilot handled the controls with light touches of both his hands and feet to keep it flying as fast as his extensive skill allowed as he flew fast and low.

Altitude took time to reach – time they didn't have - so following the contours of the ground they navigated the fastest route. It didn't make for a comfortable ride for the passengers as it jolted, vibrated alarmingly and rose and fell dramatically at times, forcing them to carry jerry cans full of water and mops and brooms so the crew in the rear cabin could swill down and remove the worst of the expelled stomach contents.

The load slung below them also acted as a pendulum, exacerbating the way it seemed to swing around with every slight turn and twist they made as he manipulated the machine to operate at its best speed.

Very familiar with the route now, the pilot and co-pilot automatically scanned the land ahead with their eyes as they both fought to keep the beast in the sky.

"Are you seeing what I'm seeing?" the pilot grunted as he bought the craft back into level flight after navigating a particularly bad patch of rough air.

"There's thousands of them...no...more than that," his friend and co-pilot confirmed.

He looked out of both the front window and side windows at the ground zipping by only a few hundred feet below where the land was thick with advancing groups of zombies, all heading in the same direction they were going. The closer they got to Warwick, the groups joined into a seething carpet of bodies.

"Report it to command. Poor buggers need to know what's heading their way," the pilot said.

He thought about the men and women he was carrying, and the hundreds he had already dropped off. Surely nothing could withstand against such numbers. Was he transporting them to their deaths?

By his side he listened to the transmission as this latest intelligence was relayed.

Overflying Warwick, he shifted in his seat to flex his aching muscles in preparation for landing.

"Shit. The whole place is fucking packed with them!" his co-pilot said, following up with an explanation of what he was seeing below him.

The concentration he needed to fly the huge machine into the castle courtyard prevented him from even flicking his eyes away to confirm what he was being told.

As he hovered, listening to the instructions from the loadmaster, he waited until it was confirmed the cargo net slung below was on the ground and clear before he lowered down to land.

No, he decided as he reduced power further on the helicopter. We need to tell them now.

Instead of the usual combat take-off they performed, keeping the power on to take flight as soon as the last boot left the rear ramp, the castle's defenders needed to know right now what they'd seen with their own eyes, and not let the message get potentially mixed up after passing through a few hands or delayed while command sought confirmation or wrung their hands over a decision.

He pulled off his helmet and put it on the control panel by his side, telling his co-pilot what he was going to do as he unbuckled himself from the restraints.

Digby, directing the last few soldiers from the helicopter where to go by gesturing with his arms as conversation so near to the roaring machine was impossible, was surprised when the engine tone lowered to be followed seconds later by a man wearing a green flight suit running down the ramp.

"Got something you need to know right now!" the pilot shouted.

Nodding, Digby indicated for him to follow, turning to run towards the main building with the pilot following close behind.

Five minutes later, after being summoned from a short break by a runner, we gathered in the meeting room where I stood, coffee mug in hand, and listened as he repeated what the pilot had told him.

"We need options," Clarke said as we all stood in silence working out what a vast horde of new zombies attacking us would mean.

I could tell from everyone's faces that we'd all come to the same conclusion.

We were fucked, and the uncomfortable, lingering silence made me think I wasn't the only one who believed as such.

Willie spoke first, a tone of defeated resignation infecting his words.

"Command needs to know…then we evacuate the women and children. How many can you get on that bird of yours?" he asked, looking at the pilot who answered immediately.

"How many are we talking about?"

"About eighty," I blurted out, trying to remember how many women and children lived with us.

"I can pack them in and take the lot in one trip if I have to. The old girl'll take it, but the round trip is over two hours…"

It didn't need to be said that there was no way we could evacuate everyone from the castle. Even if we could use vehicles to smash our way out, which was impossible anyway, we didn't have enough transport inside the walls to take even a third of us. The helicopters flying overhead could take some each, probably even more if they jettisoned their weapons and ammunition to lighten them, but still that wouldn't be anywhere near enough.

The grim reality was that, for most, there was no option of escape.

"And how the hell do you think we'll get them to leave?" I asked with a wry chuckle, referring to Willie's suggestion of evacuating the women and children.

Willie returned the smile with more sadness than he likely intended but offered no solution.

"That…wasn't a rhetorical question, mate. Seriously, how are we going to convince them to go?" I said, knowing for a fact that Becky wouldn't go.

That thought had run through my mind many times since the whole thing began when I'd pondered grim thoughts of differing scenarios.

Would we want to die together or would any of us accept being separated to give some the chance to live? I'd give my own life gladly if I knew they'd survive, but would they want to go knowing I faced certain death? My mind tumbled the options around like a washing machine until I decided the only way it could work was to lie to them, to let them think I'd be on the next flight out, and I knew they'd never forgive me for it.

I knew for certain Maud wouldn't go. She'd stubbornly stand her ground and fight to the end beside the man she'd found true love with so late in life. I couldn't speak for the rest, but I could see those with families around the table thinking about the terrible choices they'd soon be forced to make.

Unashamedly wiping tears from his eyes, Willie turned and walked to the radio where he updated command as to our current situation. The silence from the other end when he ended his transmission told us much more than any words could. They were out of ideas too.

I looked at the pilot and spoke quietly.

"Give us ten minutes. Anyone not onboard by then isn't going."

The scene at the loading ramp of the helicopter was fraught with emotion and chaos.

Chris hugged his wife Nicky who clutched both baby Hope and Sarah in her arms. She was screaming in anguish as he let her go and strode down the ramp, his dirty face streaked with tears.

Shouts of anger and desperation rose above the chinook's engines as we tried to get our loved ones to leave.

"But I'll be on the next flight," I tried to explain to Becky, trying hard not to give the lie away, but Becky knew me better than that.

"Then we'll go on that one," she screamed at me defiantly, her own face full of fear and dread. "If you think you can try and fool me with that one, then think again!"

She hugged me and shouted in my ear above the roar of the engine, ramming her feelings home.

"If this is it, there's no bloody way we're not facing it together."

To seal her decision she grabbed Stanley, Daisy and Eddie and forced her way through the crowd who were all desperately trying to get their loved ones onboard when nobody wanted to be separated.

The loadmaster who had just strapped in the four girls we had rescued from the pervert at M.O.D Kineton ran up to me.

"Any more?"

I couldn't verbalise my reply and just shook my head as it was clear that no one else was leaving. He just shrugged in reply and spoke words I couldn't hear into the microphone on his flight headset and grabbed a handle by the ramp. The noise increased as the pilot applied power, and the machine began to rise up.

Ian, moving quicker than I'd ever seen him, grabbed Chris and flung him over his shoulder and before he could react, jumped onto the ramp and dumped him on the deck of the Chinook. He screamed something to the loadmaster pointing at Chris, before leaping from the rising machine to collapse into a pile as his legs couldn't support the weight of his armour from the six-foot jump.

The loadmaster responded immediately and fell on Chris, who we could see was screaming in defiance and rage, to hold him down and stop him regaining his feet.

Wiping away a tear I helped Ian to his feet.

"You alright mate?" I asked as he winced as he tried to stretch away the pain the mad leap had caused him.

"Had to be done," he said simply, then acknowledged what we all knew but couldn't say. "At least that's one family that'll survive this shit."

Chris had insisted on staying, but Ian's act had ensured that he would live to raise the youngest member of the country's population.

Again, emotions of what we were about to face engulfed me, and all I could do was slap his back in reply and turn away to hide my own inner fears.

Could I, if the time came as I'd promised myself many times I would do and put a bullet through my wife's and children's brains at the last minute to save them suffering a horrendous death whilst saving the last bullet for myself?

Clarke walked over to me.

"Fuck me, two last stands in as many days. Am I setting some sort of record here?" he said with gallows humour.

I laughed, a laugh that verged on sounding as if I was unhinged, as we headed back to the walls, maybe for the last time.

CHAPTER THIRTY-SIX

Shane lay motionless, his rifle supported by a bipod an extension of his body. Many hours of sniping from the walls had given him the experience to pick out those ranged before him who acted differently to others, and his body count was increasing.

His keen eyes picked out another likely target, before lowering and finding its face through the magnified vision of the telescopic sight, adjusting his aim to compensate for the slight wind moving left to right, then lifting the crosshairs slightly to negate the bullet drop. Settling his breathing, he emptied his lungs and drew in half a breath to hold it before gently squeezing the trigger.

Watching another head explode like a ripe melon from the impact of the large calibre expanding round.

Gently sliding the bolt backwards and forwards Shane rechambered the rifle and began searching again.

He had two more bullets left in the magazine before he needed to swap it out for one of the full ones laid out neatly by his left hand. Spotting another one he shifted the rifle to the left and lowered his eyes once more to the telescopic sight and moved the rifle gently around until he reacquired it.

This one stood head and shoulders above the throng, passing it like it was a tiny island in a river of undead flesh. Unlike the masses rushing by it, it stood still looking ahead, and the sense of intelligence Shane got from watching it chilled his blood.

Shane checked the rhythm of his breath and held it, squeezing off the last ounce of pressure to send another ballistic cure down-range only for the thing to spin sideways as the bullet missed the head and blew the things arm off as the bullet obliterated its shoulder. Grunting with mild annoyance he cycled the rifle again and concentrated on controlling his breathing as he watched it regain its feet and look stupidly at where its arm had once been. This time the bullet flew true and its head disappeared in a bloom of red mist.

He reached for a fresh magazine and continued his hunt.

He didn't know it, but he and the other snipers were already in-fluencing the ability of the zombies to communicate. Only a few of the shots had killed ones that mattered, but those important bullets had disrupted how they communicated. The leader from each group to emerge from their nests received and reacted, pass-ing on the orders to their individual followers. When one was killed its followers glitched, confused and directionless as if un-sure what to do next. Among the thousands that attacked the walls it didn't count for much, but each of the leader's lieutenants who fell left a gap in his consciousness like security cameras going dark. Those confused followers suddenly cut off from their leader still attacked, but they reverted to being mindless soldiers in the undead army.

Every minute more zombies flooded into Warwick, filling every open space with tightly packed bodies as they waited for the next order to arrive, as groups of varying sizes surrounding their own leader merged into one huge mass of rotting flesh.

Their bodies had changed dramatically in their hibernation, those changes made by the virus as it adapted to its new goal. They were faster and stronger with far better mobility than the slow, shambling beasts of before but these changes required more energy to sustain them in their present form.

The zombies of old could survive months between feeds as their bodies barely expended any energy, but now, faster moving and with more cognitive ability, they required far more energy to keep their bodies functioning. The sustenance they needed was flesh, preferably from a live human, as even a small amount of that would keep them going for days.

The effort involved to reach the beacon – some arriving from over a hundred miles away at speeds far exceeding any human ability – sent out by the main leader, sapped their reserves requiring a brutal solution to the problem.

A hierarchy existed in the zombies. Those who had been nearer the centre of the group as they massed together against the cold winter were ranked higher than those on the periphery. As those on the outer edges had once sacrificed themselves by allowing others to tear the flesh from their bodies until only bones remained, so another such feeding frenzy ensued as individual leaders commanded some of their numbers to once again offer their bodies for the greater good. The flesh wasn't nutrient-rich enough to last long, but it revived them enough to continue, and they waited amongst the picked-clean bones of their companions for the next order to arrive.

"Are we all agreed?" Walker-Jones asked as he looked around the room where a hastily called meeting had been ordered when the news of the uncountable hordes heading to and massing in Warwick Castle had been received. All heads nodded in reply.

He looked at the weapons officer.

"Make it so. On my command, unleash hell on those undead bastards!"

The weapons officer did a brief double-take, opening his mouth before clapping it shut quickly and complying with his orders.

The CIC or Combat Information Centre on the frigate became a hive of activity the moment the new orders from the admiral had been received. The weapons officer pored over maps as he worked out the target coordinates.

"I need more information if you don't want a blue on blue," he complained with exasperation, planting his forefinger on a large-scale map of central England

Hitting friendly forces was the ultimate error in his line of business, and he had no intention of making such a devastating error now.

"Get me one of the helicopter pilots on the radio," he said, turning to a communications officer. "I need to know if they have better maps than me. I need better coordinates."

Firing from the walls, I didn't notice as one of the helicopters peeled away to hover over Warwick for ten minutes before returning to spit fire on the continually advancing zombies.

No one was resting now as a sense of impending doom weighed heavily over us. We all stood on the firing steps determined to get as many of them before they overwhelmed us. Becky and I stood with the children between us as we aimed our weapons down on the ground below us. Barrels glowed red as caution was thrown to the wind and fire rates picked up, but still on they came, running into the shield of bullets that kept us safe for the moment.

The leader sensed the time was right. The majority of those that had reacted to his command had reached him already and he knew more were continually arriving.

He couldn't wait any longer.

He had the numbers already, and he would commit the stragglers straight into battle when they reached him, further reinforcing his attack.

He sent out his signal, roaring the command to those around him.

The vibrations of tens of thousands of feet slapping the ground sent a shudder through the stones we stood on. I looked at Becky, and she locked eyes with me as she too understood what was happening.

I held back a sob as I looked down at Stanley, Daisy and Eddie. Two were mine and one was adopted, but Eddie was as much ours now as if Becky had given birth to him. My hand automatically felt for my holstered sidearm, reassuring myself that it was still there for when the time came. I slapped another magazine into my rifle, screaming a mix of rage, anger and grief as I opened up on the enemy again.

Ian and his knights had congregated by the slope of dead zombies nearest to the top of the wall. If they'd developed tactical knowledge as we expected, that would be the logical and obvious place to expect an attack, so the knights gathered where we fully expected the first breach to happen. With shields and hand weapons stacked within easy reach, they fired their rifles down, all of them deep within the thrall of battle rage.

The sound grew as whatever was approaching got closer and the castle walls shook as if an earthquake was under way, but we knew this was no earthquake.

History books recount how soldiers and cavalry shook the ground as they advanced in to battle. You could have discounted those tales as fanciful exaggeration by the victors to strike fear into the heart of any future enemy.

Now we were experiencing it, and it was truly terrifying.

A dark mass burst from the trees in a column, heading straight for the wall where the knights were positioned. Fire decimated the front ranks, but like a French column advancing on a line of British redcoats, the tactic was working.

This time though, the enemy were running and leaping at incredible speeds and not advancing slowly, one drum beaten step at a time.

Our bullets and grenades picked at the edges of the column leaving the inner core untouched. The next ranks behind kept coming, streaming over the hundreds our bullets killed, every step bringing them closer to us. Closer to the walls, and closer to victory.

Reaching the slope our firing became more desperate than ever.

The front ranks absorbed the bullets forcing those behind to leap over bodies until they too protected yet more behind them, each body adding to the slope making it easier for the rest to climb it.

As the first undead hands clawed at the parapet, Ian bellowed a command.

The knights let rifles fall on slings, replacing modern firepower with weaponry dating back a millennia. There was no ceremony as they switched tactics, no grandiose sense of a final battle to defend the ancient castle walls, just a ruthless, bloodthirsty efficiency.

Protected by shields, knights thrust downwards with spears and pikes, pinning impaled bodies in place causing a barrier of writhing flesh the zombies behind found harder to surmount, stalling the enemy advance long enough for our bullets to play havoc from the flanks.

But it couldn't last, as outstretched arms grabbed the spears and after a short, one-sided tug of war in which a living human was destined to lose, another defensive line fell to the enemy onslaught and the first zombies breached the castles walls

As shield wall and hand weapons turned the parapets slick with undead gore, the battle on the walls devolved into brutal hand-to-hand combat as the knights fought in vain to halt the enemy foothold from growing. The first few to climb over were dispatched, but more clawed hands dragged bodies over the stones. Soon the knights had been pushed back, forced to retreat a step with each kill to allow room to swing a weapon at the next, and the next, and the next foe to breach the walls.

The knights were exposed and heavily outnumbered, fighting an impossible fight against far too many of the enemy on a narrow parapet of ancient stone and they began to succumb.

Simon, his sword stuck in the skull of a dead zombie was trying to tug it free when another jumped on him to bite into his face.

Marc, a shield lashed tightly to his stump and an axe in his other hand, swung wildly, hacking into heads and necks in a regular rhythm when a zombie leapt over those he was cutting to pieces. The momentum of the attack toppled them both over the safety railings to plummet towards the ground, but even as Marc fell to his death, he swung his axe at the zombie's head and screamed in rage.

A resonating thud and the crack of breaking bones punctuated the sounds of battle.

A zombie grabbed Ian's arm and tried to drag him bodily from the line and join their ranks. Horace, who'd been using his weight to jump at and push the zombies away, always knowing when to avoid a swinging weapon as he choreographed his fighting with those around him, concentrated his efforts on the one grabbing his master.

Ian's voice squealed in high pitched terror as he smashed his shield into the face of the one that had grabbed him and tried to pull against the power that threatened to pull him off his feet.

"Get it fucking off me!"

Beside Ian, Geoff did a double-take at Ian's predicament, crushed the skull of his own foe, then swung his mace into the skull of the zombie gripping his friend.

Putting everything he had into the swing both men were treated to a vision of a dislodged eyeball and a jet of dark grey jelly following it, but Geoff had left himself exposed and was pulled out of position by the force he put into the swing.

Hands grabbed him and pulled him into the roiling throng.

Ian screamed. An incoherent sound of pure rage and hatred at another friend's death was torn from his mouth as he stepped forward and shoved with a gargantuan effort, clearing enough space to swing his huge axe with both arms as he abandoned his shield.

He stood square in front of the zombies, cleaving heads from necks with every strike until he was dragged unceremoniously backwards before he became overwhelmed by the enemy. Roaring at the hands pulling him to safety, Ian turned ready to swing the axe again, rage clouding his mind into a bloodthirsty battle-fever. Barking brought him back to reality as he half tripped over

Horace who, like Ian, had run headlong into the fight to avenge Geoff.

Jon, stepping forward to protect them, slipped on a patch of gore and fell to the ground. Before anyone could react to help, he was pulled by his feet into the throng to die screaming in pain even as he swung both his hand axes at those towering over him.

More zombies reached the walls as the knights, all fighting bravely and with a desperate rage caused by the death of their friends, were forced to retreat a step at a time.

With tears of grief streaming down his face Ian forced away the looming despair of defeat that was building inside him.

"Make the bastards pay for every inch!" he bellowed.

~

When the leader saw the first zombies reach the top of the walls he began to drool with the anticipation of feasting on human flesh.

He'd won. His unstoppable waves of undead followers had finally achieved its goal. The virus would be the dominant force over the world, ending humans brief but very destructive period of history over the planet. Plagues throughout history had tried to do what this virus was now on the edge of succeeding at.

All previous viruses had been naturally formed and all had a flaw that denied its fate. Some were too efficient and killed the host before it could spread far and wide while others lost virulency every time it reproduced. This virus had been man-made, and even though a flaw – a human error – had caused its creation, it was so close to achieving its aim.

The leader, wanting to be there at the moment of victory and have the tastiest meat for himself, stepped in to the open and pushed through the masses still streaming into the attack. They cowered from his presence and a path cleared before him as he strode forward towards total victory.

"All coordinates uploaded and verified, Sir."

The weapons officer gave a curt nod of acknowledgement before shouting to the one operating the radio.

"Tell everyone at that castle to get their heads down and get those bloody helicopters to get the hell away from there!"

He listened to his instructions being efficiently but more politely paraphrased via radio as he removed the safety cut-outs from the system and looked at the Admiral for final confirmation.

Walker Jones closed his eyes in silent prayer before saying. "Launch."

In the command centre of the castle the radio broadcast to an empty room. No one was monitoring the radios because everyone was fighting to stay alive. Nobody heard the repeated transmissions that ramped up in intensity as they went unanswered.

Shane raised his eyes from the scope and stared at what was happening at the edge of the trees, blinking to clear his vision and make sure he wasn't imagining it.

A zombie, much taller than anything he had seen before, strode forwards as the massed undead cleared the way for him.

Crowds parted around him as if he was a rock defying the oncoming tide. Its heavily muscled body swelled and flexed as it moved menacingly towards the castle.

Shane lowered his eye to the scope and its face filled his entire vision. If evil could be displayed as an image, then this was it. It had to be the leader. Nothing else he'd seen and killed had looked like this. As he watched a chill shot through his body and he involuntarily shuddered.

Knowing that this was probably the most important shot of all time, he breathed out slowly to still any movement in his body. His breath held, his finger moved to the trigger and gently took up the pressure.

Stilling his mind and body for the biggest moment of his life, and possibly one of his last if he screwed it up, Shane felt the sounds of the battle raging all around him fade away as if someone had used a giant remote control on the world.

Having only his own heartbeat thudding slow and steady, Shane cycled his breathing one last time and settled the crosshairs where they needed to be before his finger gently squeezed the last fraction of pressure the trigger required.

The .308 bullet left the barrel at thirty-one-hundred feet per second.

It took about a quarter of a second to travel the two hundred and fifty yards to a spot where Shane had perfectly judged the moving target would be when the bullet arrived.

A round hole appeared in its forehead, ejecting brain matter out the back of its ruined skull in a thick mist. The force of the impact stopped its upper body dead as what was left of its head snapped backwards, though the legs continued forwards as if they'd yet to receive the good news, making the body flip backwards to fall stone dead in a tangled heap of twisted limbs.

Shane raised his eyes from the scope to savour the sight, daring to hope he'd just fired the best shot in living history.

The undead massed around the ruined body he'd just created buzzed with confusion, milling around like stunned insects.

"No," he breathed as hope began to blossom into something more tangible. "You're kidding m—"

Shane didn't finish his thought because the world ahead of him erupted in fire.

CHAPTER THIRTY-SEVEN

There was no warning.

The missiles travelled faster than the sound they created, so when the first one hit the ground just outside the castle's perimeter fence right onto Warwick town centre, we were all knocked off our feet by the blast wave.

With my already overloaded senses now punished by the explosions I dragged my children to me and covered them with my body as I tried to work out what was going on. Protected by the wall, I felt the subsequent explosions more than heard them, as the shockwaves passed over us for thirty seconds before I came up with the only logical explanation I could conjure up.

Missiles. They had to be missiles…and the only place they could have come from was the Navy.

I knew their ships were armed with all sorts of large-scale destructive capabilities, but as they hadn't seemed a practical weapon to use against zombies I hadn't paid much attention when the weapons officer spoke about them. Also, they were in tubes on the deck so I couldn't see them while treated to a tour of the ship. No way near as exciting as the video game gatling gun I'd been lucky to play with, so I never gave them another thought.

But the zombies were still attacking – at least they were before I was knocked to the ground – so despite the continuing barrage I stopped squashing my children and pulled myself to the parapet to risk a peek over the walls.

"What's going on, Tom?" Becky asked, her shout penetrating the ringing in my ears.

I sighed with relief at not seeing a mass of undead still attacking and climbing over the walls. As far as my limited vision could see from my crouching position, everywhere below us was now a mass of tangled, jerking bodies thrown to the ground. Defying the explosions caused by the missiles still smashing into the ground further away, reducing the ferocity of the shock waves still pummelling the castle, I grabbed my rifle and pulled myself upright for a better look.

"Come and look for yourself," I replied, unable to begin to describe what I was looking at as I reached out my hand to help her stand.

Even though we'd been knocked over by the blast waves, the walls must have offered us a lot of protection as those on the wrong side of the walls seemed to have been ripped apart.

I looked over to where the knights had been fighting the zombies that had breached the walls, seeing the slope of bodies we'd tried everything to destroy had been reduced to half its height by the successive blast waves hitting it. On the walls the knights, still looking shaky, had already regained their feet and were killing the few that hadn't been scoured from the walls.

Any zombie still standing, wasn't attacking, but standing immobile as if frozen in place. As the ringing in my ears subsided and the cotton wool that made everything sound muffled dissolved, I could hear shouts of 'Stand to' or 'Back to the walls' as people tried to restore a semblance of order over the shell-shocked defenders.

Snapping out of my own stupor I turned and raised my rifle, but there were no targets of any importance to fire at. We weren't being attacked anymore, and the only ambulatory corpses I could see, looked…lost.

"H…H…Have we won?" Becky asked shakily as she clung to me for support and looked over the wall.

Woody, covered in dust and grime, staggered up to me. Despite a deep cut on his forehead, likely caused by a chunk of flying masonry, leaking blood to run down his cheek his face was split in half by a big smile, and tears were streaming down his cheeks to dilute the blood. He hugged me and shouted in my ear as he danced around joyfully on wobbling legs that pulled me around with him.

"We've broken the attack, they're done for!"

Cheers began to sound out everywhere as others came to the same realisation.

We weren't out of the woods yet, I reminded myself, as I too began to get caught up in the celebrations, but I only had to look out over the walls to reinforce the notion.

More undead were beginning to regain their feet and stand immobile amongst the carnage. There still had to be tens of thousands of zombies still alive outside our walls and out of sight from us, but they weren't attacking us, and as far as I was concerned that was all that mattered.

Order slowly restored itself when the helicopters returned, having been in informed of the attack in time to be well clear of the airspace before the first missiles hit. One of them circled the ruined centre of Warwick and confirmed the presence of a huge amount of zombies still on the outskirts, but the town centre had been levelled by the missiles and didn't appear to contain many live ones.

The report sobered me immediately, hearing that there was still danger out there.

Digby, Clarke and the sergeants quickly organised us, placing most people still on the walls to keep watch for another attack and to keep sniping at the numerous zombies still in the grounds. They were there and needed to be killed again, but at least for the moment they weren't moving and presented an easier target.

Gunfire resumed, only this time it was the controlled, measured sounds of aimed rounds and not the desperate unleashing of as much firepower as possible in the general direction of the enemy.

The defenders began the cold, methodical work of putting down all the clueless, confused survivors while others, including me, gathered in the command centre to discuss our next steps.

Clarke answered the radio which was still broadcasting from the corner. The voice of the operator sounding desperate as he continually asked for an update on our condition.

As soon as Clarke responded, the admiral came on the radio. He must have been standing over the operator's shoulder waiting for news, and the relief in his voice was evident when Clarke gave him a quick review of our current situation.

Walker-Jones had been beside himself with worry thinking that the strike he'd ordered had missed the mark, hitting the castle to cause widespread death and destruction. He was more than relieved the plan seemed to have worked.

"Thank God you're okay! I couldn't help but imagine we'd missed the mark and..."

His voice, still shaky from the panic us answering the calls, had calmed. He went quiet for a moment before continuing.

"I've just been told the Chinook is on its way to you with more reinforcements. Sorry I must go, and you must still be incredibly busy, so update me when you have a better idea of the whole situation, please. Out."

Shane, jammed into a crevice on the ramparts where a wall joined a turret, regained consciousness. Groaning in pain he tried to sit up and shake the fog of confusion from his head as he tried to work out where he was and how he'd ended up there.

Grazes and lacerations, some deep and bleeding freely, covered his exposed flesh making him look as if he'd taken a nose dive off a mountain and used his face as a brake.

The last thing he remembered was an explosion blooming over Warwick just after he'd delivered the perfect headshot to the huge zombie.

With that memory recalled it seemed to kickstart his brain, and his eyes went wide.

Trying to move, pain shot through his arm causing him to cry out and immediately regret the attempt. His arm didn't seem to be connected to his brain, and it took him a few seconds to realise that it was most likely broken or dislocated, and bloody painful.

With his other arm trapped behind him, his vision still blurry from dust, blood or concussion, and his free arm more than useless, he couldn't find any leverage or purchase to get himself out of where he was stuck.

Struggling fruitlessly Shane froze as a shadow loomed over him. Thinking it was a zombie he tried to fight back, kicking out ineffectually with his legs, trying to tap it to death with the weak kicks he managed to deliver and croaking his battle cry that sounded more like a sick frog at the thing that was about to eat him.

And then the 'zombie' spoke.

"Bloody hell mate…you okay? How did you get yourself jammed in here?" Jamie asked with a tone of humour in his voice.

He rested his axe against the wall and bent down to work out how to get his clearly injured friend out from where he was trapped. He called out, and the hulking shape of Ian loomed over Shane moments later.

"How the bloody hell did you…never mind." Ian said.

Trying to be as gentle as possible, it took the two of them a few minutes to carefully half drag, half lift Shane out of the crevice as every little movement caused him to cry out in agony.

Supporting Shane on both sides, being incredibly careful to avoid the arm he held tightly to his chest, they slowly helped him down the staircase to the inner courtyard.

"Come on, let's get you looked at," Jamie said, breathing hard from the effort

"No…Shot leader…Need to…report first." Shane hissed, his words coming out in short, sharp gasps.

Ian nodded and, reaching into a pocket, pulled out a hip flask and held it to Shane's lips.

"Have a snifter of this first to take the edge off then, if you're gonna be a stubborn bastard about it."

Shane winced as he gulped a few mouthfuls of whisky down his throat, spluttering as Ian pulled it away before theatrically shaking the nearly empty flask.

"I didn't say have the lot, you freeloading git," he muttered in mock disgust before draining the last few dregs himself.

The warm glow of the liquid spread through Shane's body, immediately forcing the pain to recede ever so slightly as his two friends helped him towards the command centre.

~

A few minutes later Shane, ashen faced and on the very edge of consciousness, was half carried into the room by Ian and Jamie.

"He has something to report, something about killing the leader," Ian declared loudly, stopping any protests before they started.

All conversation ceased and we gathered around Shane. His head lolled with the agony he was obviously in as he fought the urge to sink into pain-free unconsciousness.

"Shot the...biggest one I saw...just before whatever...blew up the world. Had to be...the leader."

The effort of speaking was too much, and he gave into the pain and passed out.

"Get this man seen to at once," Clarke ordered.

Someone ran off to get a stretcher and, after gently lowering Shane onto it, four people rushed him off to get him medical help.

Gathering around the table again, Gallon spoke first.

"I need to see if the thing he shot was the one I saw on the walls at the farm. I'm the only one who's seen it, I think. If so, then...then we may have just bloody done it."

Looking around the table he continued.

"They certainly aren't acting the same now, are they? They seem to have just...lost direction, as if nobody's telling them what to do. We need to check it out right now."

"Why the urgency, Sergeant?" Digby enquired politely.

"The risk is, if what I reckon is right, another one might take its place. We can't let that happen. If we know what they look like, then we'll be able to target them if we see another, right?" Gallon replied immediately, snapping out his words to convey the urgency he felt.

His logic was sound, and Clarke told him to go and find out.

Watching Gallon go, calling out names of soldiers to come with him, Clarke leant on the table as exhaustion caught up with him.

"What do we do now?" he asked.

Gallon stood on the battlements where Shane had been positioned, scanning the bodies piled on the ground below him through the optic on his rifle. Picking out individual bodies was near impossible as they lay tangled together, but eventually a clear patch caught his attention and he focused on it. Lying in the middle of the area, as if all the others had been scared to go near him, was the one he had seen at the Brough's.

"Gotcha, you bastard," he muttered savagely.

His eyes strained as he stared at it, recalling his memory of the other times he'd seen it. The body lying there matched his memory. It had the scraps of cloth stuck to its flesh and was larger than any of the others.

"Bloody gotcha," he said again before lowering the rifle and heading back to report. As he jogged across the courtyard the sounds of disciplined firing continued from the walls as the zombies left in the grounds were eliminated one by one.

CHAPTER THIRTY-SEVEN

As dawn broke, I struggled to open my eyes as the light level rose in the room. Too exhausted to climb the stairs to bed, I'd sprawled on an armchair in the Great Hall fully clothed and with my boots still on to grab a few blessed hours of sleep. Others around me stirred as I moved and shambled towards the kitchen to find a mug of hopefully very strong, very sweet coffee.

Maud was already up and bustling around, which was no surprise. She'd been hovering around everywhere, looking after everyone's needs when I'd collapsed into the chair.

"Have you been up all night, you daft bat?" I asked, trying to admonish her as she handed me a steaming mug.

She smiled and gave me a brief hug to acknowledge my scolding came from a place of love.

"Well, someone has to make sure you lot are looked after," she replied, trying and failing to sound her usual gruff self.

Struggling to stifle a yawn that crept up on her unannounced, she began swaying with exhaustion. I put my arm around her to hold her steady.

"If you don't go and get a few hours' sleep, I'll put you over my shoulder and carry you to your bed myself. We all need you to be on top form, and killing yourself with tiredness isn't going to help any of us, is it?" I told her kindly.

A look of intense grief crossed her face, and a tear slid down her cheek.

"It's just…it's just that we've lost so many of us and I can't…I can't not be here to look after those of us left," she said in a low, quivering voice.

"Maud," I replied, trying not to let my own emotions spill out. "If you make yourself ill, you aren't going to be able to do that. Now go to bed."

"Fine, I just need to—"

"Bed!" I said with finality.

She nodded and walked away quietly, her small form seeming to shrink even further with tiredness and grief.

As more people gathered I could hear the helicopters outside, warming their engines as they prepared to begin flying patrols, shooting the undead and keeping watch on the land around us to give us advanced warning of another attack.

Until bad weather and exhaustion forced them to land the day before they'd roved further and further away from the castle on search and destroy missions, seeking out every group of zombies they could. According to them it had been like shooting rats in a barrel as these groups, sometimes numbering in their thousands, just stood immobile as their guns ripped into their ranks.

After the helicopters had taken off and their engine noise diminished, a strange kind of surreal calm descended over our home. There was so much to do, but also there wasn't, as none of it seemed that important anymore.

No more zombies were 'alive' in the grounds as the last few had been shot during the night. A strong watch was still needed on the walls, but with nothing to shoot at this was basically now just sentry duty, with the added reminder for the need for continued vigilance piled up in a thick carpet over the grounds. The inner courtyard was a mess of churned grass, discarded ammunition boxes and crates and many other items of abandoned equipment in haphazard piles everywhere.

Only none of us had the energy, enthusiasm, or will to start cleaning it up.

A psychologist would probably diagnose us all with post traumatic shock or something, which was what I'd file under "stating the obvious".

We'd all experienced an intense period of high stress, more than a few of us had truly come to terms with our imminent deaths and mixed with the trauma of losing many of our friends and only escaping with our lives by the skin of our teeth, it was most likely true.

Outside in the courtyard, we formed small groups who gathered together for no other reason than to be near each other. Conversation in these huddles was stilted and contained no real words as we stood mainly in silence looking at each other.

Ian, Horace by his side, broke into the group I had gathered with and spoke in a voice barely above a whisper.

"Can anyone come and help me find my mates?"

That galvanised us into action. We knew that Simon, Marc, Jon and Geoff had all been killed in the savage fighting on the walls, where the knights had stopped the zombies gaining a strong foothold which would have certainly meant all of our deaths. We owed them a debt of gratitude which could never be repaid so, walking with the other knights we began the grim, heartbreaking task.

We found Marc first at the foot of the walls in the courtyard. We untangled his body from the zombie he had fallen to his death with, seeing with some kind of grim pride that he'd even managed to kill the zombie as he fell, as his axe was still embedded in its head.

We stood back as Ian, Shawn, Dave, Jamie and Alex arranged his body on a stretcher and placing his axe in his hands, laid it across his chest. Although not one of the original group, he'd still been with them from the start when the apocalypse had found them on the reenactment field where he'd lost both his wife and his son.

Ian knelt beside him sobbing with emotion. Leaning down he whispered in his ear.

"See you mate. Say hi to your family for me."

Simon, Geoff and Jon were found under the piles of zombie corpses still atop the walls.

Once we'd freed them, throwing the undead corpses over the walls without any trace of reverence, we laid blankets over their bodies to hide the horrific injuries they'd received while fighting to their last breath. Carrying them on stretchers from the ramparts we laid them reverently beside Marc, each of them gripping a weapon even in death to carry on to wherever it was they went to next.

No one was able to speak as we stared at our four friends. The knights had been at the core of our group since we had united in Bristol so many months before. Always at the centre of any mischief, always leading the fun and laughter which kept our spirits up continually. It was hard to comprehend that they were gone.

Clarke appeared from the doorway that led to the command centre and joined us, waiting patiently until individually we turned away from the bodies and noticed him. Before he spoke, he stepped forwards smartly and saluted the four fallen warriors.

"Meeting now," he said in a subdued voice as he stared at the bodies, thinking about all those who had no body left to bury after being ripped to pieces by the zombies or blown up by their own hands in a last act to save being done so.

From the soldiers at the Brough's to those lost in the convoy, each had been part of our community, and each one would be missed terribly.

~

The following morning those leaving first stood ready with bags by their side. Walker-Jones had flown in by helicopter the previous afternoon, standing dumfounded on the walls to stare at the sea of dead piled yards thick in places spread all over the grounds.

He ordered a whole community meeting where he insisted that everyone should be temporarily taken to the Scilly isles to recover, recuperate and rest. We initially refused, naturally, as we knew that the work needed to clear all the bodies from the grounds alone was an immense undertaking and as it was our home, it was our responsibility.

He couldn't order us to go, and even though we knew he had the best intentions as we'd taken the brunt of the battle for humanity. He insisted it was for others to muck in and help now. It was time to take a step back and accept help.

In the end it took Maud who he'd appealed to directly to make us agree. She knew us better than any and had been privately concerned about many of us following the attacks, so she knew it was what we needed to do despite our stubbornness.

She decided that we would go, and none of us would, or could, argue with her. Ever.

The chinook would need two trips to fly us all to Bristol where a ship waited to take us to the Scillies. We waited for the arriving soldiers to exit before we bustled onboard and sat down on the seats lining each side of the huge interior. Princess and Horace sulked as they were on leads, something they rarely needed to be.

The children were excited at the novelty of a flight not many civilians ever had the chance to experience. The children already seemed outwardly to have recovered from the fight where they'd played just as an important part as everyone else, firing their weapons as fast as they could into the enemy from the walls.

Becky and I knew differently, as all three of them had experienced nightmares the previous night, causing them to want to sleep in our bed where we'd hugged and comforted them back to sleep. Whispering as we lay awake holding our sleeping children close, we agreed that a break in the Scillies was definitely the right idea.

During the flight the children were treated by the crew to a trip to the cockpit, and after Becky was shown how safe it was, they were fitted with harnesses which were a lot smaller than usual and with a safety rope secured to the bulkhead and kept tight, took their turn to sit between the crew on the rear ramp and have the unique opportunity to fly along with their legs dangling into space.

Becky couldn't keep the worried look off her face until they were shepherded back to us where I tried to keep the look of envy off mine.

Whatever our objections had been, the two weeks we spent in the Scillies formed more treasured family memories. All put up in the same hotel, we were looked after royally by the new Scilly residents who couldn't do enough for us to make us comfortable. All of us continually had to brush of their repeated praise for what we'd done and been through for the whole country.

Our group lazed on the beach one day, enjoying the spring sunshine which was just about warm enough to discard our jumpers, watching the older children dressed in wetsuits body-board in the surf as the younger ones played with buckets and spades in the sand. I smiled, watching them enjoy the thrill of rushing through the clear water when they caught a wave, laughing and screaming with joy seemingly without a care in the world. Watching them be children again, instead of soldiers.

Both Princess and Horace jumped around in the shallows, barking with joy and caught up in the fun the children were having.

Chris and Nicky sat playing with Hope and Sarah as Maud, sitting sedately on a beach chair, kept watch over all of us like a mother hen.

Chris had forgiven Ian for bundling him onto the helicopter. As soon as they'd been reunited at the hotel, Ian had taken Chris to one side for a heart-to-heart. They'd both come back wiping tears from their eyes and Ian with a grin on his face, as no matter what had been said he knew, as we all did, that he'd done the right thing.

Sarah had taken her first few steps on the soft sand the day before, which had created great excitement and celebrations. She'd been threatening to become more mobile for months now but had stubbornly refused, as she knew that racing around on all fours was by far the fastest mode of transport to employ. Her shrieks of pure happiness as she announced her new skill to the world brought many happy tears to everyone's eyes.

"Takes you back, doesn't it?" I said quietly to Becky as I handed her a glass of wine before pulling a bottle of beer from the cool box we'd brought with us.

We lapsed into silent reminiscence, recalling the last time we'd done this on the day before the world fell apart. Now it wasn't just us, our previously small family of four on the beach enjoying the day. We were a much larger and diverse group now, but a group that considered each and every one of us as family.

Silently, we stared into each other's eyes as memories of what we had endured and overcome flashed through both our minds. I leant forwards to kiss her, and she began to cry.

I shushed her gently, filled with concern that I'd somehow upset her.

"I'm not sad," Becky protested with a weak smile.

"Then…?" I started to ask, confused by her tears.

"I'm crying because I'm happy, Tom. I'm crying because we survived."

EPILOGUE

The setting summer sun shone warmly on our faces as Becky and I leaned against the parapet and looked out across the grounds of the castle. It had become a ritual of ours that, when the weather allowed, we always took a walk together around the castle walls after the evening meal. It gave us the chance to spend some time together, away from the usual bustle of castle life. A bit of us time, which we treasured.

The only evidence left of the fierce battle all those months ago were the greener patches of grass where craters created by the mortars had been filled, and the shattered stumps of a few trees that had yet to be removed. The grounds were recovering, becoming full of life as crops now grew where the dead had laid in their masses to prove that the planet had a stronger immune system than many thought.

The huge scar created by all the funeral pyres when the dead zombies had been removed from the grounds using every available piece of heavy machinery found in the local area, was thankfully out of sight beyond the trees. Further afield the skyline had changed as the buildings destroyed by the cruise missile barrage arriving just in time to save us created gaps in what had been there before.

"The Brough's should be arriving tomorrow," I said, needlessly reminding her of something she knew but wanting to fill the silence as we gazed over the grounds.

The Brough's had insisted on returning to their farm, and even though their beloved herd of cattle had been destroyed by the zombies, they were determined to continue farming the land. After finding some dairy cows at other farms they were starting a breeding programme to expand the herd. The place was still garrisoned by a force of soldiers, but they were now volunteers who wanted to help work the land as well as keep the place secure. They were also planting crops, raising more livestock; mainly sheep and pigs being introduced to the empty land around them.

Convoys still stopped there, as we had envisioned for the place originally, to drop off supplies and rest up after ranging far and wide as they continually searched the land primarily for supplies but also on the lookout for any more survivors. The Brough's and the farms garrison did visit us regularly for social reasons. We were their nearest neighbours after all, and similar to the popping next door for a glass of wine you used to do when you got on with your neighbours, and now the need for heavily armed convoys was no longer necessary, they visited us when time allowed. Everyone still carried guns with them, just in case, but as no zombies were around, they could make the journey in a car now, albeit one that still carried extra protection in the form of a surrounding cage and a plough affixed to the front, without any real fear of being attacked.

The route from Newlyn, behind the Corn Wall, was now a well-established and much travelled route. Flying to the Scillies wasn't necessary now as, if you set out early enough, you could be at Newlyn and in a boat across to there in an easy day's travel.

"I know, darling," she said, leaning her head against my shoulder and poking a playful finger into my ribs. "It was me who reminded you of that earlier today? Walker-Jones should be arriving at some point as well if you can remember that too?"

"Of course I can!" I replied indignantly, having completely forgotten the admiral was coming.

Zombies had ranged the country for months after Shane had killed the leader, but as time went on, they began to drop in their tens of thousands from starvation. There was no food for them and their bodies could not sustain them. They had slowly died off, often lying down and twitching weakly as carrion birds and other wildlife fed on their corpses, cleansing the land to leave only bones to be absorbed by the land.

We were always in regular contact with the admiral, of course. His role had changed from a combat leader to one who concentrated on rebuilding and restoring the country. He spent his time travelling between all of our communities on the Scillies, Cornwall, Fort Bristol, the Brough's and us at the castle, working out everyone's needs and allocating our limited labour forces to where it would do the most good.

It had been suggested that if we wanted to, we could leave the castle and form another community in Cornwall or on the Scillies, but we'd rejected all such suggestions immediately and without debate, as we knew what the answer from everybody would be.

Warwick Castle was our home now.

The grounds and fields around it would provide us with everything we needed to live on as our crop growing and animal husbandry programmes expanded. It was where our extended family lived, forming a tightly knit, happy community. It was also where some of our friends were buried after giving up their lives to protect us all, and we could never leave them to be forgotten in abandoned, untended graves.

We loved the ancient, history filled walls, and knew we were adding many legends and stories that would forever be associated with the place. History never stopped being made. We made it every day we were there just as we'd made it each day before. It was our home. It was our past and our future.

It was our zombie castle.

Chris Harris is a UK-based author, well-known for his post-apocalyptic and zombie book series.
Find his website at www.chrisharrisauthor.co.uk
Facebook @chrisharrisauthor

UK Dark Book 1: The Blackout

By Chris Harris

"What would happen if…?"

Many people ask themselves the question, but how many actually do something about it?

Tom lives in Birmingham, England with his family. After asking himself the question and researching what could happen, he decided it wouldn't do any harm to be a little bit prepared. Just in case.

He discovers the world is going to be hit by a massive Coronal Mass Ejection from the sun, which will turn the whole planet dark.

He only has a few days to get ready.

Will they survive?

People want what they have, but is he prepared to kill to protect it?

The UK Dark series, out now!